**She had her head down so low he could only see the top of it.**

This was the first time in Chalgrove's life anyone had appeared crushed when finding out he was a duke.

"I'm in trouble. I've been bundled together with a duke. My employer will let me go. My stepmother will use this as an excuse to cast more aspersions at me."

Her knees were still raised, her arms crossed over them, and her chin rested there. Her eyes were closed, so he studied her face. The lashes rimmed her eyes so thickly he wanted to brush his cheek against them to see if they felt as lush as they appeared.

Then he called himself a fool.

Again, he was enthralled by a pretty face. A woman who seemed to need his help. Another woman with secrets.

## Author Note

For a long time, I'd dreamed of writing a secondary character who didn't let poverty stop her from living life with zest. Someone with a tarnished heart of gold, and who could make the world a better place—even if she had unorthodox methods that would land anyone else in deep trouble.

This character briefly appeared in *To Win a Wallflower* but she didn't have a name. I didn't plan on letting her go. When the Tyner family ancestry was being discussed, I heard, and loved, the name Ella Etta, and I couldn't forget it. Now my wanderer had a name, and I brought her back in *Compromised into Marriage*, and now again in *The Governess's Guide to Marriage*.

I hope you enjoy Miranda and Chalgrove's story, and I hope that Ella Etta steals a place in your heart as well, but do keep your silver locked away.

# LIZ TYNER

—

## The Governess's Guide to Marriage

# HARLEQUIN®
## HISTORICAL™

Recycling programs
for this product may
not exist in your area.

ISBN-13: 978-1-335-50572-9

The Governess's Guide to Marriage

Copyright © 2020 by Elizabeth Tyner

All rights reserved. No part of this book may be used or reproduced in
any manner whatsoever without written permission except in the case of
brief quotations embodied in critical articles and reviews.

This is a work of fiction. Names, characters, places and incidents
are either the product of the author's imagination or are used fictitiously.
Any resemblance to actual persons, living or dead, businesses,
companies, events or locales is entirely coincidental.

This edition published by arrangement with Harlequin Books S.A.

For questions and comments about the quality of this book,
please contact us at CustomerService@Harlequin.com.

Harlequin Enterprises ULC
22 Adelaide St. West, 40th Floor
Toronto, Ontario M5H 4E3, Canada
www.Harlequin.com

**Printed in U.S.A.**

**Liz Tyner** lives with her husband on an Oklahoma acreage she imagines is similar to the ones in the children's book *Where the Wild Things Are*. Her lifestyle is a blend of old and new, and is sometimes comparable to the way people lived long ago. Liz is a member of various writing groups and has been writing since childhood. For more about her, visit liztyner.com.

### Books by Liz Tyner

### Harlequin Historical

*The Notorious Countess*
*The Runaway Governess*
*The Wallflower Duchess*
*Redeeming the Roguish Rake*
*Saying I Do to the Scoundrel*
*To Win a Wallflower*
*It's Marriage or Ruin*
*Compromised Into Marriage*
*The Governess's Guide to Marriage*

### *English Rogues and Grecian Goddesses*

*Safe in the Earl's Arms*
*A Captain and a Rogue*
*Forbidden to the Duke*

Visit the Author Profile page
at Harlequin.com.

Dedicated to Karen,
Debbie and Laura.

# Chapter One

'Your old gran be dying.' The man stood at the servants' entrance, a faded scar on his face and his hat in his hands.

Miranda gulped in a breath. She'd believed her grandmother long gone from her life. Hoped her long gone.

'She wants to see you. To beg you to forgive her.' He twisted the hat. 'Please, miss…uh… Miss Manwaring. I brought a cart to take you to the gamekeeper's house where you lived as a child.' He plopped the hat on his head and straightened his plain coat. 'She's on her last breath.'

Miranda had never told anyone about the house. She hardly remembered it herself and she'd always known that it was better for her to have a forgotten ancestry than to reveal the truth.

One of the last lies her grandmother had told her was that she'd be back. Then she'd left Miranda alongside a road that smelled of wild honeysuckle and told her not to step far because there were spiders in the wood as big as horses. Eight legs to chase her and six eyes to see where she went.

Miranda had been terrified, but then a couple had happened along in a carriage and the woman had acted as if

Miranda was the miracle she'd been waiting for, scooped her up and took her to a house that reached the sky.

After a few months of her new life, Miranda had stopped hoping for her grandmother to return and had prayed that she wouldn't. She'd pushed those memories so far into the recesses of her mind that they now felt as if they belonged to someone else.

'The old woman, she called you Child and had tears in her eyes. She said she can't rest settled because of you.'

'I'll ask Mr Trevor if I can have the time off to see her...' memories constricted her throat '...one last time.'

Miranda rushed to knock on her employer's door, asking if she might take her half-day off now. His brow creased and he gave her permission to leave. He opened his mouth to say something else, but she ran out before he could ask any questions.

She searched out the maid, received a promise to watch over Dolly and Willie, then ran to kiss each of her charges on the top of the head before scurrying out the door.

But she had one last thing to do before going. She rushed to the stables.

The stable master kneeled, prying a wheel from a carriage, his grey hair splaying as he lunged. He stopped moving when he noticed her running. His weathered face showed concern. 'What's wrong, Miss Miranda?' He studied her.

She reassured him. 'Nothing, Nicky, but I must go away this evening. To see...someone.'

Nicky stared. 'That man who raised you send for you?'

'No.'

Her words refused to come until after she took a breath. 'Someone I used to know is dying and they asked if I might see them one last time. I could not refuse a last wish.'

'No, of course you couldn't.' He stood, compassion showing from beneath the bushy eyebrows. 'You take care, though. I'll get one of the lads to go with you. We'll never miss him. And a young woman as fine as you should never be out alone.'

She feared what a companion might see and what the lad might hear from her dying grandmother's lips.

'No. But, thank you, Nicky.' She reached out and, for a second, clasped his arms. Concern wrinkled his face and he opened his mouth to speak again.

'I'll take care,' she said. 'And I'll be back before you know it.'

Moving quickly to the cart, she thrust her bonnet on, concealing her face from the sun and anyone who might be watching.

At the cart, the driver pointed to the back.

'What is wrong with my grandmother?' Miranda asked, settling in. 'How does she know where I work? Is she—?'

'I don't know anything about her,' the man spoke, words precise. 'Just that she paid me to fetch you. She asked if I might deliver a message to her long lost grand-daughter, who is a governess, and bring you.' He took off his hat again and held it over his heart. 'One last time so that she can go on to her reward peaceful like.'

Miranda suppressed the premonition that her grand-mother's eternal reward might not be a fortune.

He frowned, making the long creases on his face more prominent. 'Right pitiful, she is. All skin and bones, and sunken eyes. It'll take us nearly half a day to get there. Best be going. Otherwise, I'll never be able to get you back before sunset.'

Miranda jumped into the cart.

She got no other information out of the man and the ride to the old cottage caused memories to resurface that she'd not known she had.

She was surprised to see the cottage still standing, its roof hardly taller than her head, the front window boarded over, but with openings between the boards. As she walked inside, she noticed shadows on the empty bed. Her eyes didn't adjust to the dim light before the door slammed closed behind her. Something crashed, hitting the wood and locking her in.

In seconds, she heard her grandmother's voice calling from the other side of the door, 'Don't be going nowhere, Child. I be bringing you a husband. One with a fortune like you deserve.'

Miranda stumbled, gulping in breaths. Her grandmother wasn't at death's door. She'd trapped Miranda in her lair.

'As soon as you are betrothed, I'll set you free.'

Her grandmother hadn't changed at all.

He could not die tonight—not on his mother's birthday.

The blow across the Duke of Chalgrove's back knocked him to his knees. Another club slammed him from behind, shoving him face down to the ground. A body landed on his back. Ruffians jumped on him from all sides.

Chalgrove's mouth pressed against the street. He tasted dirt. The shock of being ambushed had given the ruffians an opportunity to attack.

With both palms splayed, he pushed himself up, shaking loose a man who had him by the arm. A flash of irony ripped through his mind. He'd meant to visit Gentleman Jackson's.

Another attacker gripped his right shoulder—the criminal's entire weight being used to force Chalgrove's arm up his back. Pain seared his thoughts white hot and he lunged forward, shifting at the same time, and threw the man to the side.

One more man jumped at him.

He had no time to guess why he was being surrounded because all his resources were centred on survival.

Jagged breaths touched his hair. Chalgrove snapped his head back, towards the bulk behind him. He heard the crack as his skull connected with something which felt like a face. A pained grunt from the attacker pleased Chalgrove and the hold on his arm loosened.

He kicked and his foot connected with air. But as the man dived for him, the Duke jumped aside, causing the man to lose balance, and Chalgrove gave an elbow thrust that took the man to the ground.

Then a woman screamed.

Chalgrove spun in time to see a man holding an old woman. Lantern light shone on the club in the man's hand and illuminated a scar on his face.

'Stop, or she gets hurt,' the man called out. His words were distinct and he had the arms of a sailor who didn't have to climb the rigging, but could toss his companions up to do the work for him.

The woman shivered, her scarf askew. Her aged hands pleading. 'Please don't hurt me,' she cried to the man. 'I beg you.' Her voice shook. 'Please…'

Chalgrove didn't move. 'Let her go.'

The fight left his body. Arms trapped him.

'Tie him,' the man who'd been securing the old woman said. 'Hands behind his back. Once and then once again.'

The woman was released. She stumbled a few steps into the darkness. As soon as Chalgrove was tied, the old woman stepped from the shadows and took the club from the other man, throwing it to the ground, then stared at her attacker. 'You bruised me, you big beast.'

'I didn't mean to.' The man stepped backwards. 'You know I'd never cause you a moment of grief.

'I wasn't jesting when I called out for you not to hurt me, you cudgel-head. You nearly choked me.'

Then the woman's attention changed and she shuffled closer to Chalgrove, studying him.

Rage flashed inside Chalgrove. He'd fallen into a trap, yet he would never have been able to risk seeing the woman hurt.

She walked closer, peering at him. 'I said not to hurt his face.' She cringed. 'His teeth?' she gasped and her lip trembled. 'I pray you didn't bust out the man's teeth.'

He could not think properly.

*Were they knocking him about to take him somewhere for a portrait sitting?*

His head must have hit harder than he realised.

The woman walked in front of him, inclined her head closer, eyes squinted, and he could tell she examined his mouth. He saw her shoulders relax and she straightened, relief in her face.

'Make sure he's comfortable,' the old woman commanded. 'We need to get him in the cart so Jasper can put out the lantern.'

She walked behind him. A slap against cloth sounded. 'You have to keep him unharmed. We can't have him hurt. There's no time for him to heal.'

Boots thumped near him. 'This one will take a lot of feed.'

He felt a touch to his fingertips. The old woman was examining him. The skin touching him reminded him of meat put in a grinder, then left in the sun to dry.

'Ah...'

He heard a groan of satisfaction from the old woman.

'Feel these.' She spoke to one of the men as she examined Chalgrove's fingers.

'I ain't holdin' his hand,' a male voice rasped.

The old woman chuckled and he heard a giddiness in her words. 'Man's not all scarred over.'

'What'd you expect of a tailor? He's never done an honest day of work in his life.' The one who'd held the club spoke, his words as precise as a tutor's.

'Neither has you,' the rasping voice answered.

'I'm not a tailor,' Chalgrove shouted. 'I'm the Duke of Chalgrove.'

'Told you he would spout nonsense, Jasper,' the old woman said. 'Just didn't expect him to claim to be a duke. Or earl even.' Then she laughed. 'He's full of imaginations. Thinking you might suppose him a duke.'

Chalgrove heard movement again, felt what he sensed was a skirt brushing his shoulder and knew the woman stood at his side. He felt his upper arm being squeezed as she checked his muscles. 'Mmm,' she mumbled. 'Not bad.'

He hoped she'd realise he'd be gristly thrown in a pot and sprinkled with lemon.

'Look at 'em boots,' the rasping one called, close at Chalgrove's side. 'I bet I could wear 'em.'

'If you're taking his boots, I'm getting the hat you knocked off him,' the biggest brute spoke.

Seconds later, the one with the scratchy voice mused, 'He's got him a big head. Hat near wipes your nose.'

'Don't nab those boots,' the woman called out. 'Makes him an eyeful. But that hat, keep it for me. He don't need to be wearing it. I want him fine. Now, put out the light.'

The lantern wick was extinguished, leaving the scent of burning oil in its wake.

'I'm getting the cart,' she said. 'Don't let him get away.' Her steps clunked as she left.

The one with precise words said, 'I've never seen a yellow hat before. It's different.'

'Fer a flower pot?' the other voice asked.

'That hat is none of your concern.' Chalgrove didn't like being discussed. He expected at least the same respect as a man to be hanged. These ruffians would die.

'This hat smells not unlike perfume,' the careful voice said. 'What do you think, Jasper?'

He heard a sniff at his shoulder. An object tapped his leg to get his attention.

Rage flared and he couldn't speak.

'You been visitin' a lady? You prob'ly don't even have to give 'em coin or marry 'em to get 'em to tumble you. If that ain't criminal,' Jasper said, not waiting for a response. 'Poor souls like us got to pay or promise marryin'.'

'Have you ever romanced a theatre woman?' the precise one asked. 'Outside?'

Chalgrove ground his teeth together and refused to answer.

'He's nivver been with a wench anywheres but in a proper bed,' the man with the raspy voice informed his cohort. 'Nob smells like him wouldn't be able to get his twig up 'less he's in a house. Got to have a soft bed with lacy curtains and a valet to tell him where to put his goods.'

'She has a feather bed for him.' The words had a chuckle in them.

*'You're lyin'. A feather bed?'*

He heard silence.

'She's been working on this for a season. Just finished last week.'

'What are the plans for me?' Chalgrove interrupted, demanding the men enlighten him.

'I don't know,' he answered. 'Do you know?' The sound of his voice changed enough to alert Chalgrove that the man had turned his head.

'I'd nivver put nuthin' past that ol' hag. She's daft. More 'n normal-woman daft.'

'I can pay you to release me,' Chalgrove growled out the words.

He heard silence again, then felt his purse being taken from his waistcoat pocket. Coins jingled.

'We's thinkin' 'bout it,' the rasper boasted and Chalgrove knew the coins were gone.

'Let me go so you won't have to hang,' he commanded. They'd not live long enough to walk to the gallows. He'd see to that.

Again, he heard from the one with the scratchy voice. 'We had too much worries catchin' you to let you wander off. Been eyein' you for days. Would have given up, but the hag said we'd no choice but to do as she said.'

'Collecting the other one was easier,' the one with the brutish arms spoke. 'I hope the old woman will be satisfied. I'm leaving London and going where she'll never find me.'

The rasping one shuffled closer, and lowered his voice. 'We didn't have no choice. Old woman said she'd give us a curse so we'd have to stay home with our wives. Man's got to care for his jewels and the sceptre.'

'She bluffed.' Chalgrove clamped his jaw tight.

A snort answered him. 'She be a toddle on the tricky side. But, you'll be discoverin' soon enough.'

The man spoke to his friend. 'I wonder if the old woman was foolin' when she told us he was Beau Brummell's tailor? He don't fight like no tailor.'

'I'm the Duke of Chalgrove.'

Silence greeted the revelation.

'I 'spect you could be. That's a towerin' hat.'

# Chapter Two

Miranda woke from her sitting position on the bed, her back against the wall and her knees hugged to her chest. The room was so dark she couldn't see her bonnet crumpled against the wall where she'd thrown it in frustration.

Someone was outside.

She heard her grandmother shout out, telling dunderheads to be careful.

The room was black and she had nowhere to hide.

She'd not been able to escape out of the windows. All were boarded from the outside. The crevices between them let in light, but not enough to see in the moonless night.

She'd bruised her hands trying to pry the boards open, but they didn't move.

At the other side of the room, one of the biggest stumps she'd ever seen had been placed. Likely, it had been put on its side and rolled into the room. The stump served as a table and had a bundle on it. Inside the cloth wrapping, she'd found bread and cheese…a lot of cheese. Six pears. Two apples and some nuts, but nothing to crack them open. And her favourite treat when she'd been a child. Honey.

She'd put honey on bread the night before, her hunger forcing her to eat.

The water was stale and the ale ghastly. She'd left the bottles against the wall, except one which she held.

The next room was even more gloomy with fewer cracks in the boarded windows. It held a washstand, several dust-covered flannels, a bucket without a handle and the barest of necessities.

The room with the feather bed felt safer.

Miranda was sitting on a rag counterpane. She could imagine her grandmother, as innocent as a babe, putting the fabric together. Then, boarding the windows and hanging the curtains over them, whistling, and sending a man to fetch Miranda.

She waited, an ale bottle in her hand, knowing that something was about to happen. Knowing that her grandmother had rules of her own. She considered honesty something only the rich could afford. A weakness to be avoided as much as possible because you never knew when it could return to bite you. She claimed truth used too liberally led to hunger, drudgery and sometimes even death.

Men's voices. Curses. Not her grandmother.

The door opened and lantern light seeped into the room.

Hulking shapes moved in the doorway, struggling against each other. More curses. Arms and legs. She remembered the story of the spiders. Eight legs. Six eyes.

A thump when one of the men hit the floor.

The shape on the floor was moving.

She didn't dare do more than breathe.

The door closed and she heard the scraping on the other side which meant a board had locked them in.

She was trapped and with something more than a spider.

She grasped the ale bottle tightly. If she couldn't see well in the inky night, neither could he.

She would kill him before he attacked her.

She slid from the bed and crept, ever so stealthily.

'Who's there?' the man's voice thundered.

She didn't answer.

She needed to keep him talking, so she could tell where he was.

Holding her arm wide, she clinked the bottle on the wall and then moved away.

'Who's there?' he said.

Chalgrove couldn't see much in the darkness, but his senses were working double. A skittering noise. Cloth moving. A shape. He was not alone.

And he could sense it. Sense that whoever was in the room with him meant him harm. Perhaps he knew because they didn't speak. Perhaps because they were moving about, sidestepping, but not moving closer. Creeping to the side, as if they were going to pounce.

He might die, but with his last dying breath he was going to kill the person in front of him.

Working harder at the ropes, he tried again, but realised he would not be able to free himself. He didn't have time. He didn't even have time to push himself to his feet.

Then he stopped thinking about getting free, but only about surviving the next moments. He put his tied hands flat on the floor and pulled his legs close, pivoting on the floor, trying to keep the sounds in front of him. Trying to see into the void, not even knowing for sure where he was, or what was before him. A block of something at his head kept him stationary and he eased closer to it.

Whatever it was could stop the attacker.

Motion stopped. A standoff, of sorts. He had the object at his back and his boots between him and the assailant.

The sound of rustling cloth again. And he knew, knew to roll sideways just as a weapon landed in the space where his head had been. The object crashed into the block that had stopped his progress, glass shattering, and bouncing from his shoulder. Showering him in reeking ale and shards. The shape stumbled forward, making skittering noises as it tried to regain balance.

He rolled again, forward this time, launching himself in the direction of the attack, lunging with his upper torso into the inky world around him and connecting with a human shape. He used the power in his legs to push himself forward, again and again, wedging them both, until something behind the shape prevented more movement.

He heard a scream, a feminine one, and felt the claws at his head pulling his hair backwards, trying to move him away, rolling from under him.

And then a knee in his stomach. A kick at his leg and then another lunge in the darkness.

She scrambled about, searching the floor, hunting for something. Then she stilled. She breathed deep, voice guttural. 'I will kill you.'

'I think you'll find you're halfway there.'

He worked the ties. He knew. She had a weapon in her hand, probably a shard of glass, and her breathing was ragged. He could hear where she was.

'Why would you think to kill me?' he asked. Demanding.

'I will see you die before you touch me.'

'My hands are tied behind my back.' He ground the words out. 'Tied.'

He worked, loosening the ropes, he was sure. But he couldn't pull free. 'I don't want to be anywhere near you,' he said.

She paused. 'You are bound?'

'Yes.' The rope dug into his wrists and ale dripped into his eyes. 'My hands are secured behind my back.'

'Good. It will make it easier for me.'

'No,' he said. 'It won't.'

'Your hands are tied?' Her voice lowered while she contemplated.

'Keep your distance,' he commanded.

She eased to the right. He heard the movement and changed course, twisting in the same direction.

'Who did this to you?' she asked.

'Some brutes.'

'One who had a mark down his face?'

Silence. 'Yes.'

'He spoke like a learned man?'

'Yes.'

'He tricked me to come here,' she muttered. 'Said I had family who wanted to see me.'

'Why would you follow a stranger?'

'I'm an orphan, but even so, I have family somewhere. I always believed...' She stopped.

The ropes eased. He lifted his voice, covering the struggle to release his bonds. 'Someone found out and used that to trick you. But that doesn't explain why I'm here. The whole world knows who my father was and my mother would never let anyone forget that.'

Freed, he reached up. The scratch marks on his temple burned from where her fingernails had scraped.

'I'm a captive same as you.' He kept his voice emotionless and calming. He edged against the wall. With her talking, he could tell where she was and gauge her fear by the tone of her voice. The poor woman was trapped. They both were.

He settled in. It would be daylight soon, and he'd be much better able to take stock of the room and find a way to escape.

'You tell me you are a prisoner?' she asked.

'You're as safe from me as you are from your reflection in a mirror. I would say I have no wish to harm you, but after the way you introduced yourself to me, I might wish to reserve that statement until I see if you will listen to reason.'

'That is assuming you will be able to speak sensibly.'

No one in his life had ever questioned what he said. No one questioned anything he did, now that his father was gone. Oh, perhaps his mother might hide a hint of reproach in her words, but she always couched her reproof so carefully he had to sort out whether it was praise or criticism.

He wondered what sort of woman he'd been trapped with.

'Why would I need the door barred?' he kept his voice soft so he'd not frighten her more. The sound of the door being secured had thundered in his ears after he'd been thrown into the room. Now he had only mere shadows and the sound of a husky voice to guide him. 'I had nothing at all to do with your capture.'

She must understand they were both in the same situation.

'I have been taken captive by one woman and tortured by another one,' he said.

He ran a hand through his hair, brushing back the tendrils tipped with moisture. 'I suppose—there's a ransom for me. My family has surely been contacted by now and they're probably trying to access enough funds to satisfy a cut-throat. I can't guess a different reason. Perhaps the ransom will—who knows…' he interrupted himself.

'You could pay a ransom?' she asked.

'Could you?'

Silence drifted between them. 'I suppose it could appear that way. I lived in a wealthy home. Once.'

Something in her voice silenced him from asking more.

Her words were a blend of wistfulness, sadness, acceptance and maybe a question of whether someone who had funds would judge her worth a ransom.

She moved against the opposite side of the room, silent and waiting.

As the light began to creep into the cracks from the window, her face came into his sight. Softly at first, then like fog clearing and bringing the shape of a statue into view, he saw her and could not help but stare as her features were unveiled in the morning light.

He had not been tossed in with another crone. He'd been trapped with a vision.

He ran his fingers over the scratches on his face and caught himself making sure no one else was hidden in the shadows. Yes, this fragile creature had attacked him.

Her face gave little away. Emotions hidden behind an immobile façade. She studied him as dispassionately as he studied her.

The light increased and they stood immobile, trapped by the walls around them and their own contemplation while they gauged each other.

She could have easily posed for a portrait of a saint, but then he noticed the shard of broken glass she gripped.

'Do you know why you're here?' he asked. He remembered the words of the men and wanted to know what she'd heard. 'What did they speak of when they were bringing you?'

She didn't answer.

He gave a brief shake of his head, feeling the stickiness of the ale that had drenched him. 'I had nothing to do with your capture.'

He stayed at the end of the room from her, but with the force of his words, he shortened the distance. 'The ransom? The wealthy home you had. Could money be paid?'

Then she stiffened her fingers briefly, dismissing the words. 'I doubt anyone who knows me, and my life now, would do more than laugh at such a thing. Perhaps someone from my past might do so...'

Her eyes searched the room. Her stomach plummeted when she saw the size of him and the scratches on his face. If she'd known his stature when he'd been tossed into the room, she might have been too afraid to fight back. Although, from the redness of the marks, she'd been forceful.

A wave of fear shook her along with the thankfulness that he was not a ruffian.

He wore quality clothing. Not rags.

'Although it is possible I could be used for a ransom,' she admitted. 'It's hard to know what a criminal mind might think.'

She put three fingers to her temple. 'It's hard to know what a reasonable person thinks.'

Much less a woman who might slip from the gamekeeper's cottage and dance with Miranda under the full moon.

Then, another night, they would sit in the darkness with the heaven's brightness around them and the old woman would declare there were the most stars ever in the sky and the child's dance must have been the most magnificent ever created because never had the stars smiled so.

Once, after Miranda had been told to help with the washing and ran to play instead, that night the old woman had taken her outside and they had stared up at the cloudy sky. Miranda was told how she had displeased the stars because they'd hidden their light.

The old gamekeeper had been listening and guffawed.

That had been her first hint that stars were stars and the moon was the moon, and the world was not crafted to react as her grandmother wanted it to.

The captured man lifted an ale bottle from beside the stump and offered her a sip.

'I'm not thirsty.' She clutched her hands and kept her distance from him. The tightening of his lips told her he noticed.

'You've nothing to fear from me, unless you damage any more of the liquid in this room.' He closed his fingers around the bottle. 'I'm parched.' The muscles in his legs tightened when he kicked a few bits of the broken glass into the corner.

Then he popped the cork free. He took a taste and sputtered. Then he put the bottle back on the floor and gently poured a splash of water into the bottle, diluting the ale. He tasted his mixture, sipping the liquid, his eyes tightening and his swallow forced. He diluted it more, then quenched his thirst.

'I will see that old woman on the gallows.'

'Old woman?' she asked, tucking her hands behind her back. He'd seen her grandmother. 'An old woman is responsible?' She forced the words to sound easy and stood with her back against the wood. 'You saw her?'

Miranda had hoped her grandmother had stayed hidden when the ruffians had taken the man, much like when she was approached.

'Her age won't make any difference to the rope. Nor to me. And she *was* the culprit. No doubt about that.'

He held out the ale. 'You need your strength. You must drink some of this, if you can stomach it.'

'For what?' She let the wall hold her up.

'Escape. How long have you been here?'

'I was put in yesterday, but one minute is too long. I cannot remain in this cage.'

He held the bottle out to her after pouring in more

water, but she refused it with a wave before interlacing her fingers in front of her. 'I want as far from here as possible.'

Miranda didn't know what to do. Last night, she'd been afraid. Terrified when he'd been tossed into the room. But now she wasn't. Perhaps some, but not as much as she had been.

He kept to the other side of the room and she stayed on her side.

'What happened to the wealth you had?' he asked.

'It's still there. I'm not.' She held her shoulders prim.

'So you don't want to talk of your past.' He grunted. 'That's telling.'

'That's *not telling.*'

'Call it what you wish. It doesn't matter, though.' He changed the subject. 'All that matters is the settling up. In my studies, I was taught the old saying that before you start on a journey of revenge, dig two graves. This is the only time in my life I feel the extra grave would be worth it.'

# Chapter Three

Miranda understood—had understood since she'd been given away as a child—that her life wasn't to be normal.

But this was surpassing her expectations.

Before her, with an ale bottle in his hand, stood a man who overpowered the room. As the filtered light increased, the space inside the room lessened. The man didn't realise how much space he used with just the simplest movements.

She glanced around, trying to remember the past. The room had seemed bigger. In her memories, the cottage with the old gamekeeper and her grandmother had seemed big enough for the three of them and a fine home. Now it seemed so small and cramped.

The table and chairs were gone. There had also been a little stool for the gamekeeper's feet. And a chest that they'd stored things in and sometimes sat on.

She gulped. The bed. Oh, heavens, she knew what her grandmother had in mind. She pretended not to see the only furniture in the room besides the stump.

Her grandmother had said she would be bringing a husband.

She doubted the man had realised her grandmother's matchmaking methods. They were faulty. At best.

Now her companion shoved against the door, the windows, and tested the walls. He disappeared into the other room for what seemed to be an hour before returning.

After he'd examined the room three times and tried to push through the boards over the windows, he fixed his attention on the door.

'I assume we've dispensed with the proper manners we have learned since birth and they don't apply,' he said, 'as I would like assistance with the door.'

Spotting the broken shard from the bottle bottom lying beside the bed, she retrieved it, tossing the broken glass into the pile he'd made of the other pieces. 'I suppose that fledgling left the nest when I tried to knock you senseless.'

'Based on that, I'm trusting you have strength. Together we might be able to break the door.' He appraised her with a judgmental glance. 'We must get out.'

His hair hung uncombed around his eyes. The lashes rimming them could have made him attractive, she supposed, and the smudges under them gave him a reckless air. But the sharp nose, the unshaven face and the harsh mouth took away any appearance of gentleness. She could not imagine humour on his face. Or peacefulness. This man's face blended with the disarray of his clothing, although perhaps the day before both had belonged in a different world.

Now, his shirt tail had escaped his waistband, leaving behind the wrinkles to prove its former tidiness, and hanging to the length of his coat.

It should have taken away from him. Made him look worn. Instead his square jaw and determined stance made him seem bigger, stronger and more determined.

* * *

He moved to the door, pushing, shoving again, then stopping to take another drink.

She could sense him reining in his fury. His eyes had darkened and the lines forming at his mouth didn't make the slaking of his thirst seem refreshing. Instead, he appeared to be building his power so he could achieve his goal.

He moved to the door. 'Do you have any strength remaining?'

'Of course.'

'Let's try to move it.' He beckoned to her.

She watched as he hefted a shoulder near the door and positioned his legs for thrust. The sight shook her. By the way his trousers tightened, he had more muscle in one thigh than she had in her whole body. Her eyes skittered away from him, but her mind remained locked around the image of him poised to knock away the wood. A fortress of restrained power and muscle.

'Shall we?'

She heard impatience in his voice and a summons.

Miranda didn't think a man had ever viewed her so directly. But in a room of this size, he could do little else.

Quickly, she moved to the door and leaned her shoulder against it. She put both hands tentatively on the wood. His presence behind her, out of her sight, magnified him. Maleness and strength and she felt a hand claim her waist, sending bolts of warmth throughout her body. She froze. He pulled her so her frame stood at a right angle to the door. He didn't release her.

'You'll need to get some hip into it as well.' His voice rumbled over her shoulder and he moved a hand to her hip, an impersonal guide which caused every bone in her body to tense.

'Of course.' She pressed her hands tight. 'I'm waiting.'

'I'll count to three.' His hand lingered, but his voice was so matter of fact she wondered if he knew he still pressed against her. 'At the sound of one, you'll sway towards the door slightly.' His fingers applied slight pressure when he said 'one'. 'Then at two, you'll sway in again.' He pressed, then released her. 'At three we'll give it our all.'

She gave a quick nod of her head, trying to keep her concentration on the door and not her reaction to his hand. She'd not pulled her mind away from him resting his grasp on her hip. The grip was lighter than what one might feel from a waltz, but much more personal.

'One.' Pause. 'Two.' Pause. 'Three.' The words hit her mind and pulled her back to the task.

She pushed with all her might. Nothing happened. No creak. No groan—except from her arms.

'Again,' he commanded and they repeated the movement. She heard his curse. 'No use. The door and the boards over the window have been reinforced.'

All these words were spoken into her back and his voice deepened, closer to her ear.

'The door is old.' She examined the wood, then stepped away from it and watched him.

'Except the way it is placed.' He pointed to two marred edges where hinges had been removed. 'It was taken off and moved to open to the outside. So, a bar could be placed across it to keep prisoners inside. This wasn't an idle abduction. At least—the planning of it wasn't.'

That didn't surprise her. Her grandmother always had a plan. Or a machination and then a lie to go with it. Lies. Plans. Anything.

After her grandmother had left her at the road, Miranda had had to have the difference between lies and truths explained to her. Several times. But, finally, she understood. The rule that her grandmother had told her had been false—that truth usually brought bad luck with it.

He placed his knee against the door, flattened his palms, and shoved. He grunted and heaved, bringing the coat tight against his shoulders, surprising her that the seams didn't burst. But the wood still didn't budge.

Miranda put a calming hand on his shoulder. Even through his clothes, the heat of his anger burned her hand, but she stood firm.

He whirled to face her. 'I'll not let them get away with this. Particularly the old woman. She'll answer for this. She plotted this. I know it.'

'Why do you think that?'

He jerked his head towards the bed. 'When they were capturing me, they said she'd been planning this for a time. Had a bed for me. She checked the strength on my arm. It was as if she was making sure I was a right fit for the bed.' Anger flared in his eyes. 'Her neck will be a good fit for the noose.'

Miranda stepped back. Fear plunged in her. She could imagine her grandmother hanging from a scaffold.

She saw the instant he read the emotions on her face.

He raised both his palms slowly. 'I didn't mean—' He took half a step back, placing him against the wall. 'I didn't mean to frighten you. Forgive me.'

She nodded. He flattened himself against the door again, one knee raised so his boot rested against it and purposely bumped his head on to the wood.

'Truly...' his voice had a deep tiredness. He stared forward '...the captivity has taken my freedom as well as my mind. To be caged.' His voice lowered. 'And I don't even know why I'm here. I perceived I'd angered someone—

which made sense, of a sort. But now I'm convinced it is the possibility of a ransom that connects us.'

He took a few seconds before speaking 'I've been gathering support for funds to improve our water systems. Do you have any ties there?'

She glanced down, thinking, then raised her head. 'No. I am more orphan than not since the woman who took me in died. Her husband was pleased to see the last of me. I have not heard from him since I became a governess.'

To speak such personal things. Things she had never voiced before and say them to a stranger surprised her, but he didn't even appear to notice anything unusual about them.

'I can't understand it.' His brow furrowed. 'The criminals acted as if—'

She saw him study her.

And she relived her grandmother's words—speaking as if she would bring Miranda a husband. 'What did the abductors say to you?' she asked. 'How did they act?'

'The old woman pinched me. She seemed to want to check my health.' He tapped a quick blow to his own shoulder where she'd clenched it. 'I might have assumed I was in a fable, about to be poured into a pot for a beast.'

Again, he examined her. He touched his lip. A small cut. 'I wasn't to be *mangled.* And she worried about the time it would take me to heal.'

Miranda used both hands to push her hair back towards her bun. The heat and the exertion had made her hair frazzle, tickling her face, and amazement filtered into her voice.

'She...pinched you?' Miranda bit the inside of her lip. 'And seemed concerned about your...safety?'

She remembered how her mother had told her time and time again about the wondrous fortune-teller.

Miranda's mother never forgot the day when she'd had her palm read and been told that her childlessness would end. Some day soon she'd have a child in her life and she must accept and love it as her own.

The old woman saw the future so well that she'd predicted a little girl just like Miranda would some day appear. Her mother's husband had scoffed at such nonsense, then, then, not one week later, on the way home from Sunday services, Miranda was sitting beside the road, lost and sobbing.

One day, when her mother was repeating the story, Miranda realised exactly what her grandmother had done. She'd picked out a family for her. A woman who would keep a child left sobbing and alone.

No one had claimed her and they'd not been able to find her parents. Just as the fortune-teller had claimed. Miranda was a miracle, her mother insisted. A gift. And she'd refused to hear of anything else.

Miranda never told her new mother that her grandmother's palm reading was a trade she thrived at and that she'd placed her granddaughter beside the road, telling her about the toys she'd some day have.

That had been true.

Now, she comprehended that an unsuspecting husband had been selected for her.

He stood before her, glowering, and she again clasped her fingers together.

'Miss—' His eyes darkened and his voice softened, as if he was trying to take away the sting from what he might impart. 'We can't stay here waiting to find out what's in store. For all we know, a third person might be added. We can escape from this dungeon, I know it.'

He went to the broken bottle, took a hunk of the thick

glass and walked to the door. He knelt down and chipped away where the door and the frame joined.

Despair invaded her. She would never be allowed to be a governess to Dolly and Willie again. Their father often complained about how untrustworthy servants were. She had only obtained the position because of her father's ties to society. If her employer ever found out who her grandmother was, and what was happening, she would be tossed from the house. She would lose Willie and Dolly. And their next governess might be someone unworthy.

But no one could tie her in to her grandmother. No one could—as long as her grandmother wasn't apprehended and didn't talk.

She'd not told Nicky or anyone else that her grandmother was said to be dying. And the words the culprit had told had been a lie. It would be no untruth if she told everyone later that she'd been misled into going with the man. That he'd claimed a member of her family was dying and she'd believed it.

She could survive this secret, if she was released soon.

She would explain to the man with her that she could lose her position in life. Her reputation could be ruined.

All she needed to do was get them free and get them free quickly. She could return to Mr Trevor—he was a kind man, if distracted at times. And he would let her remain with the children.

Without the haze of fear disrupting her, and with hope growing, she examined the man with her.

Yes, he would be exactly what her grandmother would choose.

Likely, her grandmother would have chosen him for his boots alone. Her grandmother had once told her that she often charged fees based on the footwear of the prey. Said that was why she always wore old boots, which was nonsense. But her grandmother could assess people in an instant.

Miranda glanced again at him. Yes, she could easily see him being chosen based on his clothing. And his form.

He would likely not take it well to find out he was part of her grandmother's scheme.

'I'll get you to safety.' His voice calmed her, and she stared into his eyes and knew he would fight to save her; she just hoped later he didn't fight nearly so hard to find out who had kidnapped him, then throw her into gaol.

The sooner they escaped the better. She had to find a way to get them out. She paced, keeping far from him, which didn't give her room to manoeuvre.

'Miss…' his voice held exasperation while he used the glass to chip at the door frame '…might you be still for a few moments?'

She stopped and propped herself against the wall, her arms crossed over her chest. She pressed her hands to her temples to brush back the hair which had loosened. 'I have nothing else to do but pace and try to think of a way to get us out.'

'I understand.'

He stood, leaving the glass on the floor, and he braced his hands on his knees and bent, stretching, then raising and rotating his shoulders.

At the window, she tried to pull the boards apart enough to see out. Her grandmother was out there somewhere, perhaps even just beyond the window.

She could feel it.

He just couldn't stop moving either.

'Your employer must appreciate your inability to be still. You likely get much more work done than anyone else,' she observed.

He stopped. In the dim light, his eyes found her, sitting now at the side of the bed. 'I was born with this air. Did you gain yours from your employment?'

She took a deep breath, aware of the scent of ale and the overbearing heat.

'I'm a governess, but I was raised in a wealthy home. I just always knew I wasn't born into that life of privilege. And now I am trapped with a man such as—'

'A man such as…me?' One brow rose.

She couldn't tell him he was likely to be someone her grandmother had seen, decided on, then set about altering his life.

'You're rather proud.'

'If you say so.'

He stood, a wall inside the room. 'And you know nothing of this you haven't shared with me?'

She saw the challenge in his stance.

Her mouth opened and she contemplated him. 'I've done nothing to give anyone reason to do such a thing.' The word almost sounded like an admission of guilt to her ears.

He interrupted her—seemingly unmoved by her less-than-pleasurable glance his direction. 'You don't have any reason why you could have attracted unsavoury attention?'

She didn't want to tell him her true past. He had no right to know.

'The man who raised me isn't poor. He has always allowed me to call him Father, but it is because he thinks it makes him appear more benevolent. Besides, his first wife insisted I call her Mother shortly after they took me in. She was more than a mother to me—a near saint— but she passed on.'

Soon after her mother died, her father almost completely moved out of his country estate, until he remarried.

The man waited for her to continue.

'My father would prefer not to hear from me more than from a vast distance and my stepmother considers no location is far enough away.'

She moved to sit at the foot of the bed, back stiff and arms crossed. They could have been an ocean apart.

She watched him from the corner of her eye. He threw his head back, starting another stretch. A long, slow unfurling stretch which almost took him to where she was sitting, although he was careful not to let his arm drift close to her.

'If you change your mind about me and decide to attack again…' he said. 'I'd prefer a slap.'

'You'd likely break my hand.'

She turned away. She couldn't face him. 'It is just nonsense. A folly by a person who is mad…' She let her voice trail away. She felt words on the tip of her tongue. But this time, she had a memory trying to form in her mind and she couldn't grasp it.

He waited. The wait of someone holding themselves in check—ready to pounce at any provocation.

She stole a glance at him, afraid he could read the truth in her face that she was hiding something. 'But my father does have holdings,' she admitted, straightening the folds of her skirt. 'He's wealthy enough.'

Let him suppose this happened for ransom, but Miranda understood her grandmother's ways. A grandmother with no scruples was worse than any determined matchmaking mama. She'd tossed Miranda out once, securing her a mother. Now, she intended to secure her a mate.

'Ransom, I suppose.' He returned to his pacing. 'Why risk a noose for only one crime? Get two and save time. More rewards.'

She squinted at the pitiful ceiling. 'But my stepmother

would not pay a pence to recover me. She would never let Father do that.'

'The kidnapper is likely not to know what your family is like. And you can't know your father won't pay a ransom.'

She dropped her shoulders. 'Doesn't the fact that I am a governess tell the world something?'

'It may have just made you appear easier to nab.'

'And why were you so easy to take?'

'I tend to walk the same path most days. I had planned to stay a little while with my cousin. I had wished my mother a happy birthday and her friends had arrived to spend the night. The house became a big burst of perfumes and pomades and powders. So, I decided to be elsewhere. No one has likely even noticed I'm gone. I told the butler not to expect me home that night.'

*Butler?* Oh, that did not sound good.

The fear inside her blossomed into anger. Her grandmother's plans were evil. It was wrong to twist around her granddaughter's life. And doubly wrong to twist around strangers' lives.

'We must get out of here.' He stretched yet again, his fingertips touching the ceiling.

His next words lacked emotion. 'I just want to kill them.'

From the look in his eyes, she believed him. 'That's wrong. It's unjust. You will hold them steady while I slap them senseless and, when I am finished, you can do the same, then they can go to gaol.'

'You would not want them punished?'

'I might.' She challenged him with her face. 'I did not get to be this old without learning trust is not to be given to many. Some people start out cruel and never transform as they age, except to become worse.'

'How old are you?'

She raised an eyebrow and gave him her governess's mischief-stopping stare. 'My age is not your concern.'

'Twenty-one,' he guessed.

She didn't speak or acknowledge him.

A dash of mischief slipped out from between overdone innocence in his eyes. 'Twenty-seven?'

She glanced over her shoulder. 'Somewhere around those numbers. This parlour game is not freeing us.'

He again sat on the bed and the dip in it caused by his movements jostled her. The man overwhelmed her, yet deep inside his presence comforted. He wouldn't wish to harm her, yet she stiffened instinctively. She'd never been on a bed with a man. Ever.

He glanced at her with the same boredom her charges would have. 'I'm not reaching for you, Miss—Governess. Nor,' he added with a hint of too much sweetness, 'do I plan to.' Humour lingered in his voice. 'If I recall correctly, you are the only one with those inclinations.'

The words reassured her, even with the not-so-hidden barb. They were on the same side and she would try to find a way to get them released.

With her fear of him gone, she studied the cottage. She put her palm to the back of her neck and absently pushed up tendrils to the knot of her hair.

When she focused on him, the steadiness of his perusal startled her. She wagered she could put a hand over her ring and, if asked, he could tell her she wore a small silver band with a blue sapphire in it.

She couldn't place his origins in her mind. He had mentioned a ransom and his clothes did have quality about them. But he didn't have the refinement, to her eye, of the guests who had visited the mansion she lived in. No, she could never see this man taking tea with Willie's father, or even sharing a brandy or game of cards.

Gamblers sometimes wore fine clothes, she knew. Tradesmen who'd done well. Even some of the lower classes sometimes managed to afford well-made clothing. But he'd mentioned a butler.

'How do you make your way in life?' she asked.

He levelled a gaze at her. 'I manage properties.'

'I suspected your boots were of high quality.'

'I am thankful not to have been wearing inferior clothing and embarrass you or the criminals who took me.' Even though his eyes showed a hint of humour, the upturn of his lips showed none. He glanced at his feet. 'I never knew how much attention a pair of boots brought. I just had them made and my friends hardly noticed them. I am used to my hats being noticed. But my boots are simply functional.'

He rose, stretching his legs and tapping his feet against the floor as if to get blood flowing. 'Superior ones, though.' At the wall, he leaned against the structure, propping himself into a restful position.

He studied her and she could see the moment the question formed.

'Your name?' he asked.

'I am usually called Governess.' She kept herself firm. Once, she'd only been called Child. She dwelled on her mother asking for her name, and she'd answered Child. She'd cried when her mother had kept insisting that she had another name, as if something was wrong with Child.

Then her mother had quietened and said Miranda could have two names. Or three, or four. Several days later she had asked Miranda if that name would suit her. Miranda would have agreed to any name at that point.

'Does Miss Governess have another name?' He spoke sweetly—too sweetly.

'Miss Manwaring.' Her eyes tightened at the corners. 'And your name?'

He didn't answer her question, seeming surprised that she didn't know him. 'Will anyone be searching for you?'

'Perhaps my employer, but I cannot see him devoting much effort to it. He might contact my father—but if he does so, he will likely be told he is better for the loss.'

'Parents don't always see the joy of having children. My mother calls me Chal.' He peered at her. 'And she says it suits me because I can be a bit of a challenge. But most people call me Chalgrove.'

'Thank you, Mr Chalgrove.'

He studied her more closely than Willie did when he was planning something irritating. He ducked his head and raised it after erasing an abashed grin. 'You have put me decidedly in my place, Miss Manwaring. I, perhaps, deserved it.'

She paused. He seemed to think she should know him, yet he'd not even given her his surname, only a nickname his mother called him.

'The name sounds familiar, Mr Chalgrove.' He must be one of her employer's friends or her father's. 'But I'm afraid I don't recall our meeting.'

One side of his lips twisted up. 'I'm certain our paths haven't crossed or I would recollect it. I've given you two options, which is more than I give most people. Chal or Chalgrove. And you can leave the mister off.' He took the command out of his words with a smile. 'You choose.'

'I will not address you…' She widened her eyes. 'Unless I must. And then I will make my choice. I suppose if we are friends I can call you Chalgrove.'

'You are hanging tightly to those manners, aren't you?'

'No.' She made a tossing movement towards the window. 'They're gone.'

'Thank you for accommodating me. I had suspected that would be impossible for you shortly after you swung the bottle at me.'

'I was simply not thinking correctly. I hope to mend that and to thank you for softening the blow. The bottle will never be the same and my arm still aches.' She rubbed her arm. 'You jarred me and nearly knocked me off my feet.'

She saw his mouth relax and maybe a hint of humour, real humour, hid behind his eyes.

'My pardon,' he said. 'Any time you need my shoulder, it is here for you.' The silence grew. 'Even if you've a weapon in your hand.'

# Chapter Four

The day passed with the same joy of being trapped in a July blacksmith's forge. The silence grated on Chalgrove's nerves like the screech of iron pieces grating together and the heat mounted as the sun rose to the centre of the sky.

With a shard of broken glass, he chipped away at the edge of the wall and the door, trying to find a weak spot or make one.

As the day wore on, he swore Miss Manwaring's eyes got more luminous and her lips moistened. He blamed it on the heat, justly, he supposed. But the temperature shouldn't make her more appealing. She should melt.

Instead, she'd taken a scrap of white fabric which had to have been torn from an undergarment and was using it to fan her face.

He'd seen female undergarments tossed here and there, but this one that he couldn't see caught his attention. A plain piece of white cloth with ripped edges. He imagined her ripping the chemise, expending anger and frustration on to the fabric.

His thoughts stopped, attached to a scrap of material. A chemise he'd never seen. It was no more than stitched white cloth, with a little tear in it. Soft from washings. Warm from body heat. Plain.

His hand slipped off the glass and crashed against the wood.

He stopped his oath in the middle of the word, took in a deep breath and weighed his next sentence. He'd not been raised to speak such in front of women and his father had taught him that tempering his language was a sign of strength.

'My thoughts, exactly,' she said. 'Although I am not speaking them.'

'Might make you feel better.'

'No. It wouldn't. It would only make me angrier. I've tried it. I keep my anger all tamped down inside me and usually let it out and scrub it away when I'm bathing. The other servants think I'm an extremely serene woman who is overly concerned with cleanliness.' She sighed. 'There is not enough bath water in the world for this.'

'True.'

He studied the planks in front of him and realised he needed to tamp down all the visions of her bathing even further than he'd hidden the chemise images or he might accidentally cut off a finger.

He needed a horseback ride or a long walk…those were his ways of working out the imaginations he needed to keep in control.

His fist slammed against the wall again when his hand slipped a second time.

'Perhaps you should put that aside for now,' she suggested.

'I'll take more care.'

He had to. For her sake, if for no other reason. And there was an extra grave he needed to dig. But, first, he had to catch the culprits who'd trapped him and this woman.

That was not revenge. It was justice. No one should ever scare Miss Manwaring. It wasn't right. But she was handling it well. Not cowering in the corner or crying or screaming. It almost seemed as if she were mentally digging a grave as well.

If it weren't for the snap of her wrist and the set of her jaw, he might assume she felt no discomfort.

The heat did uncover more of her, but not on the outside. She didn't complain, reek of perfumes gone stale, or droop in an unbecoming way. True, her clothing wilted on her, bringing more of her shape into view.

He forced his mind on to the task and continued picking away at the wood. He'd made a small notch in it, nothing to be proud of, but he could not sit idle. The movement helped ease him. What else had he to do? Otherwise, he'd think of the chemise. The woman sitting with her back straight. And the way her clothing softened around her, bringing out curves and femininity and he angered even more that he hadn't, in some way, protected her.

She should not have been taken. He should have made the streets safer somehow.

She stood and stamped her foot, and began another search of the room.

He could tell by her movements she'd not cinched her corset tightly. She wore it for propriety's sake and not because she wished to attract attention. She wasn't bursting at the seams of her dress—she was hiding her body neatly inside, or so she supposed. Prim and proper to the core. Cleansing all her unkind inclinations away and tidying the very best ones and attiring herself in them as if she awakened pure as an angel each morning.

He closed his eye and rubbed fingertips over it. Inside

his head, he unleashed a string of the most vile profanities that he could think of.

Then he placed the glass on the floor and examined the room again. Letting the woman distract him wasn't going to help either of them. But how could he ignore her?

'Your pacing isn't helping,' he said. 'It'll only tire you and you might need all your strength to escape.'

She waved his words away and kept walking.

'You're exasperating me,' he claimed.

'I know,' she mumbled, stopping in front of him, bringing the scent of lavender to him. 'I'm paid to be annoying.' Her voice sounded different now. More human. 'It's how I earn my keep. Don't complain. It makes nothing better.'

'Do those words work for the children?'

'At night, I tell Dolly the angels need their rest as well, so she must be still to make their watching over her easier. I tell the boy a devil lies under his bed and if Willie steps one foot out before morning, he'll get pulled into Hades.'

'You do?' He stilled, examining her face.

'No. I only think it,' she spoke wistfully. 'I tell him we will have questions if he does not fall asleep. I do love him dearly, even if...' Her brows and lips rose at the same time. 'He is so unpredictable, and can be a...a challenge.'

'And I supposed I was the exception.' He noted the sunshine in her voice when she spoke of the children. 'Questions? What questions do you ask your little charge?'

Even though the walls surrounded them, when she spoke, they faded away.

'In what year was the Bank of England founded?' she queried, eyes narrowed.

'You ask a child this?'

'1694.' She rushed ahead. 'You should pay attention to your studies. Who became the Tsar of Russia in 1689?'

'Peter the Great.'

The room didn't seem so forbidding and the space enclosed them in a companionable way. 'He always answers that one correctly as well. I tell him Peter the Great was over six and a half feet tall and, when he travelled, he used someone's stomach for a pillow. Willie loves to think about a rumbling pillow. And the tsar's cane he thumped people with. Although I don't think I should have ever told him about the cane. He decided he wished to be the tsar of Russia.'

'You're a governess, not a tutor. How did you learn such things?'

'Books. My father read a lot. And he exchanged books with friends and I would often read them as well. I could read quickly and he likely didn't notice me even borrowing them.'

She walked the room, testing each board he'd already tried dozens of times, searching for an escape.

If he could get only a few boards loose, she would be small enough to crawl out to unlatch the door from the other side.

'Any progress?' she asked, wiping her brow.

'Little.' He leaned against the wall. His back ached. His shoulders. His knees. The ale had helped, but the effects were fading.

He studied the wood, combing for anything he might have missed before, but the shadows of her movements caught his eye.

He'd watched her pat her bun every few minutes, straightening her hair like some sort of spinster crown, with a little shiny bauble in it. She didn't want her hair to be mussed—this governess who didn't seem a woman who would let a man take out the pins and let her dark hair fall to her shoulders. He would say she'd never been kissed, but with those lips, he knew she had.

She stalked the walls of the room, still searching for an escape. She paced, two to three steps, then ran her fingers over the wall. Paced again, examining lower or higher after the next few steps. He wondered if her hands had stroked each surface of the walls several times.

And if he watched the liquid grace of her hands moving over the wood, his body stirred with arousal.

He'd not slept since before his capture. The hours of being awake, the imprisonment and the woman in the room with him made him aware of his back being against the wall. It wasn't just the physical action of it, but the little currents of air and thought and circumstance that forced him to contemplate every strand of sight and movement that he could take in.

He understood one feeling that hadn't entered his consciousness before. Somehow, this woman, seemingly no stronger than a puff of wind, comforted him.

No one comforted him. Not by words or actions. Perhaps a strong drink might brace him, or a forceful word might send someone scurrying from his sight, but no one had ever comforted him because he didn't need it. He didn't need it now. He would deal with the circumstances he could control and withstand the rest.

She was the one to be reassured.

'I will get us out of this. I will do it,' he said.

She stopped. Stared. Concentration firm. Her head moved closer. 'The door is barred. So are the windows.'

'I know that full well. I just want to assure you that I was taken by surprise. That was my error. But, be that as it may, you needn't concern yourself.'

She crossed her arms, and tucked her chin under. 'The door is closed.'

'It's just a door. Wood. It will give way. Eventually. Then I will see justice done.'

She perched on the edge of the bed and stared at the window. 'I'd rather have a good axe right now than justice.' She faced him again. 'A hammer even.'

'I am not particularly handy with tools, but I could use a weapon. We will be out within twenty-four hours. I will see to it.'

She blinked twice. 'Could you perhaps go for twelve?'

In answer, he blinked twice, and somehow felt relieved that the solace he'd found in her presence had turned into an irritation.

He smiled. 'I will take your suggestion into account.'

He had to get some rest soon, or he would be picking an argument with his shadow.

Striding to the so-called window, he checked again that the boards had been reinforced from the outside many times over.

He had to get them out soon. It would be hard for his family to gather money. His mother knew nothing about the family finances. She didn't even know the name of his man of affairs.

'It's against the law to pay a ransom,' he said. 'Though I hardly think a kidnapper would concern herself with that.'

'I don't think she wants funds. I think it's more about… some kind of justice.'

'I could see myself angering someone, many times over. But you?' he asked, then waited. 'Whom do you think you angered?'

Miranda comprehended that she was being scrutinised. She stared at him from her resting place on the bed. 'I try not to anger anyone.'

'You've kept one secret from me…' Chalgrove resumed his efforts to whittle away the wood '…which I think you should share.'

She didn't wish to know his next question, but she didn't want to hide from it. She waited.

'What do you know that you're not telling me? You're aware of more than you're saying.'

She reminded herself of her promise not to lie. 'Nothing to get us out of here any sooner,' she said.

With the merest movement of his eyes, he acknowledged her response and she could see the transformation inside him reflected on his face. Distrust.

The man she gazed at now was as stalwart as a fortress and his compassion would only be meted out as he decided it was deserved. And she saw none for her, but she didn't lower her chin.

'Fair enough.' Almost a bow without moving more than a few muscles. 'For the time being.'

He moved to the bed frame and, in the light, she took him in. Noticing more than she'd seen before.

His feet were bare now and she didn't think they'd ever been without stockings. But it didn't diminish him. Only demonstrated the sinew and skin beneath the clothing. And perhaps the rawness. The animal part of him that was comfortable without adornment.

The cords of his feet weren't attractive by any means. More—almost primitive. And she realised she'd never seen a man's bare foot before. Never. But she liked the appearance of them. They were more different from her own than she would have suspected.

She repositioned herself, then found a place to sit on the edge of the stump. 'You can rest if you wish. You've been striding back and forth. There's so little room in here, it only takes you about one step before you reverse direction.'

He grasped his coat, removing it. Taking off the waistcoat. Shoving the tails of his shirt back into place, which didn't help much. Then he sat on the bed.

He stretched across the bed, from the top to the opposite corner, and she saw he was totally unconcerned about her presence. His posture was the only way the bed could accommodate his length without his feet hanging from the end.

His back to her, he grasped her pillow, curled it into his arms and relaxed.

She felt certain he fell instantly asleep. The way he breathed, rhythmic, calm.

His muscular arms encased the soft ball of feathers and he kept the pillow tight.

The man didn't appear gentler asleep, but more like a spring ready to uncoil at the slightest sound or movement.

She scrutinised him, the well-made clothing he wore hugging him like a second skin. No peacefulness softened his face, but it was easier to examine him when he wasn't aware.

In the dim light, the shadows darkened the beginning of a beard even more.

The man her grandmother had captured for her was becoming primitive.

They had to escape.

She had to escape.

She was losing her strength and he was gaining it. Even as she watched him sleep, she understood that he was doing so to gather his resources. He would awake solid and more potent than before.

## Chapter Five

The singing voice came from just outside the boarded window.

Chalgrove was at Miranda's side before she knew he'd moved.

She shut her eyes, but when she opened them, her grandmother stood, staring between the slats of the window.

'Ah, Child,' the old woman spoke to Miranda. 'How do you like being my guest?'

Miranda stared, seeing the aged eyes of her grandmother, the wrinkles around them surprising her, but anger overrode it. 'May the sins of your past rise up and may you never shut your eyes without seeing the faces of those you've wronged.'

'But, then,' the old woman sang again, 'do you think I might be seeing your face? I think not.'

'You would see my face every moment you are awake.'

The old woman laughed. 'Shame. Shame, Child, to speak such to your elders. And you teach the little children, but you know nothing.' She fluttered her ringed fingers. 'Nothing at all.'

Miranda felt Chalgrove moving forward.

She grabbed his arm with both hands, then threw her body between him and the window.

'How could you do this vile thing to me? To him?' Miranda choked the words out when she frowned at the old woman's face. 'You're vile. Evil.'

'No, Child. That is not my name,' she mused. 'Have you forgotten it? But does it really matter?' Then she straightened her posture and laughed. 'Vile. I'll take it. I like that word. I should use it on my calling cards. Besides, I care for you like no one else.'

'You're a menace. You're—'

'And who are you, miss?' eyes flashing, her grandmother asked. 'I nabbed a woman of quality, but before me, you stand as if you would like to tear out my heart. That is not the way you were taught. I am sure of it. The woman who raised you did better than that. She would have been embarrassed at the sight of you now, yesterday and last year, too. You take the table crumbs when you should have the feast.'

'How I live is not your concern.' Miranda lunged for the window, but the old crone moved away.

Miranda kept staring at the window. 'Let us go. You've taken me from my employment. You've stolen this man from his family. You've hurt people who've done you no harm.'

'Have a care, Child. I do only good for you. I am a matchmaker. Besides, the stars told me to do this. And I must always do as they say. Blame them.'

Miranda reached down with her free hand, lifted her foot and pulled off the buckled slipper. She held her right arm aloft and hurled the makeshift weapon towards the woman's head at the window. It bounced from the wall.

The face disappeared for a few seconds, before returning to view her, glowering. 'Ungrateful.'

'The poor souls in Bedlam are less daft than you,' Miranda shouted to her grandmother.

She removed her other shoe, but held it in her hand, pointing the toe at the old woman. 'You must release us. You have no right to keep us. At least release him, then you and I will talk.'

'I cannot release either of you. Not yet. I have to see that you fulfil your destiny.'

'What destiny?' Chalgrove spoke.

The old woman ignored him, and Miranda did as well.

The hag used the same gesture as Miranda, pointing a finger towards them. 'That slipper is better than any I have ever worn. You should thank the person who caused you to have such fine garments.'

'I do. I thank my mother.'

'Your mother?' The crone's brows lifted. 'The lady did right by you, but then she went and did that evil thing. She died. I cannot forgive her. Then you became a little mouse who skitters into the corner of life and will not take as she should. You give everything away. Even your life as you spend it behind doors with someone else's children.'

'They are precious, the children. I love them with all my heart.'

'They are someone else's. Now, toss the slippers out so I might see what fine things you wear. The opening is wide enough you can push them through.'

'Come retrieve them.' Miranda didn't lower her arm.

Chalgrove tugged Miss Manwaring closer. Then he freed her waist and grasped for the shoe, but she twisted, keeping it firm in her hand.

It would not do well for both women to be throwing shoes at each other.

Miss Manwaring lunged within Chalgrove's reach, then

threw the shoe, making the old woman dodge again. The shoe bounced from the wall.

'See what a prim and proper miss you are.' The old woman's lips pinched and she held a slender loaf of bread at the window. 'Are you hungry?'

The scent of fresh-baked bread wafted to him.

'Toss it here.' Chalgrove leaned forward, taking it with his left hand as the old woman slipped the food towards him. He kept Miss Manwaring in his grasp.

'The fine life you've had didn't make you strong,' the woman shouted to Miranda 'Made you weak. You're little more than a flower growing among the grass. You should be a rose, a thistle, anything high and proud. Not on the ground for feet to step on.'

Chalgrove tossed the bread on to the stump and Miss Manwaring slipped from his grasp and rushed to the window.

The old woman moved away.

Miss Manwaring gripped her shoe again, hand shaking, and Chalgrove hoped the old woman didn't step closer. Right now, it wouldn't be in their best interest for the governess to try to knock out the old woman.

He pulled Miss Manwaring away from the window.

The woman squinted at Chalgrove. 'What happened to your face? Did those clods do that? I will kill them.'

He patted the scratches Miss Manwaring had made.

'Kill them,' he answered without hesitation. He snugged Miss Manwaring close again. The woman was practically writhing against him in an effort to push herself towards the other so she might try to thump her with a shoe. This was not how he would have planned an encounter with her. This was not comforting.

'Miss Manwaring.' He tried to pull the shoe from her

hand and she moved her shoulder, and used her body as a shield, keeping him from taking the shoe.

They stood, bodies locked together, a silent struggle, and the old woman… The old woman smiled.

'The lady is correct,' he said. 'We need to be released. We have families.'

'Ha!' she sputtered. 'She has no family. She cares for children who are not her own, knowing any day she could be dismissed. Never sitting under the sun—the stars. Never leaving her prison except on her half-day off to buy sweets.'

Miss Manwaring gasped. 'You've been following me.'

The old woman muttered, 'You never check behind you. You should.'

He tightened his grasp, trying to calm Miranda, sliding his arm to her back, and pulled her close.

'Woman,' he spoke. 'Might you introduce yourself?'

She scrutinised him. 'I'm telling you nothing.'

'Why would you risk so much to kidnap us?' he asked.

'I cannot tell you all.' She laughed again. 'But no one tells all. The miss in your hand, she has her secrets as well.'

'She is entitled. We all are.'

'Then I am entitled to my own.' The crone's eyes twinkled between the slats, then her expression hardened. 'I didn't want this burden. It's not how I planned it.'

She peered overhead, speaking to the heavens. 'Twenty-odd years ago, I finished my chore. I carefully planned. I read the fortunes. Oh, so many. Asking questions of everyone. Finding out all I could.' She made a rumbling noise from her throat that would have sounded like a snore if she'd been asleep. 'Then, the little miss… She cares for others' children instead of her own. This I didn't foresee.'

'My mother took care of me,' Miranda cried out. 'I find no fault with her. I made my choices.'

The old woman sputtered. 'Lies. Lies. You lie to yourself. You're supposed to lie only to others. You are to tell yourself truths. You have it all backwards.'

'I do not. I do not lie. To anyone. I do not lie to myself.'

'The rich ways you are around make you weak and dishonest to your birthright. You give away what you should have.'

'Step closer and you will see how weak I am.'

'Miss Manwaring.' This time Chalgrove pulled her so close that he lifted her from her feet for half a second and could feel the deep breaths she took even closer than his own. 'Can you please let me speak to the woman?'

She hushed and settled against him, and his senses reacted, unaware of anything but Miss Manwaring's softness.

He pushed the awareness aside and carefully moved away. 'Why have you done this?'

The old woman's face didn't waver. She raised her eyes to his. 'If you want to blame anyone, then…' She paused, sadness flittering in her eyes. 'Blame me. It's my doing. I'm daft. Born so and I've perfected it over the years.'

'You're not only addled, you are despicable,' Miss Manwaring interrupted. 'You would abandon—'

'My… My…child.' She nodded. 'Yes, I do good works. It is sad you do not have the eyes to see what is good and what is bad, and have them as mixed up as you do truth and lies.' The old woman moved away. 'I have more fresh bread for you. But you're not hungry.'

'I am,' Chalgrove said.

She pushed another chunk of bread into the window. Chalgrove released Miss Manwaring so he could slide forward enough to pull the loaf into the room, then he put it beside the other one on the stump.

'I'm not getting close enough for you to grab me,' she said to Chalgrove. 'Besides, I would still be on the outside and you would be on the inside and you would not be free. You must keep me alive for that.'

'How much ransom are you asking?' Chalgrove demanded.

'I ask for no payment from you. I give my riches to you,' she sneered. 'You think you wish to give me money? I will earn more than you could ever pay me.' She waved a hand around her head, as if giving a royal wave. 'You'll see.'

His fingers tightened at Miss Manwaring's waist, the caress seeming to calm her and to spark a need within him to protect her.

The old crone tilted her head sideways, censure in her voice. 'You two are both so haughty. Both so stubborn. Both a trial to me. But better together.'

'Explain.' He spoke softly, a thread of power underlining his words.

Her jaw went slack and the deep eyes studied him through the wooden slats. With one word, she argued, 'Haughty.'

'Yes. I agree,' he said.

'Meddling old witch,' Miranda mumbled.

'Miss Manwaring.' His quiet words fluttered the tendrils of hair at her ear. 'Might I speak with the woman? You can throw my boots at her afterwards, if you wish to.'

The crone cackled. 'Yes, little one. Your silence would be appreciated.'

'Manipulative. Conniving. Tossing people here and there just…' Miranda grumbled.

The old woman threw her head back, laughed. 'I am all you say and I thank you for the praise.'

'The buttons on my coat.' Chalgrove knew the gold would fetch a good price—though not as much as they were worth. He'd had them made with his coat of arms imprinted on them. They might be traced back to him. 'Take them. Sell them. Buy more food. You barely brought us enough for one meal.'

He reached out, secured his coat, ripped a button from the fabric and held it near the window. She reached in and he tossed the button into her palm. She quickly pulled her hand away.

'I'll take this one, but keep the rest in case I need them later.'

'You can have them all,' Chalgrove said.

The woman peered at them both through the slats. 'I don't want them. All I wish for is for my dreams for Child to come true. And they will. One way or another.' She fixed one eye on Chalgrove. 'When I am convinced that her true worth is recognised, I will set her free.'

'How much ransom is our true worth?' he asked.

She bit the end of her fingernail free and spat it to the ground. 'I said nothing about funds. Gold is heavy and weighs one down and banks can't be trusted with their paper nonsense.'

She stilled and tapped her fingers over her lips, eyes wide. 'I am losing my mind. I could have asked for a ransom. A small bag of gold isn't that heavy.' She took a step back, almost whispering. 'I am getting too kind-hearted.' Shaking her head, she reassured herself, 'No. I am getting old. That's all it is.'

She shrugged her shoulders. 'No ransom, but you may freely give me a gift. After she is betrothed.'

'Be…trothed?' He stared.

'Yes,' she said, head erect so that her face was impossible to see through the opening. 'I am a woman of herbs, of fortunes, revenge and kindness. It's time for her to wed. She's almost eighteen.'

'I am not almost eighteen. I am well over eighteen.'

'Shush,' she shouted the command. 'I'm going to get you a marriage proposal, but you must learn to keep your mouth shut.' She scowled at Chalgrove. 'So, she's twenty. We cannot hold a few years against her.'

'No,' Miranda called out. 'I'm over twenty.'

He clapped a hand over Miss Manwaring's mouth and captured her fist as she raised it towards the woman.

'It doesn't matter,' Chalgrove snapped out the words. Then he muttered in Miss Manwaring's ear, 'Let's not quarrel with her.'

The old woman peered in again. 'You're getting married, Child. It is all up to you how long it takes. When you come to your senses and you both agree, I will let you out.'

She turned away from the window and grumbled as she walked away. 'Why am I the only one who knows what is best for everyone? Now I will have to get more food. The stars are letting me down. Everyone hates me and I know more than anyone else.'

After the woman left, Chalgrove released Miss Manwaring, picked up her shoe, and handed it to her. 'What was that all about?'

'She kidnapped us. Both of us. What else could it be about?' She waved the shoe.

Chalgrove stared at the wan face in front of him. 'She wouldn't take the gold buttons on my coat.'

'She took one. She'll think about those other gold buttons and decide that she must have them, and return for them.'

He questioned her by raising his brows. 'We may need to see her again.'

'We will. A bad penny always returns.' Miss Manwaring hugged herself and he expected her to crumple in front of him. Instead, she jutted her chin out and held out the shoe towards him. 'I am a governess and I am unwed, and there is nothing wrong with that. I have the best life of anyone I know.' She stopped, scowled at the shoe, then continued. 'Until an old woman decided to take it all from me. And I'm really older than twenty and my age is no one's business but my own.'

He tried to see inside her, then he glanced to the window and scrubbed his knuckles against his unshaven jaw. The old woman had expected Miss Manwaring to remember her name and Miss Manwaring had claimed her right to secrets.

'Where did you first meet?'

'It was a long time ago. I was a child and I've not seen her since. She's so unsettled that she's been following me.' She closed her arms around herself. 'And I never suspected a thing.'

He had the feeling he'd been drawn into someone else's fight and wasn't sure which side of it he should be on.

The air chilled Miranda. She felt as alone as she had been when she didn't know what had happened to her grandmother and was worried about the big spiders in the woods. The time before her new mother told her that she would always have a place to stay and she'd promised it. They'd both believed the promise.

Chalgrove took her arms in his grasp and scrutinised her face.

'You're shaking.'

'I know. But I'm not afraid. Just angry.' Memories of being a child and being left abandoned resurfaced along with the realisation that she finally had a life of her own and now the old woman had appeared to destroy it.

'We'll get out,' he said. 'We will. I will see to that. She's bound for a noose the second I get free. Doesn't matter if she won't tell me her name or not. I'll find out where she lives and let the law take care of it. They don't have to know her name to judge her guilty.'

Chalgrove peered at her face.

Miranda waited before speaking. Her grandmother was twisted, dishonest, but had helped her survive childhood.

She should be punished for taking them. But not hanged. 'She's daft. That doesn't mean she should get the noose.'

'Miss Manwaring.' He spoke so softly and precisely it was almost as if he said the letters instead of the words. 'She needs to be hanged. Who knows what she might try next…or tomorrow…or tonight?' He paused.

'I just want to escape,' she said. 'I want this behind me. I want my life back.'

'Why did you throw a shoe at her? To taunt an asp is never a good thing until after it's dead and cold.' His next words were smooth, precise. The tone a king might use when asking a question that could influence a decision. 'You know her, don't you? The two of you have met in the past.'

'It didn't end well.'

'Tell me what happened.'

She put a hand on her hip. 'Isn't her kidnapping me enough? She sent one of her minions after me and they brought me here.'

'But when did you first meet?' he asked.

She waved her hand at her side, dismissing her words. 'The woman is a fortune-teller at the fair. She is a swindler.'

She couldn't tell him how her grandmother had used

the fortune-telling as a way to find out who might take in an unwanted child and give it a home. She couldn't tell him. Everyone accepted her as Manwaring's ward, even if she and Manwaring did not get on well.

Her employer let her work in his house and care for his children, all based on her pedigree as her father's ward, an orphan with no family. If he found out she was really the granddaughter of a woman who kidnapped people, her employer, as she had already feared, might have concerns about letting her so close to his children.

'Did she steal from your mother?'

Miranda drew in a breath. 'No. But I discovered she'd read my mother's palm many times before I was left along the road. I tried to tell my mother once that the woman was tricky, but my mother wouldn't listen and told me not to question things. She said everything had worked out the way it was supposed to.' She frowned.

Her grandmother had disappeared after dropping Miranda off. Had never again read her mother's palm.

The housekeeper and her mother had talked about the fortune-teller once and Miranda had listened. Apparently, in the years before Miranda arrived, her mother had visited the fortune-teller several times at the fairs. When the old woman had told her mother that she'd some day have a child, she'd been uncertain about how that would unfold, but the moment she'd seen Miranda, she taken her into her heart.

Miranda had assumed her grandmother had forgotten about her immediately after leaving, relieved to have her burden gone. Then she decided she must have died, or she would have returned for a scheme, or candlesticks, or a few gold coins. Some false tale designed to get riches from her mother.

But she'd not returned and Miranda's mother had died.

Then her stepmother had arrived and Miranda had determined she would get away from her father's new wife.

She had got away and found respite and two beautiful children who she loved and cared for as her own.

Chalgrove stared at her, impassive and, in its own way, intense. She couldn't forget her grandmother watching her with the same determination right before she left Miranda with a warning about spiders.

# Chapter Six

Chalgrove watched her eyes when she spoke. Eyes dark, but not afraid. Her chest heaved with deep breaths, but she had no fear in her eyes. None.

Miranda knew something he did not. An innocent would not want to protect someone so deranged. He wondered if he'd misjudged her as he had the woman he'd loved.

He sat on the bed.

He'd met a man named Manwaring once at Tattersall's and they'd both admired the same gelding. They'd crossed paths several other times. A robust old man—a mite insipid, perhaps. He couldn't bring to mind more, although they'd talked for a quarter-hour or so. And the man had funds. His daughter surely wouldn't be a governess. But she said she'd been disowned.

He caught her perusal of him. Nothing else moved, except the rise and fall of their chests and their contemplations as they gauged each other.

'Well, Miss Manwaring. We might be together longer than we'd hoped.'

He would find out more from her, not only by asking

her direct questions, but by speaking with her and watching her actions and seeing what she tried to avoid.

He rubbed his wrist, but truly he was feeling the place where his hand had caressed her. 'How did that mindless old fraud capture you?'

'A man told me… He told me someone I used to know was dying and that her last wish was to speak with me. I thought… I guess I didn't think. But I trusted him and he shoved me into this room and locked me in.' She shivered.

Her face wasn't as plain as he'd perceived at first. She had a pert nose and a certain grace when she moved. Her form, well—with those prim clothes—she tried to hide herself, but that would only work when she stared in her own mirror.

Her slender fingers straightened her skirt. He wagered he could get her to rearrange her skirt or straighten her hairpin again with very few words. Yet it was as if she tried to make herself less attractive instead of more alluring.

He wanted to let her think he was satisfied with her answers. Perhaps lull her into believing that he trusted her.

He ate some bread and left some for her. He decided to see if he really could get her to re-fluff herself.

He remembered the old woman at the window and she'd smiled, as if things were going as she'd planned. And she'd called herself a matchmaker. She was as daft as any soul in Bedlam. He shoved the knowledge from his mind. It didn't matter. She might be witless, but she was cunning and they were trapped.

He let his lips relax. He needed to find out what Miss Manwaring knew that she wasn't telling him and he wanted to thaw the ice around her. 'You've a good arm. If the window hadn't been so boarded up, you'd have clouted her with the shoe.' He added assurance to his words. 'Wellington would have been proud to have you in his army.'

Sure enough, she glanced away, adjusted the hairpin, fiddled with her sleeves, then patted her skirt.

He felt comforted for some reason.

He wondered who'd given the pin to her. She wore nothing else of colour or fashion.

Her eyes moved to him and he could tell she didn't believe he had confidence in her.

'I do not encourage the attention of lawful people, much less criminals. This room seems to become smaller every hour and I am thinking we will have to gnaw ourselves out of here.' Her eyes flickered over him. 'I didn't want this to happen. To you or me. I assure you.'

'When that bottle came at me from out of the darkness, I didn't take that as a sign you wanted me here.' Then he checked the scratches on his head, acknowledging her force, and indicated his shoulder. He moved to the light, and the thin fabric of his shirt showed a darkening underneath. 'I would have woken up dead this morning if you'd had your way.'

'My apologies.' Her eyes dipped.

'It doesn't hurt,' he said. 'But I certainly couldn't show this bruise to my friends as I could when my horse kicked me. They might ask how it happened and I can hardly tell them about a woman with a waist half as big as the bottle in her hand and as spirited as any ten Viking wenches. They'd be wanting an introduction.'

'I want no such introductions and I am nothing like a Viking wench.'

'You need no such introductions. And please don't tell me you aren't as spirited as ten Viking women.' He patted the bruised area. 'My pride might be hurt.' He delivered the words in a way to bring a smile to her lips, though she quickly replaced it.

'Did you have a governess who taught you boxing along with your stories of Peter the Great?' he asked, voice soft, intent on finding out more about her.

She studied him, gauging his words and her own. He'd not deluded her. She saw through him as easily as a pane of glass.

Still, she answered.

'Miss Cuthbert, a dear companion who reminded me of a pigeon when she moved about the house. We have remained close, but after my father married again she was not welcome in the new household. I miss her. She found me the governess position.'

He paused. 'She taught you well.'

She accepted his words and a barrier fell from between them.

'It was like losing my mother twice in the same year. Mother died, then Father brought in a new wife and Miss Cuthbert had to leave. She wasn't precisely sacked, but she said she could not countenance living under the same roof with my stepmother. After all, I didn't need a governess and Miss Cuthbert had become a companion to both my mother and me. She helped so much when Mother passed.'

'What happened?'

'The maid went to wake Mother and she was already gone, but her health had always been fragile. Miss Cuthbert said seeing me grow had kept Mother alive more years than she would have lived otherwise.'

She paced to the opening and peered out. 'This is easy compared to losing her.'

Miranda had returned to the bed, her back against the wall again and her knees up so she could prop her arms on them. The room had no chair and, somehow, sitting the way she did seemed more proper than any other way.

He'd not wanted to speak after she'd mentioned the horrible year of her life and neither had she.

She'd spread the skirt around her, covering her stocking feet. But she'd had no wish to put her shoes back on after using them against her grandmother.

She no longer felt like a governess with all the proper gestures. She felt like a beggar. The beggar her father's new wife had called her. Begging for freedom and the return of her life.

'The old woman wouldn't be feeding us if she wanted us dead. That is, *if* she is sensible.' He broke the silence.

Her grandmother was all machinations and trickery and whatever else at hand. She wouldn't let them starve, but the food she gave them might be stolen.

Miranda had once walked through an orchard with her grandmother at night, filling her basket.

The gamekeeper, who they'd lived with, was the biggest poacher of them all and she'd sometimes had to stay with him while her grandmother went to fairs.

One night, they'd all traipsed out and he'd kept the dogs quiet so they would not alert anyone that the orchard apples were being picked, which had amused her grandmother.

Her grandmother had once taken in and fed a little mouse with a broken leg, but then after it had got well, she'd let the cat into the house to catch the mouse.

Yet she would leave crumbs of food on rocks in the wintertime for whatever creature might find it. She claimed to be feeding good fortune.

Well, the fortune had dissolved for Miranda and might have grown tentacles.

The old woman wanted Miranda to get married and

so she'd locked them in a room, not caring about repercussions.

'Might anyone search for you?' she asked.

'I'll not be missed until the Earl of Kenton's house party.' He gave a quick shake of his head. 'I'd been with my mother yesterday for an early celebration of her birthday and I was going to a cousin's house to escape the evening festivities she had planned for her friends. I had mentioned to my cousin I might visit, but I'd not been certain. He'll think I stayed at my estate.'

'You are to attend an earl's house party?' Her stomach would have fallen to the floor had it been able.

*This unshaven man was a friend of an earl?*

'Yes. His wife is my aunt.'

*Related to an earl.*

'Well…' her throat scratched to get out the words '… I'm sure they will miss you soon.' Although it was highly doubtful they'd know where to search for him. 'Did the old woman know who you are?'

'The men were told I was a tailor.' He stopped and leaned his back against the wall opposite Miranda, his hands behind him. 'Beau Brummell's. If I am to be a tailor, I suppose that is the one to be, although I understood Mr Brummell himself has moved to France.'

'Did she say why she took you?'

'I'm not sure.' He pushed himself from the wall. 'She laughed when I asked. Although the men who helped her said I was to be held for ransom.' He paused. 'Which is strange. I control most of the family funds,' he mused, as if talking to himself. 'The person to kidnap would be someone I care about. I can bundle funds together much more easily than they, which is no secret. I even have an elderly aunt, Agatha Miles, in London, who is coddled by the same servants who've been with her for her lifetime. She could have been a much easier target.'

She swallowed. 'You're very wealthy?'

He stopped, his body still and his gaze on her face. 'I'm not just Chal. I'm Lord Chal. Lord Chalgrove.'

Her jaw dropped and she didn't even hear the end of his sentence. If the truth came out, the whole truth, she would never again find work. She might be considered an accomplice. It would be easy for a man such as this to have witnesses against her. The courts could do as they wished to please an influential man. A lord.

The trials were held one after the other and, at the end of the session, the criminals were led to the gallows. No long waits. No long goodbyes.

'I care for the Duke of Chalgrove's properties because they're mine. My father died about five years ago.'

Then she remembered hearing of the old Duke of Chalgrove and how his son had taken the title, and she'd forgotten about it because it had happened in the year her mother had died. She'd completely disregarded it. She dropped her head, bumping her knees with it. 'I am going to die.'

'You *know*. You know more than you're telling me,' he whispered into the room, but the words had as much portent as a shout. He realised she knew more than she admitted, but not everything. She'd not known who he was.

'You should be overjoyed to be with someone who might have friends to sway others to help rescue us.' His voice lowered. 'Yet you give the impression you're displeased.'

She raised her head, her eyes on his. Face pale even in the shadows.

'Miss Manwaring?' His eyes studied her.

She let out a deep breath.

'Why aren't you happy that I'm a duke with the resources to have justice done?'

'I am. Happy you're a duke. It's the situation that's upset me. The old woman doesn't care how close she dances to the noose.' She moved back and pulled herself into a tighter ball, her arms circling her propped knees and her brow against her arms. 'Your father died the same year as my mother. And I may have seen him once. A man who stood rather like some sea god with flowing white hair and people would bow and shake as he walked by.'

She whispered. 'Thank goodness he is dead.'

'Miss Manwaring.' He could say nothing else. Her rudeness was unthinkable.

She jumped. 'It would be very difficult for him to know you were taken and not know where you are.'

'He'd be tearing the world apart to find out what happened.' As the current Duke of Chalgrove planned.

This was the first time in his life anyone had appeared crushed when finding out he was a duke. She had her head down so low he could only see the top of it.

'I am in trouble. I've been bundled together with a duke. My employer will let me go. My stepmother will use this as an excuse to cast more aspersions at me.'

Her knees were still raised, her arms crossed over them, and her chin rested there. Her eyes were closed so he studied her face. The lashes rimmed her eyes so thickly he wanted to brush his cheek against them to see if they felt as lush as they appeared.

Then he called himself a fool.

His fascination with Susanna had not taught him anything.

Again, he was enthralled by a pretty face. A woman who seemed to need his help. Another woman with secrets. 'You had no more choice in this than I.'

'No one will believe that.'

He wondered why she would think such a thing. Unless she, too, had thought he was a tailor and was in on the plot to kidnap him. She might be brave enough to help in the abduction of a tailor without influential friends, but a duke might cause her pause.

Apparently, it did.

And based on the shoes flying about, her cohort had betrayed her.

Miranda could almost feel the heat wafting from her skin like steam from a pot, but that felt better than the dread roiling inside her.

The Duke had turned away. The Duke of Chalgrove.

She didn't know why she'd not recognised him at first, but then she'd only seen his father a few times.

Plus, this duke had not been shaven when she'd first seen him. She'd always, somehow, assumed that dukes woke up clean shaven, perfectly groomed and perhaps occasionally needed their hair dusted, not with powder, but to remove the earth that had surely been stirred up as people scurried around to do their bidding.

This man did not fit her vision of a duke.

He couldn't seem to stop himself from moving. She expected that he also retraced every word she'd said, searching for all he could figure out about the situation.

She'd watched his back as he worked. The thin lawn of his shirt, sometimes dampened by sweat, did nothing to hide his muscles as he strained to find an escape. She knew at times he had concentrated so hard he forgot she was there, mumbling curses.

He'd once stopped and pulled a splinter from his thumb with his teeth. The way his eyes had darkened and his teeth snapped, he'd appeared wilder than anyone she'd ever seen. Dukes did not have feral glints in their eyes.

Oh, goodness, perhaps they did. Perhaps they were just like her grandmother, except on the other side of the societal ladder. They kept to the top rung, her grandmother on the bottom, and everyone else was trapped between them. And now her grandmother was shaking the ladder.

An irritation flashed in her. She didn't want to be at either end of the hierarchy.

She just wanted to hang on to the ladder and be left alone.

She recognised that little things about him had seemed to change now that she knew he was a duke. It didn't seem possible. He appeared bigger, stronger and more capable. And he was scruffy, especially since he wasn't wearing the coat with the one button ripped away.

But now she saw the truth. He acted as a leader would.

He'd not been able to stop trying to escape because his life was his to control. Always. Now it was not and he could not accept it.

Whenever he rested, he did so by moving about the edges of the room, searching again for something he might have missed to free them.

'You've tried the floor, walls, the door and both windows. A thousand times over.'

'The alternative is to do nothing,' he said. 'Which will result in nothing. I will find a way out. If for no other reason than to keep her from having the last laugh.' He paused, but then sat on the bed. 'You're correct, though. This is not a game of movement, but of strategy. To move accomplishes no preordained result if it is not planned properly.'

Her grandmother worked by the same principles, but she claimed the stars told her which way to move.

'If something she imagined told her to do something wrong, she should not have listened. Because she didn't listen when you told her to set us free.' Miranda waved her hand about, her voice becoming falsetto. '*I must do this or that because the stars tell me.* Well, if the moon had told her to stick her finger in a fire, I dare say she would have doubted that.'

'Perhaps not,' Chalgrove whispered. 'Perhaps, in a sense, that is what the stars told her and she did it.'

Chalgrove kept his sight on the door. He didn't want her to see his mistrust.

She let her knees drop and fell to the bed.

She stared at him, determined, it seemed, to convince him.

'I'm content with my status of governess. I have had men express an interest in courting me, but I see no reason to leave a comfortable life. Granted, it isn't always easy. But I have children to care for—a family of my choosing and their choosing—and my life is considerably better than a wife's might be.'

He watched her eyes. He accepted that someone had expressed interest in courting her. She had an expression that captured a glance and stretched it into longer ones.

'The men who asked to court you—how did you meet them?'

She shrugged away her answer. 'At the shops. I take the children out for walks, even though I always have Nicky with us. He drives the coach. He's got a whip and it's not for the horses, he said.'

'Protective?' He could understand someone wanting to take care of her. She did appear fragile. Willowy. But from the thrust she'd landed on his shoulder, he would gauge her sturdy.

He only had her word she was a governess, though. And servants sometimes moved to the wrong side of life.

'Very. He understands I am a gentle woman. These are extraordinary circumstances.' She spoke the words rapidly. And she also declared them as if she'd also expressed them, at least to herself, many times. 'I work hard to be proper at all times. It is my employment and my livelihood. I must.' She tapped her chest. 'And the little ones. They are my heart.'

Her eyes softened when she mentioned her charges.

'I must get back to them.' Her lips quavered. 'The children... They are my happiness.'

'It is a perilous thing for anyone else to hold your happiness.'

'True. But as soon as I held Willie... I saw him in his nurse's arms and he had two little teeth, more drool than smile, and I just fell in love with him. There are hours when I don't love him, but still, he has my heart.'

She'd not even needed to say it. He saw the love reflected in her face and heard it in her voice. So, she did care for the children.

'He's a mess.' She smiled, shaking her head, and the emotion he heard in her words magnified. 'And Dolly. She is a treasure and the despair of her brother as he doesn't like to share attention. But Dolly is too precious to even know when she is getting notice.'

She paused, reflecting. 'I cannot be upset about the misfortunes of my life because it brought me my mother, and then, when she died, it brought me Dolly and Willie. So, I hold no one responsible for the past. But I don't want an old woman to take my future away from me.'

She slid from the bed, reaching for his coat on the floor, but then she stilled and glanced back at him. 'It concerns me to see such a garment tossed aside. I feel it should at least be off the floor.' She indicated a peg. 'May I?'

Instead of answering, he strode to the peg, then wrenched it free and held it.

'Why did you do that?' she asked.

'I realised it might be held in place with a nail and presumed that might help us.' He tossed the peg aside. 'But the nail has rusted through. Broke easier than snapping a twig. Easier than losing trust.'

'Trust?' She lifted his coat. 'I would have trusted the old woman to take these buttons. But she didn't.' She slipped a finger beneath the rip in the coat. With his strength, he'd torn the button from the fabric.

'I once knew a woman who would have happily snipped them off and pouted at my mistake of not wearing more,' he said.

'You were tricked?'

'I courted a woman whom I cared for. She was already married. I didn't know it. No one else knew, except her husband, I suppose.' He shrugged.

That had sweltered inside him for months, like banked ashes kept from waning, which could still cause pain.

He'd been so convinced Susanna was a jewel. But afterwards, he'd recalled so many little things that should have warned him. He'd recounted them over and over and been amazed at how easily he'd brushed them aside as they occurred. He'd been deceived by an alluring woman and he'd fallen into her machinations.

'It's different. For a…duke. You have to marry. I don't.'

'I don't have to marry. The Royal Dukes can take their time. I can be the same. I have many friends. I have my family. My mother. My cousins. My sister. She says I am the twin of her heart, except I am of the wrong gender, the wrong size and the wrong sensibility, and rarely see things as she does.'

'It isn't that you don't have people to show you care in your life. It sounds as though you might have too many. You don't feel the need for a wife because you have numerous people who love you.'

'Life isn't about love. Susanna didn't put me off marriage. She made me wary of my ability to see the truth.' She'd misled him so completely. 'My perceptions were flawed. I truly had faith Susanna was more than she was. I overlooked her mistakes easily enough.'

He moved to his feet, remembering the love Miss Manwaring had in her eyes for the children and realising that even Susanna had cared deeply for a little dog he'd given her. 'This talk accomplishes nothing. We're imprisoned and thinking of things we don't need to concern ourselves with. Escape is all we should consider.'

## Chapter Seven

Miranda watched him stride into the other room.

In her mind's eye, she could see him brush the flannel over his bearded chin, around his neck and into the hollow at his collar.

She pulled the pillow over her face, trying to close out the visions of him, but the gesture didn't work.

She noticed him in a way she'd never been aware of a man before.

He was titled and she was certain that increased her awareness. Even though her father had lived among the peerage, he'd always kept her secluded from his life.

He'd really not wanted her observed. After all, she was his ward, not his child. He'd never accepted her.

She'd not particularly cared. He'd been gruff with the servants, not spoken to her governess and had been condescending to her mother.

The only thing she ever remembered her mother openly going against him was in her insistence that Miranda be *their* ward and a part of their family. Although Miss Cuthbert claimed her father didn't have a bad opinion of Miranda, she strongly doubted it.

When Miss Cuthbert left, then heard of another governess post and wrote to Miranda about the employment, Miranda obtained it before telling her father. She presented it to him as a fait accompli.

His jaw had flexed when she told him and he'd agreed it might be best for her.

Within days, she'd started over in her new life. None of the servants seemed particularly welcoming at first, but she didn't care. Getting away from her stepmother had made Miranda feel like singing and kicking up her heels.

She had sung and she'd danced with the baby in her arms. Willie's mother usually spent Sunday afternoons with him, and spare mornings here and there, but she was completely happy to keep Miranda close at hand.

Miranda had been so thrilled to discover a new child was on the way.

Willie's mother hadn't recovered from the second birth. But Miranda hadn't had time to mourn her as Dolly had been a fitful newborn and the first wet nurse hadn't stayed. Willie had also been demanding because he'd been used to constant attention. Miranda had had a morose employer, Mr Trevor, a little boy with an over-abundance of energy and a baby who needed cuddles much of the time.

But in those circumstances, she and the staff became closer. They all rallied together, working to bring Mr Trevor back among the living, to keep Willie quiet and Dolly settled.

One night, after a particularly rough day, Cook stepped out of her role and brought Miranda teacakes after the house quietened. Miranda had been surprised, both that Cook had noticed Miranda hadn't eaten and that she'd strayed upstairs, and taken on the duties a maid would normally assume. Cook had claimed that she'd not wanted to see Miranda faint away with a babe in her arms, as her own daughter once had.

They'd talked long into the night, alternating who carried the whimpering Dolly, and Miranda had realised she had a family.

Now, she gazed around the room at the meagre surroundings. She'd lived in poverty and in wealth. While she liked the tidiness wealth brought with it, she hardly noticed her surroundings, only aware of the people around her and their goodness or badness.

Chalgrove stepped back into the middle of the room and scrutinised the walls, windows and doors, before his regard stopped on her and locked with the intensity he might have used if she'd had the key to their escape.

Her hair, Chalgrove noticed, haloed around her head, pins loose.

He could easily understand why she was a governess, particularly after she got misty-eyed over a little one. Miss Manwaring would be good with children. It was the comforting feeling he'd sensed emanating from her. The children would like that. Hell, grown men would like it.

He'd never really reflected much about having children, but now that he was with Miss Manwaring he realised he'd want someone like her as a governess to his children.

It would make marriage easier, not having to worry about who took care of his offspring, or what kind of mother his wife might be. If Miss Manwaring would be a governess to his babies, his wife would never even have to check on them. He'd not even need to take much care in their raising until they were... Until his children were old enough to be in society. He would need to introduce them to the people among the *ton*.

'Children are fine enough, once they speak and if they are well mannered.'

She jumped as if he'd slapped her.

'My father would agree.' Her lips and her chin went up.

He had been slapped in retaliation. A novelty. Oh, his long-time friends would offer verbal jabs and punches, but a woman didn't do such a thing. He wondered if she'd jab again. He wondered if he could see those eyes flash.

Softly, he took in a breath. 'Babies. They're such a nuisance. Squabbling little things that take too much care. A woman's work. Not suitable for a man.'

Her lips thinned. Her eyes narrowed.

'Babies are best kept secluded from society. The crying and all.' He spoke softly. The fury increased and, if her eyes were any indication, it was directed at him.

'I'd really consider you overqualified to be a governess, having been raised in prosperity. I'd suppose this Miss Cuthbert is more suitable to taking care of the smelly little beasts.'

There was silence between them and her eyes reminded him of a lit fuse reaching its end where the powder would spark and flash.

'I suppose you could be correct, Your Grace. Thank you ever so much for that wise observation from a man who was once a smelly little beast.'

He'd never heard the words 'Your Grace' spoken quite so directly, except on the rare occasions of ire when his mother addressed his father so. He tightened his lips to keep the smile hidden.

'It is fortunate you have not married,' she muttered.

'And do you agree with my assessment on children?'

'I think they do sometimes grow up into narrow-minded adults and that is a shame.'

He scratched his cheek. His narrow-minded adult cheek. 'Tell me one good thing about a babe less than a year old.'

Her chin jutted his way and her body followed. 'Their

little wisps of hair. It is the softest thing. Better than any silk when it brushes against your cheek. And it has a soft scent. That is what love smells like. And then, when you hold them in your arms, if you have a heart at all, it just melts with love.'

'Does it?'

'If you have a heart.'

'I suppose I've never held a child. Perhaps I will some day, just to see if I have a heart.'

'It would be a waste of your time, I'm afraid.'

'You are very sensitive about those little babies, aren't you?'

'I suppose I have ancestry of the lowest class, because I noticed quite a few of the servants smiling when they saw Dolly and even now as she's older. It is the joy of childhood. She doesn't yet know she's better than everyone else.'

'Oh.'

'Willie does. He was born that way, though. I suppose it is because he is a male, Your Grace.'

The words were softer this time. She'd rested her gauntlet after testing it a few times across his face.

'Perhaps it will be enlightening to hold a child. And see what love smells like.' His eyes held hers.

'Don't be surprised if the baby wets on you. They tend to do that.' Smug eyes. Lovely ones, and he'd bet his last pence that if he ever held a child, it would wet on him. It just would and the awareness jumped between them. She would have the last laugh on that.

'And you still like them?' he asked.

'Of course. It would be impossible not to. For me.'

'Some day, I will hold a child and, if it wets on me, I will think of you.'

'Please do,' she said, eyes smiling, accepting his surrender. 'Babies are very good about sensing when a stranger is holding them and not good about hiding their feelings.'

Their eyes met and locked. In that moment, he imagined them in a room, a child between them and the laughter over the baby's actions.

Both jerked their gaze away at the same time.

If they didn't get out of the little room, he'd soon be as daft as the old woman. He needed to get his mind off the governess who held that babies smelled like love.

He changed the path of his thoughts to their escape. He had to get them free.

'When you were brought here, did you notice anything about the door? How it might be barred?' he asked. 'Was it a simple board slid into a U-shaped holder at each end?'

She took in a breath and shrugged. 'I rushed in. I didn't pay much notice.'

'How did they get you inside? I assumed you were taken just as I was.'

She stopped. 'A man came to get me in a cart. He said someone I used to know was dying and she wished to speak with me.' She clasped her hands, brushing a thumb over her wrist. 'How could I refuse a dying woman? I thought she might have something to tell me about my birth. My parentage.'

He could see her point, but still, she wasn't revealing all she knew. She wouldn't be keeping secrets unless they were harmful.

For some reason, the knowledge saddened him. She was betraying him. He just didn't know how.

Progressing to the door, he prodded the wood, taking out his frustration on it. He found a dark shape when he inspected the crack in the door facing. A board crossed on the other side. Barred, just as he expected.

'If I had a small rope—the door is lax enough at the

hinges so when I heave against it, pushing to the side, a crack opens up the height of it. I can see through the crevice.' Then he crouched on one knee and examined the base of the door. He knelt completely, peering closely at the threshold.

'With a string, if the hole is big enough, perhaps I could get it outside the door from above, over the board, then let it dangle down and trap the end to pull it up, looping it under the board. If I lifted one end and it slid, then it could tumble to the ground.'

She braced herself, interested. 'Corset ties are small, strong, and might be long enough to be used to pull the board up from the outside.'

He crouched on his knees, scowling at the wood. 'I've nothing to snag the tie so I can drag it inside. Even the spoon she left for us is too thick.'

She pulled out the butterfly pin in her hair and walked towards him. He stood and watched as she held out her hand and offered her hairpin. 'Perhaps this will help.'

She tapped the sharp end lightly against her finger, smiling into his eyes. 'My mother told me to always keep it handy when strangers were about.'

He took it, held it carefully in both hands, rotated it slowly and inspected it. High quality craftsmanship. Those sparkles weren't glass. They were diamonds of a nice size.

'Your mother gave this to you?'

'Yes.'

'We can use it, but we may break it. I will have it repaired, later.'

'My mother would not care. It might help me and that is all that would matter to her.'

'Susanna would have made me promise to buy her a new one if I damaged this one.'

'Maybe she truly loved you. Her husband could have been a mistake.'

'I am sure he was.' His voice was resigned. 'And he told me too much about myself to convince me that Susanna had true emotion for me. She—' He stopped. 'I suppose she cared enough in her own way. And she would have married me if she hadn't had one marriage in the register to a man disinclined to turn up his heels—who knows, we both might have been content.' He tapped his hand on to his knee. 'He told me he'd made sure his brothers knew of the situation, so if he was found floating in the Thames, Susanna would be punished before anyone could work out who the body was. Said he'd told her the same many times.' Susanna would be huddled in the corner crying if she were in the room with them.

He grasped the pin tightly. 'Let's try the corset tie.'

She moved to the second room, untying her corset. A few minutes later she stepped out, triumphant, holding them high. The ribbons dangled to the floor and he ignored the delectable roundness of her dress, but it was too late. He'd already committed her shape to memory. She wasn't as willowy as he'd thought.

He pulled his concentration back to the task of escaping.

'It's getting dark. Unless one of her cohorts is standing right at the door, he won't see anything—unless the board falls. If he notices earlier, then we'll be aware there's someone out there when he stops the string. But if I get the bar to drop—' His voice dipped. 'Even if he sees me, it'll be too late.'

He took the corset fastening and looped a huge knot in the end. Then he poked the unknotted end through the crack at the top of the door, working the tie to the other side, until he stopped as only the large end remained. He slid the knot down the inside of the door, stopping when he reached the barred area.

'Can you see enough under the door to snare the string?' he asked.

Carefully, she pulled out her hairpin and slipped the straight end of it outside. She levered the pin one way and then the other while he dangled the string after each movement.

'I felt it.' She lifted the end so she could scrape the point against the earth, trapping the string and sliding it inside.

Bending down, Chalgrove scooped the tie, sliding it up, along the crack. When he raised it to the level where the bar rested, he had one end of the ribbon in each hand and the tie was looped outside around the board.

Slowly, he lifted both hands, fingers tense.

'It's not rising. I'll lift the end as high as I can, until the board tilts out of the string. Then the downward force should make the board slide out of the other side as well.'

He lifted, putting all his strength into it. *Snap.* The tie broke and he stumbled backward from the momentum in his efforts.

*Merde.* The board was wedged too tight. His efforts were from the wrong side of the wood and the sideways pull had broken the string.

She'd moved out of his way when he'd caught his balance. Now they stood side by side.

'I should have had a new corset made a long time ago. I knew it.'

'I doubt it would have worked,' he admitted, 'even with a stronger ribbon. The wood is too tight and perhaps there is something wedged to hold it in place. Or perhaps the bar slides into iron brackets.'

Her shoulders dropped.

He grasped them. He hated disappointing her. 'We'll get out.'

They stood silent and he had to repay some of the comfort she gave him.

'This was just a first attempt. We'll be free soon.'

Then he moved so close he could scent her hair and his jaw tightened. He wagered her hair smelled the same as a babe's. It did. It must. No wonder she liked them.

'Don't worry, Miss Manwaring.' He touched her elbow. Eyes gazed up at him. 'I am. Worried.'

He clasped her arm tightly, reassuring her. In that moment, he recognised that even though the old woman was likely her cohort, Miss Manwaring wanted to be released as much as he did. 'I'm missing something to get us out of here. I'll find it. Then we'll be freed.'

Her face was a mixture of despair and sadness. He could not bear it. 'My pardon,' he said, then he put an arm around her, keeping a blanket of air between them, yet nudging her to the bed so she could rest.

They both sat at the edge, shoulders touching, and their purpose intertwined. The silence grew between them, adding a feeling of camaraderie.

'You don't act like Susanna,' he said. 'She would be weeping. I don't miss her any more. I haven't in a long time.'

'I've had a beau and know what it's like to be disappointed. I didn't want to wed him, but I was so intrigued by him that when he left my life, it was as if I mourned him. He made certain that his hair always had a wave over his forehead. He had sweet words for every occasion.' She wound the corset string around the fingers of her left hand, interweaving it. 'What was odd was that I felt sad after it ended. If he had been an upstanding man, I would have guessed I was recovering from love. I suppose it was the friendship I missed. The stolen moments. Or perhaps the flowery words and the dreams of my future.'

'Stolen times can be compelling,' he agreed. 'I find them so.'

'You must have many women hoping for your notice. I would imagine you are practically tripping over women who coincidentally find themselves in your path.'

He saw no reason to deny it. He recognised it on some occasions and found it flattering. He certainly had with Susanna. Then he'd shied away from it, hiding the annoyance that flourished in him when he saw the fascination with his title.

'I don't want another Susanna in my life and my mother was pushing for me to marry. So, I suggested she find a wife for me.'

'That was daring of you.' She unwound the string and tossed the ties into the corner.

'Mother has trouble with decisions. She can't make up her mind between two shades of fabric for a ball gown. Now she doesn't complain that I can't find a wife. She only bemoans that she can't find one for me.'

'What if she did and you didn't like the woman?' Miranda perched at the edge of the bed, back straight.

'Easy enough. I would just ponder about a flaw I'd suggest and Mother would notice it and continue the search. She expects perfection. She mistakenly credits me with it and she wants the same in my wife, yet she can see the flaws in women easily.'

She rubbed her hands over her arms as if she were cold. 'There is another reason that prevents me from marriage,' she said. 'Willie and Dolly. The children I care for. I can't marry and remain their governess. Their father would forbid it and, even though Willie can be so annoying, I do care for them greatly.'

'So, your heart is full.'

She nodded. 'I do have a family and they need me very much. I need them, too.'

He couldn't imagine living without being surrounded by blood relations. The ties that his family brought had enclosed him all his life.

'You don't feel alone?' he asked.

'In my mother's house, I was always the ward. Deep inside me, I knew it. While my mother loved me and cared for me, and was all that I could ask, I could sense that… sometimes she didn't feel happy. She could be moody even behind her placid face and perfection. I knew it and I stayed closer to Miss Cuthbert on those days. Where I live now, I am the governess. For the children, that is a stronger word than mother. They don't remember their real mother, but they will remember me.'

Light flickered over her face when she turned to the window.

'The children and I have that in common. I know nothing of the woman who gave birth to me and I've told them sweet stories of their mother. Every scrap I can find out about her.'

She shut her eyes briefly. 'More terrifying than being abducted, or losing my own life, is the possibility of losing the children.' Pain flashed across her face.

He would see that she was released. But if she had been in league with the old woman, it would be harder than she realised to return to the children she loved.

He mulled over his family. His mother. Sister and cousins. They normally faded into the background of his life. Always there. Always caring. A continuous, permanent connection.

If he could not secure their release soon, each day would bring less of a chance for freedom. He surveyed the room with the intensity of a warrior planning his next onslaught.

## Chapter Eight

Miranda watched as Chalgrove went to the window, knelt down, put his palms flat against the wall and pressed his eye to the opening. 'Clouds might give us a strong rain,' his voice so quiet she could barely hear the words. 'What do you think?'

She moved to the opening beside him but, when her shoulder pressed his, awareness of the fortress beside her heightened.

'If you turn your head down and stare overhead.' He reached around her and put his hand on her shoulder and moved her into place at the opening. The movement took her so much by surprise, she tumbled.

He immediately clasped her waist in both hands.

'Forgive me. I didn't mean to jostle you.' He didn't remove his hands.

'I was unsteady. The situation has unnerved me.'

She put her face against the opening, feeling the cool air and the few sprinkles of raindrops blowing in.

*And him.*

She didn't move and his hands stayed as they were.

Another drop of moisture blew against her face and the sensation jarred into her. The wind cooled her face, filling the room with the scent of rain, and the temperature had dropped. The air had chilled significantly, and she fought a shiver, but it wasn't from the cold.

Even as she remained outwardly unmoving, the sensations in her body swirled and vibrated with such awareness she couldn't believe her skin could contain them. And maybe it couldn't. She brushed her thumb inside her clasped hands and felt a sheen of moisture on her palm.

The smell of the rain on the ground hit her nostrils and a light spray of it blew into the room, sprinkling her cheek.

She had to move, or Chalgrove would realise the effect his presence had on her. She couldn't give him the knowledge.

The wind blew—louder than the sound of her heartbeats in her ears.

Suddenly he jumped and she turned face him. A drip of water ran from his forehead to his nose.

'I think the roof might leak, Miss Manwaring.'

As he spoke, the rain slowed, but another breeze blew in. He strode over, picking up his coat and draping it around Miranda's shoulders.

Miranda didn't move, especially her eyes. The coat enveloped her, completely covering her hands. She raised one, flapping his sleeve. Her mind kept taking flight and letting her mouth pick its own words. 'You seem sturdier than I would have expected you to be.'

'I was born so. I've worked as a labourer alongside the farmers and they had trouble keeping up with me.'

'Why would you do that?'

'A lark. A respite. A challenge.'

Tension remained in his shoulders, but he expelled a breath. 'Susanna was no longer in my life at my request. Everything seemed bleak. My favourite uncle had unexpectedly passed away and my aunt was in reduced circumstances. I found a home for her, but the life I'd expected to build with Susanna had been an illusion. Only memories remained. Of her. My uncle. My father. At that instant in my life, I felt I had no respite except for an empty country estate where I'd grown up. I decided to go back.'

He'd hated the part of himself that had mourned Susanna and he'd feared replacing her with another copy of the same, with only a different outer body.

Moving to the estate had hit him harder than he'd expected. His father was gone for ever and now the walls didn't seem like a home, but like an elaborate crypt.

He'd been planning to return to London, but his estate steward had been struggling along with a broken leg, a poorly made crutch and gritting his teeth with every step.

Chalgrove found himself asking questions, learning from the man and walking the estate. When the tenants struggled with a physical chore, Chalgrove had pushed himself to prove, if only to himself, that he could do as well as they and he'd helped.

The physical labour had felt good, bolstered him and cleansed his mind of Susanna. The work was a novelty at first, then a salvation and then something to soothe him.

The fencing lessons he'd taken, the sparring and the riding had given him an edge he'd not known before.

At first, he'd found the usual deference at his estate. Then, as the months changed, the deference had as well— it transformed to a new kind of respect he'd never had before.

He'd slipped into a different culture which had existed right under his nose, yet he'd been oblivious to it. The same place he'd spent most summers of his childhood and which had the peaceful demeanour of a pond surface had come alive, vibrant and pulsating with different aspects of humanity. He'd not known of the bickering and squabbles and romances and jealousies that flourished and faded and sometimes flared into fist fights.

Over time, his estate steward had altered towards him, no longer telling him how wonderful everything was, but listing concerns he'd been undecided on and asking for a decision. His decision had been appreciated and esteemed, not from his position, but from its merit.

'A duke doesn't get invited to country dances if he doesn't let it be known he wants to attend. I wanted to dance and drink and laugh with the men. I didn't want my friends to know of my foolishness of falling under Susanna's spell. The tenants didn't know me. I could act that all was well with them and, within time, it was.'

'You got over her quickly?'

'I demanded it of myself. Another thing that surprised me and illustrated the shallowness of love.'

Then, when he'd returned to London, he'd moved on to the camaraderie he'd found at Gentleman Jackson's and found less enjoyment in his old habits of drinking the night away without deeming anything important but laughter.

He'd stepped into his true heritage as easily as he'd stepped into the clubs in the past and the life of the tenants.

His fingertip steadied her elbow. His grip couldn't have been lighter, yet he felt so much more than just the fabric of the sleeve. It was almost as if he could feel her heart beating and absorb the love she felt for the children.

He flashed a smile, changing his tone. 'I can shoe a horse as fast as any blacksmith, but I still flounder at the simple task of putting on a saddle.' He laughed silently without humour. 'Someone had always taken care of that for me in the past and I'd never comprehended it. The beasts blow out their stomachs to fool me into thinking I've got the cinch tight when it's loose. Some horses act as if they are too privileged to let me ride. A horse doesn't understand if a titled man saddles him or a stable boy. Or he does and prefers to show the titled man his place. They're good at showing me my place and you've not seen eyes twinkle so bright behind a serious face when a stable boy helps a duke to his feet.'

Her eyes mirrored the smile in the stable boy's.

He left the window and put as much distance from her as he could in the enclosed space. Miss Manwaring reminded him of the life he'd found in the countryside. The vibrancy of it. The feeling of being strong and alive and able to conquer anything.

Anything but an old cottage.

With his coat around her, it seemed she could scent his shaving soap and that his arms surrounded her. She should give it back. She really should. The air wasn't that chilled. In fact, the coat made it a little too warm in the room. Or just right.

Hunger moved her forward to the food.

She ate one of the apples, its tart taste refreshing her, and some of the hazelnuts, trying to escape from the feeling of being too close to him, yet unable to remove his coat.

He sat on the bed and examined the sole of his foot. 'Horses are just like pieces of glass. Shards of glass don't care whether it's a titled man or a stable boy who steps on them. I suppose I should be more careful.' He laughed, but he didn't gather his boots.

When Chalgrove laughed, Miranda couldn't take her eyes from him. His face changed, infused with the innocence of a youth.

This was a side of him she'd not seen before, perhaps a side of a person she'd never seen before. He merely laughed. Carefree.

The sound was enough to make her giddy—drunk, in a sense. He must never laugh again. A woman had no defence against a sound so entrancing.

They must escape. She must.

The night was falling, clouding up, and the air chilling rapidly. Light barely illuminated through the opening.

'The sun is going down. You don't have to concern yourself about me. But when I sleep or you sleep, you must let me stay between you and the door. You're safe with me, Miss Manwaring, and if anyone comes in that door in the night, I'll stop them.' He rose and moved to get something to eat.

His consideration impressed her, but she knew her grandmother had no plans for any altercation in that room. Conception of a great-grandchild, perhaps…

Chalgrove steadied her when she stepped too close to the stump and almost stumbled.

She buttressed herself against whatever foolishness had invaded her. Soon she'd be no different from her grandmother and believing that stars could talk. They had to get out before her grandmother's wishes came true.

## Chapter Nine

He couldn't afford to be exhausted. Too much depended on his strength. He didn't know if he might need to use force to protect her, but he must be prepared.

He ignored as best he could the protest from muscles which wanted to spring into action and moved to the window, trying to see out as much as he could.

Miranda stepped closer.

She removed his coat and held it out to him. He reached out, but stopped. The scent that was like a child which she compared to love might be on it. The soft scent of her skin. His arm dropped.

'You might need it,' he said. They remained motionless, her holding out the coat and him not moving to take it.

'It's too warm.'

'The air is getting colder,' he insisted.

'Not that much and I can wrap up in—'

She didn't lower her arm.

He took the coat, clamped his teeth together and turned away. Yes, she could wrap up in the covers. 'By all means.' He erased all emotion from his voice and suspected that she heard he'd done so.

She scurried to the bed. He heard the movements and

imagined the covers were being neatly divided into two piles. One for the male in the room, the other for the female.

The stubborn part of him caused him to put his coat on and the wool surrounded him with a feminine scent, but he refused to feel it. He would not acknowledge it. He wouldn't. It was too soft, too fragile, and could seep into him.

He waited, inhaling softly.

He sat on the bed and, sure enough, a bundle of covers lay beside him. He pushed them to rest with the others.

The old woman had done well on the softness of the bed, but she'd sorely misjudged on size. He no longer cared. He lay down and stretched, letting his feet hang from the end because he would not encroach on Miss Manwaring's area.

He wasn't really attracted to this governess. He was having some problem caused by celibacy, he supposed. His friends had warned him, explaining that to avoid women was to court disaster. The needs would build up inside him and then he'd lose all sense of logic and propose to the first woman he saw.

That had been proven correct in a very large way.

After he'd been so duped, he'd not wanted to risk that type of experience again.

He had truly misjudged her. Her husband had showed up one day, concerned about Chalgrove cutting his wife's funds. He hadn't. A small lie Susanna had told.

He'd been so blinded. And she'd been lying to her husband as well.

She'd lied. She'd laughed. She'd cried. And if there were more emotions she could have shown to her advantage, she would have.

He put his arm across his eyes, but he couldn't keep from being aware of Miranda. He peered out.

He saw the outline of her arms stretching over her head and heard a yawn. Then she began her little fluffing ritual. First, she righted the pin which she had retrieved and felt to make sure her hair remained in place. Then she straightened her sleeves and brushed down her skirt.

She didn't really seem scared. Inwardly, he sighed. She might end up transported, which would devastate him. He couldn't let her be on a ship with criminals, no matter what she'd done.

'You are not as frightened as I would have expected you to be,' he said.

She let out a huff. 'It is as you said. If it were about murder, we would be dead. So much effort would not have been spent on holding us. And we are going to get out and I will never, ever see this cottage again.'

She picked up the broken glass he'd discarded and began chipping away at the door.

'Save your strength. It can't work fast enough.'

'I know. I just have to try.'

He spoke, scrubbing his knuckles over his chin. 'I can hardly wait to see my valet's face when he sees me. It will almost make the whiskers worth it—if he survives the shock.'

'You sound as if you care for a...a servant?'

His eyes challenged her. 'I've spent more time with the man than any other except my father and uncle. In my youth, he was a footman who did not like to be surprised with rocks in his pillow.' He smiled. 'He knocked on my outside window in the dark after telling me a ghost story one night. He waved a white cloth against the glass on occasion. My mother finally discovered Wheaton was telling me the stories and forbade it. She said it caused too many imaginations.' He rocked back on his heels. 'They were not all imaginations. A few years ago, Wheaton told me he nearly broke his neck climbing that tree outside the window in the dark with a broom in his hand.'

'That was cruel of him to do to a child.'

'He really didn't like grass snakes. He'd told me they sent ghosts to people who caught them—after I'd put one on his shoes while he was wearing them. I forgot about the ghosts…when I found another snake. After two snakes, he took measures to make sure there wasn't a third.'

'I cannot imagine a servant acting so.'

'You have not met Hector Wheaton.'

He lay, listening to the scratches and scraping sounds she made. Every few minutes she would give a soft grumble, or groan or complain about the wood or the tool. Her squabbles with herself charmed him.

Night had fallen completely and he hadn't planned to sleep, but realised he had when her movements awoke him. The bed moved as she crawled between him and the wall. He'd never had a woman get into his bed so stealthily. For some reason, he found humour in her plan to enter the bed quietly. She might as well have jumped on it. Keeping the bed still was impossible. The light mattress moved like a dinghy in high winds.

He could tell she had positioned herself away from him and her body rested board straight.

If he tapped her side and shouted, she'd probably not stop jumping until she ricocheted off the ceiling.

He lay immobile, not wanting to let her know he'd awoken.

The governess soothed him more than any tavern songs, or boisterous friends or nights with his family.

She was delicate and yet not. A woman who'd walked

out of an uncomfortable life and made a new one that suited her better.

He didn't sleep, but lay there thinking about her as if she were a country away and a lifetime from him.

In the darkness, thunder cracked over the cottage and she jumped, wakening.

'Without thinking, he clasped her hand. 'It's just thunder.'

She stirred, but didn't speak.

The wind picked up again and the rain started softly, then increased, and drops pounded on the roof and into the room.

He rose, standing barefoot on a damp floor, and took a step where a puddle had formed. A puddle made from the leaks in the roof.

'Off the bed,' he said, jumping nearer her. He tugged her arms, lifting her to her feet and on to the floor.

With a heave, he pulled the bed, stationing it under the leak in the ceiling. He jumped on to the mattress again, gauged the strength by pushing with both palms, then with a fist, slammed the spot where the water ran in. The rotted wood gave way.

His hand could fit inside the hole he'd made and, in a matter of minutes, he'd rammed the remaining boards to and fro enough times to weaken them, showering himself in waterlogged splinters and the odour of rotting, wet wood.

Grabbing the largest piece he'd broken loose, he used it as a battering ram, increasing the opening. Pounding against the roof, cracking reverberated with the water rushing down. Water drenched his hair and rotted wood splintered as it landed on his cheeks.

He slammed the board upwards again, making a large

rupture. Water flooded over him as he opened the planks to the torrent above him.

He couldn't see the sky, but he could feel the freedom.

The opening had widened enough, but was slippery. He'd pounded away the damaged rot and found a strong section that he couldn't loosen.

Reaching up, he clutched the slippery boards, jumped and threw himself upwards. He climbed on to the top of the house.

'Toss up my boots,' he said, 'and put on your shoes.'

He grabbed the heels as she shoved them up and slid his feet into his boots.

'Let's go.' He crouched at the opening, lying on his stomach and reaching in to take her hands.

She lifted her arms and he raised her through the broken timbers with enough force that he had to roll and she sprawled over him.

'I could have planned that better.' He held her for a second, then released her. 'But I hope you don't mind that I didn't.'

He manoeuvred to give her a chance to right herself.

Standing, he tugged her hand, keeping her near. Water drenched them.

'Take care,' he said and steadied them, ignoring the pounding rain and concentrating completely on the task in front of him.

When they got to the edge, he didn't pause, but twisted and lowered himself, jumping to the ground.

'Now,' he called out, arms raised, and she tumbled into his arms.

He didn't give her a second to think, but gripped her hand and pulled her into the woods.

'Follow me.' He guided her among the trees, close to

the two ruts which had more weeds than any well-used road would ever sport.

Thick trees lined the cart path.

Brambles pulled at her, tearing her clothes, slapping cold, wet splashes on to her skin.

Mud tried to suck her feet into the ground, but she kept running. But not fast enough. She couldn't keep up with Chalgrove's legs.

Breathing became harder, then almost impossible. She put a hand at her side and stopped, pulling herself free.

She let her breath catch up with her. 'I am not a race-horse. The briars catch on my dress.'

He pushed a limb aside and backtracked, stopping at her side. 'You're right to slow down. We'll have a break in the downpour eventually. But it's almost daylight. The ruts are hard to see in the dark and I don't want us to stray off the road.'

'How will we…?' She tried to pull more air into her lungs and forced herself not to shiver. Water pelted down on her.

He held her, concerned as she struggled for air. 'I doubt she'll try to recapture us without her helpers. But we might stumble across her camp. We need to keep quiet, although they'll not be able to take us back. They can't have planned on us escaping and I can't imagine more than one guarding the place—or even one, in this rain.'

'I can't believe anyone's out in this. I know she isn't.' Miranda said the words without thinking and she didn't really know why she felt so certain except—except she knew that the old woman wouldn't be standing in a downpour.

She would be snug somewhere. In a cart with a stale oilcloth over her, or in another house nearby.

Miranda had lived in the house they'd just left. She

should have kept in mind the direction to the nearest village, but she wasn't sure in the dark which way they should run.

He pulled her closer, under a large tree, shielding her from some of the rain.

'You're shivering,' he said. 'I didn't think it would be so cold for you.' Taking her hand, he sat and pulled her on to his lap. Wrapping his arms around her, he shielded her from the rain with his body.

'Your nose is cold.' But having his arms around her made her heart beat faster and filled her with warmth. She clasped his chest, snuggling tight, sharing his body heat.

The rain lessened, but neither of them moved, waiting until daybreak, sitting huddled against each other.

He dislodged her as the light began to shine around them. All the rain had stopped and the chaffinches began to call. Pulling her to her feet, he scouted the countryside and the fresh scent of the morning gave promise.

'I don't even know for sure which way to go, but we'll keep moving in the same direction.'

They arrived at a turn in the road, with a side path going away from it.

Chalgrove paused.

'It's that way,' she said, pointing.

Chalgrove stepped to Miranda's side. He put a hand at her shoulder, the smallest clasp, yet holding her motionless. 'When were you here last?'

'As a child.'

His eyes, intense, ignited her senses in the same way a spark flared gunpowder. She lowered her gaze, taking in the cheekbones, the column of his neck, finishing at the bristles of his beard. She could see the corded tension of his neck.

'I will find out.' His words left no room for doubt. She'd spoken to Willie in just the same tone when he had been caught outside with one of Polly's dolls ablaze and a lit candle at his side after he'd heard the story of Joan of Arc.

Chalgrove stood in front of her. 'You are better off explaining it from your point of view than letting me learn of it from a magistrate.'

'The fortune-teller spouts nonsense and curses and fables of unicorns. And when she talks in her sleep, I'd say she even lies then.'

'How do you know this?' He moved closer, so close she could scent the wet leather of his boots and the dry warmth of his face.

She couldn't meet his eyes.

'Don't expect me to be able to tell you her machinations. I can't.' She stepped away and her arm slid from his. She couldn't even fathom her own mind, much less anyone else's. 'How can I understand a daft old woman's intentions? I've not seen her from the time of my early childhood until she locked me in the room. She was old to me even then and she told my mother's fortune.'

His eyes narrowed. And she shivered inside.

Without speaking, he took off walking again.

She kept up until she got out of breath. Tugging on his arm, she caught his attention.

He stopped and, after observing her, took her to the wooded area beside the ruts and pulled her close, waiting. They were caked in mud and he embraced her, keeping her aloft, yet letting her rest.

'You know she will hang.' He dropped the words in the air and they formed images in Miranda's mind.

Miranda could feel her own feet dangling. Her father and stepmother had attended a hanging. Her stepmother had returned home with a whole basket of tales and had recalled the first vibration of the trapdoor, who stood where, what they were wearing and every utterance. The condemned man's last words had been repeated at least twice.

Soirées did not get as much attention.

'I know you want to have justice.' She closed her eyes, speaking softly. 'I am alive, though. I am unharmed and, should I be able to resume my duties, I want no more of this. I don't want to see the woman killed. She's addled. She must be. I have no coin to steal.' She pleaded, hoping to convince him. 'What good could come of her death?'

He reminded her of a stone wall, each rock chiselled into place so firmly it couldn't be moved.

'Satisfaction.' His brows creased. 'Others being safer.' A soft breeze blew through the leaves, chilling her, and he must have noticed because he pulled her even closer. Her palm flattened against his chest and he didn't feel like a stone wall any more, but more like a blanket.

She gazed up and found him watching her.

'If I were to leave this be, who's to say what she'll do next?' His voice was soft, gentling.

Miranda could hardly think to speak. 'I know she's addled,' she repeated. She clutched his arm, letting her hand rest on his sleeve, savouring the closeness between them. 'I know I should hate her. But I don't.'

'My freedom was taken. And nearly my teeth.'

She waited, trying to come to terms with the fate he intended for her grandmother, but she couldn't.

'Does it really matter to you?' Words spoken tenderly, but with something else beneath them.

Miranda didn't speak. He knew it did.

The knowledge caused her to waver and he held her. He rested his chin against her hair, embracing her.

'Let's move on.' Chalgrove spoke ever so softly against her hair. A pang of regret settled inside Miranda.

He released her, except that he clasped his fingers around hers.

His hair was finger-combed. The rain had caused his locks to curl around his ears. His shirt had lost all starch. His mud-caked boots were no more presentable than her shoes. He had passed needing a shave and sported enough hair on his face to begin a beard.

His eyes softened. In that moment, she knew he was going to kiss her. His mouth was nearer and her breasts warmed. She waited, lips parted, the moment bringing her body alive with yearning.

But he stopped and his mouth moved into a rueful smile instead of a kiss. He stepped back, his hand releasing hers. 'Forgive me, Governess. We'll have time to sort this out when we arrive in London.'

The sensations he caused didn't completely melt. But he'd called her Governess for a reason. He'd wanted to erase the attraction between them.

He looked into the distance. 'The magistrate will gather as many constables as it takes. I have the means to hire an army of men.'

It was as if he warned her.

All the warm sensations he'd given her evaporated.

Now, she just had to hope he never found her grandmother, or discovered their relationship. Not that her grandmother could keep anything quiet. A woman, who from the best of Miranda's recollection, never hid in the shadows and enjoyed calling attention her way.

Her grandmother had even complained when she'd had to stay inside the house, blaming the walls, the weather and, again, the stars…even in the bright of day—for bringing such a curse on her. The stars got credit and censure for everything that happened. But no magistrate would ever go after the stars.

Chalgrove would not take it well that her grandmother had abducted him and he already understood they had some connection.

She'd not forgiven her grandmother either. Hardly. But the old woman had once kept her fed and clothed. Plaited her hair in the mornings.

Miranda wanted to keep her alive. And she didn't want to see the woman in a gaol. She was tougher than all the other criminals and would likely be playing her tricks on them, but still…her leathered skin wouldn't be a match for a rope.

She followed his movement, reaching out to his coat, grasping one of the buttons and gazing up. 'You must know I would never have wanted this to happen.'

'I do.' He brushed his knuckles across her cheek and gave a soft shake of his head, and the power of the touch infused her.

She smoothed at her dress and avoided his eyes, then realised, by doing so, she raised more questions in his mind. But her mother had tried and tried to impress upon her that women of quality told the truth. Impure women's words were glossed and shined, and arranged for their own use—their words like pictures on the walls of their minds. For decoration and display and to capture attention.

She didn't want to ruin her reputation, cast aspersions on her dead mother for taking in a waif, then lose Willie and Dolly at the same time if her employer judged her a risk. Even the children's reputations might be hurt because she'd lived with them and been in their father's employ.

'I don't want to see her hanged.'

'You should.'

'She is daft.'

Suddenly, a memory she'd hidden eased into Miranda's mind. Of her, and her grandmother, setting out, walking on that very road, a bucket with bread in it, and going to the fair and, on the way, sleeping in a carriage stall beside a tavern, smelling the sheep dung from the pasture nearby.

A grand adventure and they'd returned with a pack slung over her grandmother's back full of purchases bought with the money made telling fortunes.

Miranda lugged the refilled bucket home, dirtier, more tired, and feeling just as big as her grandmother.

That had been a glorious day. She'd felt richer than she'd ever been since, knowing about the purchases in the pack and knowing that they'd all be eating well for some time.

Her grandmother could spin any thread of conversation into a fine feast, but she'd pushed her luck too far this time.

Miranda quickened her steps, not wanting to linger in the past.

Chimney smoke filtered through the trees, the burning wood aroma mixing with the scent of the wet woods around them. They both stopped at the same time.

'We'll be back in London within hours and justice will follow.'

He took her hand and turned her so that their eyes met. It was as if he gave her one last chance to tell him what she knew.

But she couldn't speak.

The kiss was a whisper against her lips. A whisper of goodbye. An end of their time alone.

Then, still holding her hand, he strode away and she could barely keep up with him.

## Chapter Ten

They'd taken less than ten steps when she heard a dog bark. 'I can see the smoke.' She raised her chin.

'Walk in the woods alongside the road,' he told her. 'Follow me from a distance, so if we aren't greeted well you'll still be hidden.'

She hesitated, but moved to be covered by the trees, and the rain and mud scent of the road was lost among the smells from the chimneys and stoves from the morning meal preparation.

As they rounded a curve, they came upon a clearing with a larger house and two smaller ones further along, plus a church barely big enough to hold more than a dozen people.

She saw Chalgrove stop and study the woods until he located her, but instead of waiting, she ran towards him.

'Wait,' she called out.

She touched his arm and pointed to the next house. 'That one has a child who's already spotted us. A boy with a dog is watching us.'

'I see the dog, but no child.' Chalgrove put a hand to shade his eyes.

'He jumped behind the tree and now he's running into

the house.' She could see the little boy dart away, trousers too short and barefoot feet.

'I guess since we've been announced, we should visit there.'

She nodded. 'The grass is worn away under the tree from children playing. A family who lets their children play instead of working all day would be gentle.' When she heard the words she'd spoken, she realised she'd been repeating something her grandmother had told her from long ago. Words she'd never thought of since her grandmother had abandoned her.

Together they walked to the house, following the worn path.

Before they could get to the door, a thin woman opened it, with two girls at both sides of her faded skirt and a little boy propped on her hip, and a whiff of their breakfast surrounded them. The woman nodded briefly to them.

Chalgrove smiled at her. 'I'm Lord Chalgrove, and I hoped we might talk with your husband. I've been robbed and we escaped our captors on foot. We're needing assistance to return to our homes in London.'

The woman clutched her children closer, fear flashing across her face.

'Don't worry. They were after me. They'd planned this for a long time and I will be able to have them apprehended quickly once I return home.'

She stepped back so they could enter. This house was half again bigger than the cottage, but still small. Surprisingly, a homemade sofa sat at one wall, but Miranda surmised the furniture had been made so it could also be used as a bed.

The woman called to the boy, 'Get Papa.'

He nodded, eyes wide, and was out the door before she'd finished speaking. 'I don't know what we can do for you, except take you to London.' She gave them a tentative smile while she wiped her hands on her apron. 'My husband has to work from daylight until dark in the field because of last night's rains. One of the fields is under water and they're hoping to open up a dirt bank they'd built because it's causing a flood.'

She indicated two chairs, then picked up the youngest girl and held her on her hip.

'I'll see he's paid.'

'Oh, no.' She shifted the baby. 'We must assist you. It's our duty. We would want someone to do the same for us. Just last season, Elbert Daddle broke his leg right before harvest and my husband worked to cut his hay as well.'

While Miranda waited for the husband to arrive, Chalgrove reassured the woman that the culprits were after him, most likely in the hopes that they could steal more money.

A few minutes later, a man entered the room, hay sticking to his clothing.

In seconds, he'd agreed to arrange travel to London.

As soon as she reached London, she'd get back to her post. She'd explain to Mr Trevor that she'd not been able to return as quickly as she'd hoped and he'd understand.

No one could trace her back to her grandmother. Only she knew the connection. She'd treat this as a nightmare, best forgotten, except...

She stole a look at Chalgrove. He still talked to the woman and he had her entire attention.

Even the children watched him. Rapt.

Unkempt, he still had the confidence of a king, and charmed like a fallen saint.

Her grandmother had chosen well. Miranda couldn't take her eyes away from Chalgrove, but she'd have to forget him. And soon.

* * *

The surprise in the driver's face amused her when he stared at all the fine homes as they trundled along, travelling closer to their destination.

Then she realised the servants in the houses had bigger living quarters than the wagon driver was used to.

After Chalgrove directed him to stop in front of his house, Miranda glanced at him, but she didn't have to commit Chalgrove's face to memory. It would always be there.

'I'll travel by hackney to my post.' Miranda stared at the ducal residence, regretting the moment of saying goodbye to him.

'No need.' His voice could have lulled the wind. The words were too calm, showing nothing of underlying emotion, yet hinting of tempest beneath them. 'I'll see you're taken care of.'

He jumped from the cart and told the driver to wait.

Chalgrove secured funds from the butler for the driver and the man took the money after a few refusals. Miranda knew it would be more real coin than the tenant would see in a year.

Before she knew what he was doing, the driver was leaving without her. She turned to Chalgrove, again feeling lost beside the road.

He must have sensed it or seen it written on her face. 'You're not alone…' He paused, taking time with his words. 'No matter what you've done, you'll still have me. I'll make sure you aren't harmed.'

She clung to the words and the compassion in his eyes, but she could also see the mistrust.

He swept the back of his knuckles against hers, spending a moment longer than was necessary, giving her strength.

'You must come inside,' Chalgrove said. 'My mother will see to your care and you'll have the best. This is much more comfortable than an old cottage, I promise you.'

Chalgrove offered her his arm, seeming to know she needed support to enter his home. In that second, a smile teased his eyes. 'You won't need an ale bottle, or even a duelling pistol, but I'm sure Mother can find a pair for you if you'd like. Father once had to get rid of the powder because she'd been reading novels again and she'd been begging him to let her learn to shoot.'

She hesitated.

'You'll be safer with me,' he said. 'No matter what has happened in the past.'

She bolstered herself with his words, understanding that he could help her grandmother better than anyone else could once the magistrate was involved. But she would have to win him over.

Wearing clothing she'd slept in, she walked through the doorway of the finest home she'd ever seen.

A high-pitched screech from a woman's lips sent shards into Miranda's ears.

'What has happened to you?' An older woman hurried down the stairs, squinting, feet moving as fast as her delicate shoes and tight corset would allow. In a quick appraisal, Miranda could tell this woman never sacrificed fashion for comfort. Even the weight of the dress should have hampered the woman's movements, but she didn't slow as she rushed towards him.

He stepped forward and she stopped in front of him, clouding them both in scent.

'Your face?' She put her knuckles to her lips, while staring at her son. 'What dire circumstances have you been in? Were you thrown by a horse? Knocked unconscious?' She put fingertips over her lips. 'And has your valet seen you? I hope not. This would terrify him.'

She patted his cheek. 'I didn't realise you could grow a beard,' she mused, eyes teary. She let her hand rest on his arm, holding on to reassure herself.

He bent to give a kiss to her cheek. 'Since I was a young man, Mother.'

'What happened?' She appraised him again. 'Your clothes are destroyed.'

'I was detained…'

'Detained?'

'Locked in an old cottage. Have you received a ransom note?'

The older woman swayed and Chalgrove caught her, keeping her upright.

'A ransom?' he repeated.

Her eyes fluttered. 'No. No note. You cannot be serious?' She clasped him in a hug, then moved away, stretching her arms, holding him back so she could examine him.

'Very much so.'

'Send for the magistrate and constables,' she called, suddenly alert, running to the stairway and bending over the banister. 'And a physician.'

The sounds of footsteps running up the stairs were followed by a woman calling out, 'A physician as well?'

His mother put a hand to her heart. 'Yes. I may need one.'

The maid rushed away.

His mother's chin quivered as she turned around and rushed back to her son. She noticed Miranda for the first time. 'And was this miss…abducted with you?'

'By coincidence, we shared an ordeal.'

'Oh, my dear.' His mother seized Miranda's arms,

studying her, now completely taking her in. She trapped one of Miranda's hands in both of hers.

She examined Chalgrove. 'How could this happen?'

'I was walking to see Edward and fell in with the wrong crowd, face first. A man had crouched in the shadows, with a club to knock my feet from under me.'

She appraised Miranda, but chose her words. 'Was— Were the two of you taken together?'

'We'd never met before we were captured…individually,' Chalgrove answered. 'We came here because I wanted to be certain Miss Manwaring had your chaperonage immediately so that no aspersions are cast on her character. She has been my sustenance during the ordeal.'

'Sustenance?' His mother's eyes widened.

'A friend. She helped me find the way back to London and I don't want her to be inconvenienced in any way.'

'No one would dare insult a guest in my house,' the Duchess reassured Miranda.

Then she focused on her son again. 'I cannot… I simply cannot accept that you were taken and I did not get a premonition. Of any sort. My life went on as if everything was as normal. What if you'd not escaped? What if you'd been buried alive? What if you'd been thrown in the Thames with rocks tied inside your clothing?'

'Rocks, Mother?'

'Yes, I read about it in a novel. You must put rocks in a bag along with the poor soul you wish to dispose of. Dreadful. Or you could have been sold into some sordid group. *Gift to the Egyptian Princess* explained how such things happen.'

'Mother, you must start reading poetry. Something soothing.'

She clutched her chest. 'I cannot be soothed knowing someone could have hurt you.'

'I was detained, Mother, but all is well now.'

'Your coat is dreadful, and...' she carefully examined his clothing '...your hat?'

'Sadly, it's gone. The criminals took it.'

'The hat? You're sure?'

'Yes. Taken.'

Her voice rose. 'By thieves?'

He nodded.

The older woman's shoulders sagged. 'Such desperation.'

She moved to touch his cheek and her eyes softened. 'Chalgrove, I am so happy you are well.' She sniffed.

Then she continued, putting on a brave front, even though her lip trembled. 'You must tell me exactly what happened.' Then her eyes darted to Miranda, and one eyebrow raised. 'You're sure the two of you weren't captured—together?'

'No, Mother. I was near Gentleman Jackson's. She was taken from another location.'

'The world is a sad place. I told your father it would come to this.' She took one of Chalgrove's hands and one of Miranda's. 'But you're both safe now.'

'Mother...' his voice held a patience which suggested years of practice '... I'm home. Happy. Hungry. And with a guest. Let us show her the best hospitality. I'm sure Miss Manwaring would like a room and a maid to attend her.'

'Well, I've sent the servants scurrying, but I'll find someone for her.'

His mother placed a hand on Miranda's upper arm, giving a light squeeze of support.

'Miss Manwaring, my personal maid will attend you. I'll also see if we can find a suitable gown for you to wear while your clothing is cared for. It will be an honour to have you.'

Then she bustled away.

Chalgrove whispered so close to Miranda that his breath brushed her ear, filling her with warming sensations. 'We'll speak later. After you've had a chance to get settled.'

The sound of footsteps on the stairway caused Chalgrove to pull away. He spoke to the servant who arrived. 'See that Miss Manwaring wants for nothing and that she does not even have to lift a finger to summon anyone. Let me know of all her requests because I want to be certain she has the finest care.'

His voice lowered, almost caressing, and he said. 'She's very dear to me.'

Miranda's heart thudded. She didn't know if he meant the words, but her traitorous body accepted them as if he'd had them engraved in stone.

The servant's shoulders straightened. Then she gave a brisk nod as she led Miranda into the hallway.

They moved up the stairs and stopped at a room, and the maid opened the door for her.

The room did have the flair of a princess's dream. At the top of the walls, a vine of roses traced the space and each bloom seemed created on a different day in the life of one flower, from bud to vibrancy to fade. The vine continued on, with another rose of a different hue.

All the linens in the room were of different shades, but coordinated with the similar flowers that were running along the top of the walls. Windows stretched tall, but didn't fight for attention. They were covered in flowing curtains, the pastels matching hues from the roses.

The tester bed rested serenely among the gentle covers, snuggled in among the other furnishings, all soft and gentle, with smaller roses painted on the canopy.

No silver or gold or gilt, but only a few glass figurines

sat on the surfaces, and the framed paintings were as serene and gentle as the rest of the room, and their frames had been painted pastel.

She'd never seen a room so delicate, or even realised one could exist.

She pivoted to thank the maid and realised another servant had arrived. The second person curtsied and said she had but to ask and it would be done.

Chalgrove had put her in his house and she doubted she could move one foot outside the house without being observed.

The servants fluttered around Miranda, seeing that she had warm bathing water for a hip bath, a dressing gown and the choice between an herb-or rose-scented soap, and told her they'd be back after securing her a clean garment and to ring when she was ready.

She bathed, trying to wash the memories of the past from her body and the knowledge of Chalgrove's touch, and trying to immerse herself in the confidence that she would be able to return to the children soon.

After rising from the water, she donned the gown and called for the maid.

The servant helped with dressing Miranda's hair. Later, the other brought in a day dress and left again.

The gilt that had been saved on the room adorned the dress. The garment was lovely, even if it was a few years behind fashion.

Golden thread ran in patterns on the capped sleeves and on an off-white band below the bodice.

'An old one of Her Grace's daughter's. She never wore it because it didn't fit her well,' the maid explained, 'although she kept it thinking it would fit her again.'

Before Miranda had completely dressed, Chalgrove's

mother whooshed in, her skirt gathered in one hand so she could move rapidly.

She waved the maid away and started talking the second they were alone.

'Were you taken prisoner by bloodthirsty cut-throats? You can tell me, dear. I will not swoon. Chalgrove is trying to spare me the details, I'm sure, for fear I'll be too weak to withstand it. But I *will* have the truth and justice. Justice is best served quickly and swiftly.'

His mother ran a hand under her own chin, mimicking the movement of a sword across the neck.

'I appreciate your help. But, please, don't put yourself to any trouble.' Miranda relocated closer to the wall, hoping to extricate herself from the questions and the overpowering presence of the Duchess. The move didn't work.

'I need to be on my way so I can put this behind me. I want to get back to my duties. My employment.' She certainly didn't want her connection to the old woman to be discovered.

'Don't worry, my dear. You're safe at my home. Chalgrove has everything under control. We have sturdy footmen and good stablemen. We have a small coterie of assistants and we'll find those *cut-throats* before you know it, then you'll not have to worry again.'

Chalgrove's mother's smile fluttered and lodged into a vengeful curve.

She took her handkerchief and dabbed at a tear which never materialised. 'They'll have a quick drop.'

'I would like to reassure everyone I'm well.' Miranda spoke in the same voice she used to soothe Dolly after promising her that Willie would not feed a baby rabbit to the cat.

'Oh, I do like a dutiful daughter.' She edged forward. 'Now I must spoil the surprise. I asked Chalgrove about your family and I have already sent a note to the Manwarings inviting them. People often think it's grand to visit a duchess. Novelty for them.' She laughed. 'Sometimes, I jest with them that we put on our bejewelled slippers just the same as anyone else.'

Miranda stared at the Duchess, a woman whose wishes were almost met before she spoke them and who had grown accustomed to getting her way. Chalgrove's mother had a spirited streak and she was very much like her son in that.

Miranda would find a way to leave quietly and, once she did, she would be putting Chalgrove behind her for ever. But she had no other choice.

She remembered the look in his eyes when he'd promised she wouldn't be harmed. That would be a memory she would cherish for ever. Even if she could remove everything else of the ordeal from her mind, that gaze would be held close.

Chalgrove listened to the rasp of the razor over his cheek as he removed the scruff.

He had to become presentable quickly. He needed to discover Miss Manwaring's secrets. The woman was becoming too enmeshed in his thoughts and he needed to remove her from them.

He'd sent for Wheaton immediately, but he'd not been able to wait on the valet before he had begun shaving. Now, Wheaton waited behind him with a flannel, watching. Chalgrove nicked himself and swore.

No ransom had been requested. His mother hadn't been contacted in any way by the culprits. It was almost as if he'd been taken for no reason. He'd been gone over twenty-four hours, imprisoned and taunted by a mad woman.

The culprits had had time to request a ransom. What

good would it do to take someone, yet let no one know he was gone?

Perhaps it was a case of mistaken identity. He would have the magistrate speak with Beau Brummell's tailor. He glanced in the mirror and spoke over his shoulder to Wheaton. 'Do I look like I could be a tailor? I was mistaken for one.'

Wheaton bowed as he spoke. 'They do not dress as well as you are attired, Your Grace.'

Chalgrove took the flannel and dotted the remnants of the soap from his face, before returning the cloth to Wheaton.

He strode to the door.

He'd asked his mother to keep Miss Manwaring nearby and now her parents were invited to visit. Miss Manwaring didn't think her stepmother as devious as to kidnap them, but she might not see the truth of the other woman.

Plus, his companion knew more than she admitted and he intended to do whatever was needed to do to find out.

'When we finish, I want you to send someone around for a hat for me. One like the one I wore last. If you need to go for it, I don't mind. As long as I get another one.'

'It was certainly a fine hat and quite the crack. I'm deeply distressed it is gone. It made you one of a kind. A true find. But...' he paused '...perhaps not up to the standards required by a duke. I am sure the maker meant well, but if it had been a small amount less elegant, it would have been suitable for a tailor. Perhaps that is how you were mistaken for a tradesman.'

Chalgrove paused.

'An exemplary hat, sir. I am proud to work for a man who has the best of taste.'

Chalgrove took an extra second to stare at Wheaton.

'Have I ever got angry at you for giving me your honest opinion on my clothing?'

'Never. I am completely awash with amazement at how faultless your taste in fashion is. It echoes my own.'

'But the hat was…suitable for a tradesman?'

'I would never assume such a thing. Ever. But a man of the criminal sort is not as discerning as I.'

'You're a good valet. You've been my valet for five years. In my life for all of my life. You could have been sacked had anyone discovered you were trying to scare me when I was a child.'

'I was foxed that night, sir. It seemed like a good idea at the time and you'd become adept at filling my life with all matter of reptiles and rodents. I needed the job and you were a trial.'

'You can tell me the truth, now. Surely.'

'If you insist. You are still a trial—but one I am blessed to have.'

'Hector.'

One shoulder fell and the words seemed pulled from him. 'Your Grace, I know you enjoy flaunting hats to see how they will be received, but that may have been nearing a step too far.'

If it had caused him to be mistaken for a tailor, then perhaps Wheaton had a point.

'When the magistrate arrives, make certain I am informed immediately.'

'I will see if he is here now, sir.'

Privately, he would make sure the man hadn't heard of Miss Manwaring before. But he already knew the answer to that.

At least, he hoped he did. He'd been misled once by a woman's beauty and, in truth, his old sweetheart was nothing compared to Miss Manwaring.

He remembered pulling her through the roof and taking her into his arms after they'd tumbled.

Even with the rain, the roof and the uncertainty around him, he'd been aware every moment their bodies had touched.

## Chapter Eleven

Miranda had no doubt that her parents would visit the Duke of Chalgrove's mother. Her father's wife wouldn't risk offending anyone of the peerage, and few in London would be able to resist any request from a duchess. It just wasn't done.

Two different trays of food had been brought to her, along with two volumes of poetry, and she'd been asked what sort of book she preferred reading, or if she would like another letter posted.

Another knock sounded. The maid, her head bowed, raised her eyes as she entered. 'Miss,' she whispered in her excitement. 'The magistrate has left, but he's sent his best constable and he wishes to speak with you.'

'I— Are you sure?'

'Yes, miss. The master and the constable have been speaking in the library for some time now. They requested you.'

'Oh.' Miranda stood and smoothed the skirt of the borrowed dress. She moved carefully, trying to calm her breathing, and her hands. She wanted to run for the door, yet she had done nothing wrong.

And the one person who had been devious, Miranda didn't have the heart to have her captured.

The only mother Miranda had ever known, the woman who'd found her beside the road, had always told Miranda that her arrival might not have been in the preferred method, but that a blessing didn't always travel the conventional route.

She'd claimed the fortune-teller had been so wise. The woman had told her that a child would come into her household and she must love it as her own. She'd said she'd known then it would happen and she'd prepared herself for Miranda's arrival.

Miranda's mother had smiled and hugged her, telling her how pitiful her new daughter had looked sitting beside the road, with tear-stained cheeks, and together the world had shone brighter for both of them.

Her mother had called her an angel, a gift, but Manwaring had always distanced himself, as if he saw her as nothing more than a bit of refuse that his wife had brought home. Knowing him, she found it surprising he'd allowed her into the household. But it would have taken a colder man than he was to have left a child to starve.

She pulled at the bodice of her dress, trying to make it more sedate. A governess would never wear such a revealing gown and with gold threads. The sleeves fluttered as she walked, reminding her of little wings. The corset she wore had been borrowed from a maid. The shoes, her own, had been cleaned, but were still damp.

The dress suddenly felt too ornate for her. She felt like a child wearing a mother's ball gown.

She would have slipped out the back door and made her way to her employer's house, and the servants would have welcomed her with open arms. But she doubted she'd have

been able to get to the front door without someone noticing, questioning and reporting her activity to Chalgrove.

And he would have followed her, or sent a constable.

She paused, knowing he wouldn't send a constable. He
would arrive himself. A tiny spark of happiness nestled in
her because a bond had grown between them enough she
could believe he would have to see for himself where she
was. She could believe him when he said she wouldn't be
harmed. He meant it.

But he'd not promised anything about her grandmother.
Except justice.

Miranda couldn't leave without arousing his suspicion,
or without the awareness that the moments between them
would never be the same again.

As soon as her governess dress dried, she intended to
put it back on. Perhaps then she would be able to have the
strength to find a way to convince him to forget about the
abduction, then walk out the door and say goodbye to the
moments she'd spent with Chalgrove.

She followed the maid to a door, waited as she knocked
and entered after the girl opened it for her.

The library had few books, but if a room could have a
learned air without books, this one did.

Rays of light filtered through the oversized windows
and the scent of cleaning oils hit her. Oak wood gleamed.
The pieces of furniture more solid and designed to last longer than the trees that had been felled for their construc-
tion would have lived had they been left to the elements.

The room had no hint of a woman's presence except for
the solemn painting above the fireplace of two children.
The boy had a book tucked under his arm. The girl sat in
a small chair, her doll at her side, dressed in the same perfect dress as her owner. The children were being trained

to take their roles in life, or the artist had been advised to paint them such.

Chalgrove stood in the room, more than a mere duke in this house, more a sovereign of the residence. Gone was the stubble, the rumpled clothes and the man she'd first known. This man took up space in a room the same as he had at the cottage, but he could command a bigger room. In the little house, he was out of his element. In his world, he ruled. He knew it. Every thread of his clothes knew it. Less emotion was showing on his face than would have shown from a portrait.

Her eyes wouldn't turn away. This stranger was the same man she'd seen only hours before. She searched for the bond they'd had, but she didn't know if it still existed or if he'd shaken it off with his bathing water.

Her heartbeat chugged along, but she had to remind herself to breathe easily. She *had* been captured and *was* innocent. And she should want the culprit caught—only she didn't.

She gave a curtsy to Chalgrove. Her first for him.

A shuffling movement at the side of the room caught her eye. The spindly man eyed her more closely than she'd watched Chalgrove.

The constable's clothing was sombre except for a checked waistcoat. If she'd seen him on the street, with his drooping eyelids and his thin, tilted nose, she would not have judged him friendly, even with the curling hair framing his face, and would have given him wide berth.

But he smiled at her, his teeth almost too big to fit inside his mouth, and waved a hand for her to be seated.

She took a chair across from him.

'I wish we could have prevented your ordeal, Miss Manwaring,' the constable intoned as he sat and gave a quick snap at the hem of his waistcoat to put it in place.

Chalgrove strode to the window, as if he were more interested in the scene outside than any happenings in the room. His movements alerted her more than if he'd casually sat. The coat he wore contrasted with the shirt underneath. She wondered if he wore the almost mismatched colours to state his power. To tell others he could wear what he wished and to speak of it with him might be unsettling for the speaker.

'Please recount for me the happenings of the day you were taken,' the constable interrupted her reflections.

She told him her story, only mentioning that she'd expected to find a dying person who could tell her the circumstances of her birth.

He chewed the inside of his lip as she talked.

'Do you know who might have done this?'

She swallowed. She glanced at Chalgrove. He'd not altered his movement. 'At first, I deduced, erroneously, I'd been abducted by the Duke, although I didn't recognise him as such. He was dishevelled from the circumstance and I perceived him to be of a criminal sort.'

Chalgrove's lips tilted in amusement.

'Continue.' The constable leaned back, giving the appearance of someone more befuddled than proficient. But she doubted the magistrate would assign anyone to help the Duke who wasn't the best.

Her eyes returned to the older man. 'I was obviously wrong and I understood it was possible that I had been captured in expectation that my parents might pay a ransom. I am not wealthy, but with my father's estate, it could have been assumed he would disburse funds to have me safe. And my position as a governess made me an easy target. It wouldn't be obvious that I normally travel with one of the other servants from the house.'

'I see.'

'And the Duke, he would have easily been assumed to be worth a large sum of money. A criminal could think holding two might be no more risk than one.'

'Go on.'

'Go on?' She raised her shoulders. 'I'm a governess. I don't know the workings of a criminal mind. I was hoping you might shed some light on this situation. What is your conclusion?'

She saw a glimpse of more teeth. 'I don't have one.'

She raised a brow.

'Too early. I don't draw conclusions, anyway. I draw solutions.'

Chalgrove took a small step and the movement signalled his entrance into the conversation. 'I have men visiting the small cottage to see if anyone reappears. If they do, they are to be brought here.'

She touched her throat. She could imagine her grandmother in the Duke's house, screaming curses, blaming everything on Miranda and causing a ruckus suitable to Drury Lane.

'Let me ask—do you know of anyone who might wish you ill?' The constable's teeth appeared to grow larger as his eyes grew smaller.

'I can't think of anyone who might dislike me enough to kidnap me.'

'Do you have anyone who dislikes you at all?' His features took on the expression of a clergyman ready to start collecting names of the purgatory bound. Then he grinned, and he might as well have sprouted horns.

'Well…' she gave him a pointed blink to let him know she didn't appreciate his probing '… I would hope I am well liked by all who meet me. My stepmother and I have no great love for each other, but I assure you, she is *not* a kidnapper.'

'So, what's the verdict on His Lordship? He bear up well under pressure?' the constable asked.

She stiffened her back and heard a laughing snort from Chalgrove before he spoke. 'I am deeply offended. And do not answer, Miss Manwaring. It's not pertinent to the crime.'

He nodded.

'Shouldn't you be taking notes?'

He scratched his head. 'I have an amazing memory, Miss Littlemore.'

Her frown let him know she didn't appreciate his jest regarding her name.

'Ah, Miss Manwaring, I find a little humour makes my task easier. Particularly if it is at the expense of others. An irritated person says more.'

'Does it help you catch the culprit?' she challenged, temporarily forgetting her wish.

'Not at all. But we have no shortage of the criminally minded so I am always in demand.'

He stood. 'Every crime is not solved in a day. And with one of this magnitude, we can't make a mistake, not that I feel it is possible.'

She waited.

'And what is your employer's name?' he asked. 'I wish to see if he noted anything out of the ordinary.'

'I would rather he not know of this.'

The constable's brows rose. 'And I would rather him not have anything to know of. His name, please. If you do not give it, I will merely ask the Manwarings.'

She gulped, but tried to hide everything she felt. 'His name is Carlton Trevor. He is such a reticent man. But please...' She heard the pleading in her voice. 'Please do not worry him more than you can possibly help. He up- sets easily when something varies from the usual and he cares greatly for his children. I fear I will lose my position if he knows of this.'

He waved a hand. 'Don't worry about that. I can be subtle. I have never been up until now, but I'm sure I can be.'

'Be subtle,' the Duke commanded. 'I would not want Miss Manwaring to lose her job for no reason.'

'I will,' the constable said. 'He'll never even know he's being questioned.'

'Please don't upset him.'

The constable grimaced. 'Perhaps it would have been easier if you'd been taken alone. It's not every day someone nabs a duke. Word is sure to spread, what with it being an abduction crime. Capital offence. No choice but to make an example.'

'Let's see that it doesn't,' Chalgrove said. 'It would be easy enough to say Miss Manwaring was merely led into a trap by a cutpurse who convinced her a friend was dying and, when no funds were to be had, locked her in a cottage.'

The constable gave her a bow, spoke with the Duke, assuring him that he would personally oversee the other constables who would be dispatched to solve the crime and they would bring this to a quick end. Then he took his leave.

*Crime. This was a crime. Of abduction. A capital offence.*

No matter how much she'd hated her grandmother for leaving her beside the road, her grandmother had given her treacle, taught her to spit and braided her hair much more gently than even Miss Cuthbert had.

She rose. She didn't want her grandmother hanged. She touched her neck. Nor did she want to be standing at her side.

# Chapter Twelve

Chalgrove stood just at the opening of the door as he closed it behind the constable. She could tell he was thinking of the cottage, and the old woman, and her role in the ordeal.

'I'm pleased you stayed, Miss Manwaring.'

With the warmth in his words, the bond between them appeared again. It was as if he was no longer the Duke, but the ruffian she'd seen the first night in the cottage.

With the most delicate touch, he took her arm and led her towards the seat the constable had vacated. He couldn't be aware of the fluttery longings he caused in her body.

She waited before sitting, not caring how long it was proper to examine him, and he accepted her appraisal without any censure. They were not enemies or lovers, but she hoped they were more than friends.

In those seconds, she didn't see him as a peer and she could tell he wasn't judging her as a subordinate. They were two people who knew each other and, even though they had entirely different backgrounds, she was certain that, perhaps in some way, they could follow each other's mind without speaking more than a few syllables.

She also suspected, that, for the rest of her life, every

time she heard his name she would listen. She wondered if he would do the same.

'Am I to be questioned again?' she asked.

'A few minutes in your presence would be a pleasure for me. You don't have to assume that I only wish to ask questions.'

'But it's true.'

'Not entirely. We met in unusual circumstances and I would think that brought extreme emotions to the surface for you. It did for me.'

'Not good ones.' She'd been terrified. The darkness. She didn't think her grandmother was capable of murder, or anything that would cause harm, but she'd been afraid when a man had been pushed into the room. Her grandmother had said she was bringing her a husband and, for once, she knew her words hadn't been a lie.

'All the same. We've shared something of life and death. Perhaps that is nearly like a...' he shrugged '...marriage?' He watched her face.

'No.' She pulled her shoulders back. 'I would not think that. It was survival. Instinct. An attempt to stay alive.'

There was the slightest twitch behind his eyes. 'Who knows? Perhaps a struggling situation can show two people either at their best or their worst and it is much more telling than a few sweet words at a soirée when all have on their best society gloves.' He touched his forehead. The red scratches were visible. 'You had on no gloves.'

A pang of guilt touched her. 'I would never have done that if I had known you had no more to do with the situation than I did.' Except, he didn't have a mad grandmother in his family lineage. That would be best kept private. Mr Trevor would not take that well. Chalgrove would not take that well either.

'My employer will accept that I was gone longer than

he expected, but he will not understand if I am in London and have not returned to my post.'

'I'll send a note around to the residence expressing gratitude for your help.' One side of his lips quirked up. 'I assure you, your employer will be most happy to do as I ask.' He seemed to be letting her in on a secret. 'Peerages are a currency all their own. I can't change that so I might as well use it for good reasons.'

'I would appreciate it, but you don't know how nervous Mr Trevor is. He insists that I not let Willie run too fast.' While Willie was only one breakneck instant from being a hellion, his father was just as close to being too cautious for Willie's own good.

'I'll soothe his fears,' he reassured her.

She could see a trace of the methods he might use on her employer when he moved closer to her. His eyes softened. 'I kissed you and I held you in the rain. Those moments were almost as intimate as making love. I didn't want to let you go that morning. Did it not mean anything for you?'

'It can't. I have to put it in the past. To forget it. For my life to be given back to me.'

Chalgrove spoke. 'I don't feel I can put this behind me until the people who took my freedom are punished.'

'It won't undo what happened,' she continued.

'Even if it did, I would still want them punished.'

They stood so close, she couldn't ignore the marks she'd put on his face. Three scratches at his left temple. She wondered if he'd carry the scars for ever.

He caught her appraisal. 'It's fine. A memento of our meeting. My valet suggested he could change my hair to cover it, but it's not big enough to matter. The valet said the scratches are in good alignment and will add character if they don't fade completely. I suspect he is hoping I will be scarred.'

'I was terrified.'

'I beg your pardon for that. I should have introduced myself.'

She doubted she would have trusted he was a duke at first, rather perceived it another trick. 'You did. Eventually.'

'I don't blame you for the marks, I blame the old woman.'

'I can't judge her happy with her life.' She didn't back away, feeling she could sense his reaction better if they remained almost touching. 'Circumstances must have made her what she is.'

'Why would you care? Why would you even think of that?'

'Probably because I have been a ward almost since I can remember. I loved my mother dearly, but I don't take the riches I have as my due.' After her mother had died, some of the servants treated her with a little less respect. And when her stepmother arrived, the gulf widened more.

'Riches?' He studied her. 'You're a governess.'

'Yes. But I am not selling apples on a street corner, or worse. No one said life was to be easy for me. If the Manwarings hadn't taken me in, I might be one of the most unfortunate people. I *was* one of those people.' She would have followed her grandmother into a rough life.

'What do you know of your life before you became a ward?'

'I never talk of it any more.' She'd not even talked of it when her grandmother had left her, believing her grandmother when she told her that she must never ever mention their connection. She'd detailed the perils that would happen if anyone found out her background.

It wasn't the first time she'd been warned to do exactly as she was told. Her grandmother had said it time and time again.

The sound of someone speaking from below stairs floated to them.

He moved and, with one arm extended, shut the door. Then he stepped closer and lowered his voice.

'I will discover who she is and where she is, and the courts will take care of the rest.'

'I didn't know anything about the abduction until I found myself in the room with the door shutting behind me.'

His face tightened. 'They should be punished for that alone. Not to mention for the fear you felt when I was added. And that is why this puzzles me so much. I wonder if you were double-crossed and I wonder if the fascination I have with you is because I don't truly know who you are.'

His words jarred her. He thought her in league with the criminals.

'I don't know who I truly *was*,' she said, words terse. 'But I know who I am. And that is a governess. And I am about as fascinating as any other governess.'

She grasped her skirt to leave and he touched her waist, stopping her with a light touch. 'Never let yourself believe that you are like any other person. You aren't. Not to me. I know the woman asked if you'd forgotten her name.'

He believed her capable of a crime. She opened her mouth to tell him of her grandmother, but then she froze. Once the words were out of her mouth, she would have no control of how he reacted to them. She remained silent.

'I saw the shoes flying,' he said. 'And yet I still promised you would not be harmed for this crime. I have given you amnesty. The criminals punished you enough. Now you have a chance to repay them for that.'

Chalgrove had only promised to keep her unharmed, not her grandmother.

'When you said you would not harm me, did you also believe at that time I might have been cheated by the criminals?'

'Yes.'

'So, did you mean the words?'

'You will not believe how fast and quietly the culprits can be punished. The magistrate promised me. The others will be taken care of quickly.'

'You can't.'

He went to the desk, reached for a paper and held it out to her.

She saw her handwriting and gasped. 'That's the note I sent Nicky after I returned.'

He held it to her. She took it. The sealing wax was unbroken. She gripped the missive. 'Why wasn't it sent?'

'The servants are to check with me before anyone or anything enters or leaves this house. A simple rule that I insisted on right after we arrived.'

The paper crumpled in her hand before she realised it. Chalgrove held her life and her grandmother's just as easily. Who could say if he might change his mind?

She took in a breath and met his eyes. Her courage might mean the difference between whether her grandmother lived or died.

'I'm just letting Nicky know that I am fine. He would worry.' She firmed her jaw and met Chalgrove's eyes. 'I care for him a great deal. He is the closest thing I have ever had to a father, in truth.'

She slipped her finger under the seal, slit it open and held the words towards him. He waved them away, but she didn't move.

Finally, he slipped the note from her hands, their fingers brushing. He folded it and strode to the pull.

After the servant rapped on the door, Chalgrove bade them enter. Once the maid stepped in, Chalgrove handed the missive to the girl. 'See that this is sent immediately.'

Then they were alone again.

'Do you know where the person is who took us? You will only prolong the process by keeping silent,' he asked.

She moved closer. 'I wouldn't tell you if I did.'

'That man you just sent the note to might have had something to do with our abduction.'

She shook her head slowly, from side to side. 'No. Not Nicky. You've not met him. And you can't punish everyone I've ever spoken to. There's not enough room in the gaol or the gallows.'

'Miranda. We're alone in this room and you can tell me the truth. You and I both know you've not told me everything you're aware of.' He let out a sigh. 'We're not enemies.' He shook his head. 'We can't be. You've already tried to kill me once and I thought we'd got past that.'

He took her shoulders in his hands. The touch, gentle, surprised her. And she was captured as a baby bird would be if he'd clasped both hands over the creature.

Miranda felt her heartbeat increase.

'Who are you protecting? And whomever you're protecting, don't trust them enough not to do the same thing again. You can't.'

Her stomach plummeted. She clasped the lapel of his waistcoat, holding herself steady. She could imagine her grandmother repeating her mistake. Capturing her again.

The moment lingered between them, then he took her chin in his hand and kissed her, soft and slow, moist and burning. A sensual explosion of taste and tenderness. An awareness of his masculinity and a connection she'd not expected.

He stopped, letting silence move into the space between them. He touched her cheek, as if he tried to soften his next words.

'Your parents are on their way here,' he said. 'They'll need to see that you're safe.'

The illusion she'd had of her life returning to normal evaporated.

'They're not my parents. They're the Manwarings, summoned by the Duke of Chalgrove. They daren't refuse.'

'You believe that the Manwarings had nothing to do with the abduction,' he said. 'But I need to believe it.'

'They didn't,' she said. 'They wouldn't expend the effort.'

She'd grown up with a father who hardly saw her except at rare times. Who truly didn't live in the house, even after her mother had died and her stepmother had moved in.

She was little more than a silhouette in his life. A hint of a child to satisfy her mother. Much like an overly large jewellery piece he might give his wife and then expect her to wear it on special occasions.

The Duke took his hands away. 'So, you choose not to have a family—'

'I choose to have true friends. Not all my friends are always proper and they may annoy me, but they aren't false. I choose them carefully and I am friendly, but keep the ones at arm's length who have small hearts—'

She paused. 'I know a governess is not truly a member of the upstairs, nor truly a servant. But I have made friends as much as I can with the servants of the household. I have used every scrap of wiles I have and done my best to charm every breathing soul in that house, and the ones at the shops who I see and the people around me at Sunday Services.'

'I would think you do not have to work hard to charm them.' His chin gave nothing more than a twitch of negative.

She nodded. 'I do. As I know they are all concerned about their own life and their own path. And most are selfish and truly care nothing for me. A few do. And those are the ones who I would not want to worry about me when it is unneeded.'

She'd already been beside the road once. She'd got a mother, but then when her mother had died, her home became someone else's. Even her room had been changed to another one because her father's wife said Miranda needed privacy. She could still hear the purr of her stepmother and knew the woman would happily deposit her along another road if she could. Her father would put up no protest.

'Why do you choose to live among the shadows? Your father is more entrenched in society than you let on. I've attended several soirées with him present. Your father and I belong to the same club.'

'Without his acceptance, I fit nowhere. That world doesn't need me. Only in the world of the servants am I useful. I may not be accepted by everyone there either. But I am more acknowledged than I was in my father's household.' She touched her chest. 'I spent most of my life in their world and some of them know I wasn't born there and have no concern with it. Others think I am presumptuous, but those are not my friends. With them I *am* presumptuous' She chuckled. 'A haughty governess of unknown parentage. Rather feather ruffling to some.'

Her mother had been reclusive and sickly and hadn't wanted much to do with society, and the glittering world had been an unfamiliar place to Miranda. In fact, she and her mother had tended to spend more time with servants than anyone else.

But the woman who'd moved in after her mother's death had been so different.

Her stepmother had wanted to shine and her daughters to get all the attention. Miranda was a hindrance.

'Society doesn't accept me.'

'Perhaps if you tried to enchant the people of society as much as you do the servants and shopkeepers, they would. You could captivate anyone. You really could. And you do. I would guess the distance you keep around yourself makes you more intriguing and you cause people to want to breach the wall around that surrounds you. To be your friend.' He clasped her hand.

She raised her chin. 'That is preposterous. I worked hard to be friendly.'

'You may have worked hard to put yourself in their path, but in honesty you admitted to me that most of them are selfish and your true friendship is only given to worthy people.'

From a young age she'd realised she had to be careful who she could trust. Even so, once when she'd broached the subject to her mother of finding her grandmother a hint of sadness had shown in the woman's eyes.

'I'd like it if you didn't think about such things,' she'd answered. 'I'd like you to always think of me as your mother. Your only mother.'

It had seemed unfair to question anything after that. It had felt like betrayal.

She imagined Chalgrove's life.

He'd always known who his father was. His mother. His place in society.

Never once would he have had to question any of those things.

When his father died, he'd immediately stepped into the role prepared for him.

When her mother died, she'd been afraid her father would toss her out and, when he'd brought home a wife, she'd almost wished for it. Then she'd planned an escape.

Chalgrove had no idea what it would be like for her to try to enter society's world. Her stepmother had worked even harder than her father to keep Miranda in the shadows.

She'd thought she would never see them again, but now it appeared she would.

Miranda studied his face and almost felt she could tell him who her grandmother was.

But then she saw a flicker at his jaw and she batted those illusions away, and made an excuse to return to her room. She couldn't let him use her emotions to trap her grandmother.

## Chapter Thirteen

Miranda walked to her room feeling as if she'd been nearing a sugar-spun dream and a nightmare of darkness at the same time.

She remembered the salty-sweet taste of his lips. The promise of her safety. Words he could easily change.

When she arrived at her door, she saw a maid poised to knock.

'Oh, I'm so glad to find you, miss. Her Ladyship would like to speak with you.'

'Please tell her I'm suffering from the effects of my recent trauma.'

The maid's composure wavered. 'I will, of course, if you ask. But I do not recommend telling her.'

'You don't?'

'No.' She whispered, 'It is best to do as she wishes. I recommend you find her. She has never experienced the possibility of her suggestions being ignored and could take great affront.'

'If you're trying to tell me she may pitch me out, don't worry. I don't wish to encroach on her hospitality, anyway.'

'Oh, no, no, no. She's a gentle sort. Gentle. She rules

this house with the softest touch, but even soft touches can pinch.'

'Please make my kindest excuses, then, as I must get some rest. The events have near swept me under a rug.' Miranda entered her room and touched the rail of the four-poster bed. 'I'm exhausted.'

'I understand and will try to inform her.'

The knock barely sank into Miranda's consciousness, but the jostle at her bedside woke her.

'Oh, dear, you must be tired.' Her Ladyship stood over her.

She actually pulled the covers up and gave a few pats to tuck Miranda snugly in bed. 'I waited as long as I could and then became concerned you'd been abducted again from right under our noses.'

The Duchess shuddered, brushed a hand at her breast and then inhaled. She moved to the pull and tugged it. 'I talk to my son and he tells me almost nothing and makes it sound like a misunderstanding, but his clothing was in tatters when he arrived home, then the magistrate appeared and sent a constable. There are probably three men watching the house each time I look out of the window.'

Next, she sat on the bed. 'I hope you are up to talking about your adventure.'

Miranda had a feeling it wouldn't matter if she didn't feel well. The Duchess wasn't going to rest until her curiosity was satisfied.

'My son is trying to spare my sensibilities—or the ones he thinks I have,' the Duchess said. 'He will not divulge anything much except to say you both were taken from different places by several men and a woman and held in a small home. He said the cottage was warm and dark, but otherwise not bad.'

'True.'

'He said you weren't compromised?'

'No. Of course not. He was ever the honourable gentleman.'

'Well…' The older woman lowered her voice. 'He's remarkably handsome and you are lovely. A mother needs to be reassured no harm has been done and, if harm had been done, I would want to help repair any damage. I could not tolerate Susanna and feared constantly he might marry her. I pretended not to know how much time he spent with her—and she was ruthless. At least that is what I heard and surmised.'

'Are you sure he would want you to discuss this with me?'

The Duchess batted away Miranda's concern. She raised one eyebrow. 'Well, he did allow me to alert him to any potential future wife. So, he is sensible.'

Miranda bowed. 'Please understand, Your Grace, it is difficult for me to speak of it as well. At first, it was dark and I didn't know what would happen. Then, your son managed to save us.'

'That's Chalgrove. He's always lived up to his heritage. Except…where his private life is concerned. The women he finds attractive have been appalling.' She blinked and contemplated Miranda. 'Perhaps we could discuss you instead.'

Miranda pushed herself to the opposite side of the bed.

'When all is said and done…' Miranda composed her words carefully '… I'm suited to be a governess. I have two charges to care for. Their mother died soon after the younger was born, and… You must understand. I love them dearly. I must get back to them.' She reflected on the Duchess's absorption in her words. Miranda raised her chin, the problem solved in her mind. 'My employer is quite kind. The children come first in my life.'

'They do?' The Duchess's brows rose. 'Even though they are not your own?'

Miranda nodded. An idea glimmered in her mind, but she immediately pushed it aside. She could not dwell on having her own children. Chalgrove's children. She couldn't dream of snuggling his child close and wrapping her arms around it and its wispy little feathery tips of hair.

She had to keep her attention on Dolly and Willie. They were here, they were motherless and they needed her. 'I love my charges.'

The Duchess ducked her chin. 'What a fresh idea and what we all hope for in a governess. I mostly left Chalgrove on his own until after university. He's his father's son and we surrounded him with people who would take good care of him. I want that to continue. I wish for him to have a wife who will be at his side and I have a lady to assess, Miss Antonia Redding.'

The Duchess's cheeks plumped as she smiled. 'After all, he needs someone nearby who he can trust to have his best interests at heart. Someone who will hire a...um... good governess.'

The Duke's mother smoothed the bedcover beside her. 'It's rather like a chess game, only you're playing for life. It's part of the game. Move the pawns, bishops, knights, whatever, to try to get a mate. Check. You'd think it's much easier on my side of the table, but not really. Until this incident, it had not occurred to me that anything could happen to him. It's even more important now that he have an heir.'

Tapping her fingertips together, she added, 'I have several more prospects to evaluate for him—and, yes, my son comprehends I'm choosing his wife. He is such a dutiful son that he trusts me in this.'

Someone knocked and the Duchess called out for them to enter. A maid came in. 'Emerald,' the Duchess whispered. The woman bobbed a few times and left on the run.

Chalgrove's mother whispered, 'I do have the best servants. They do make the occasional mistake of letting me go about half-dressed—and this has been trying. I forgot my necklace this morning because I was thinking of who might be my best daughter-in-law and reading over the letter again my sister had written about the young lady.'

'Reasonable.'

She took one finger and patted down the skin at her eyes. 'Egg whites.' She rotated to Miranda. 'An old trick of the Quality. Have a maid brush just the slightest amount while holding your skin firm and blow. Once dry, it gives a youthful smoothness.' She jutted her skin in Miranda's direction, waiting.

'Very, very smooth,' Miranda agreed.

She stopped her preening. 'Sometimes I wonder if I'm not searching too hard to select a daughter-in-law. I suppose I'm wrongly considered meddling—perhaps from the top of my perfect coiffure to the tips of my specially made slippers.' She moved back and raised a hem.

She stopped at the door and it seemed to magically open for her, a servant listening at the other side. 'But, Miss Manwaring, I do want you to know I thank you most utterly for your part in the rescue of my son. He has a rakish side. Inherited his fashion sense from his father, though. Nothing can be done about it. Luckily he can't hide those eyes he inherited from me.'

She laughed. 'My eyes and smile. They were my fortune because it allowed me to have an asset a man would notice, much like I might notice a title.'

The Duchess inspected Miranda. 'I'm duty bound to find Chalgrove the best wife and one he can be content with. I wish them to suit, just as my husband and I once did. All marriages should be so perfectly formed. We were perfection together and our parents decided we would make a good union when I was just a child. I am forever grateful.'

She sighed. 'I will find my son a wife. If I'd have known it was going to be this difficult, I would have taken interest in the education and training of several suitable female children right after he was born. Then he could have chosen from my protégées.' Her shoulders drooped. 'Sadly, I had no idea how short the time had become for him to marry. The ordeal you had convinced me. I can only pray Antonia is the one for him.'

She gave a sniff before speaking. 'You'll be a governess again in no time. And I will finish my project soon. I'm planning a few exploratory soirées.' She sighed. 'Not enough hours in the day. But my son entrusted me with this duty. It is endearing when people realise you can observe their life objectively and make decisions for them.'

'Your future family member will be fortunate to have such a caring mother-in-law.'

'That's so kind of you, Miss Manwaring.' She finger-combed a few curls framing her face. 'And you truly do not mind being unwed?'

'No.' Miranda spoke gently, not putting any unpleasant emphasis on the word. 'If I were to marry, my employer would have to let me go because I was hired to put the children first. They are my life.'

'Ah… Well, please join us as soon as you can. Your parents are here. I hadn't realised that the Manwarings are in society and it occurred to me that perhaps you might be suitable for a bride for Chalgrove. But if you wish to remain a governess, then it is your choice. Besides, Antonia is so well recommended.'

She moved through the door. and a maid stretched her arm in and pulled the door shut, right before she gave Miranda an encouraging smile.

## *Chapter Fourteen*

Her father's wife stood, her silver hair swept back so elegantly it classified as a crowning glory, a crumpled handkerchief in her hand. Her father remained a half-step behind his wife. He dressed more as an old Puritan than a man of society, his only idea of ornamentation the huge signet ring he wore. His hair had thinned and the lines on his face doubled since she had seen him last.

Her stepmother wore a gown with oversized sleeves and extra rows of flounces at the skirt, but she had managed to pull it all together into something fashionable.

Tears were in her eyes, but that didn't surprise Miranda. Her stepmother cried at every meeting, every stumble, every chance. She cried when happy, when sad and when she wanted to make sure her tears hadn't deserted her. And, if attention strayed too far from her, Priscilla's tears could almost work in the same manner as a bark in a church.

Priscilla rushed to grasp Miranda's hands. 'Are you… all right?'

'I'm well.' Miranda gave a smile and let herself be pulled into her stepmother's arms. A fragrance of perfumes and medicinals washed over Miranda and she clamped her teeth together behind her upturned lips. Her stepmother had never hugged her before.

'I'm so glad you're safe.' The woman pulled back a little. 'I cannot think how this could have happened in this day and age. We should never have let you work. Never. I feel we must shoulder the blame, but you insisted and how could we stop you?'

Miranda removed herself from the suffocating grasp. Her stepmother would have made a deal with the devil, or with Miranda's grandmother, to get her daughters abducted and put into a room with Chalgrove.

Her father, hands clasped behind his back, had bowed his head. When he lifted it, she noticed a wetness in his eyes.

'Father?' she asked, surprised at the emotion.

He walked around his wife and took Miranda's arm. 'I'm pleased you weren't injured and you're back,' he said.

Miranda saw the tense glance his wife gave him.

'Thank you,' she said, shocked to see that he did care for her.

He pursed his lips, gave her weak smile, and blinked the tears away. 'You may come home to recover if you wish.'

His wife gasped and Miranda felt her stepmother's nails clench into her skin and tighten now on Miranda's arm.

'I believe you've met the Duke—' Miranda pulled herself away from the talons '—and he was instrumental in our escape.'

Her father nodded. 'Chalgrove and I have met.'

Chalgrove waved a hand for them to sit, and the ladies eased themselves on to the hardback chairs. Her father took the overstuffed chair, back straight. Lips firm.

Chalgrove moved to the desk, purposeful. Behind the

welcome on his face, she saw a tightness in his shoulders and his hand tensed on the surface of the wood.

'I didn't realise you knew the Duke,' Priscilla spoke to her husband.

'We've talked horses together. Bought myself a fine gelding on his suggestion.'

'Well, we must express our gratitude for him saving your ward.' Priscilla gripped the handkerchief. 'You must let us know everything that happened. Everything.'

'Miss Manwaring has been pivotal,' Chalgrove spoke. 'Without her I would not have found the road to London after we escaped.'

'Yes. She's sturdy,' her stepmother analysed her.

'I fear this ordeal may have taken a toll on her,' Chalgrove said, his words calm and soothing. 'I also am afraid the criminals may wish to harm her to prevent the possibility of her aiding in their trial when they are captured. I'd hoped your family might stay here a few days while we search for the criminals.'

For the only time in their acquaintance, Miranda saw Priscilla drop the handkerchief.

'Of-course-we'd-be-delighted.' Priscilla spoke as if it were one word, before her husband could more than open his mouth.

'I'd hoped for your consent,' Chalgrove said. In those words, Miranda knew he'd had no expectation of any other response. 'My mother will be pleased to have visitors as she enjoys company so much.'

'Well, I don't know...' Her father hesitated. 'I'd planned to leave tomorrow to attend business at one of my estates. Apparently, a tree fell on a carriage house—of all things. And the man there thinks he's in need of an army to do the repairs.'

'All the more reason for the ladies to stay here,' Chalgrove responded. 'I have already alerted the most trusted servants to be on their guard because of how Miss Manwaring has been threatened recently. That is enough for them to know. No one will be able to get in or out of this house without my knowledge. Your daughter will be safe.'

'Awfully sporting of you to protect my family like this.' Her father's lips thinned and he seemed to want to say more before averting his eyes.

Miranda thought he might need the handkerchief.

'Of course, I could do nothing less.'

Chalgrove might have had the intensity of a hawk in his gaze, but the mouse's squeak came from Priscilla as she jumped to her feet. 'Oh, Your Lordship, your graciousness is beyond compare. I so appreciate your deep kindness to our daughter.' Affection glittered in her eyes. But behind the affection, Miranda saw smug calculation.

Priscilla bent and gave a quick squeeze to Miranda, who pulled away. Her arm still burned from the last touch Priscilla had given her.

Priscilla recognised the reticence and a puff of air blew out her cheeks. Miranda felt the blade of an invisible knife sliding down her spine.

'Now we're reassured she's in good company, I suppose I should get on my way.' Her father stood.

When their eyes met, she felt he looked at her as a daughter—something she'd never expected in her lifetime.

'I'm pleased you made the trip,' she told him.

He gave a one-shouldered shrug. 'You're safe now. All's well.' He held out his hand to his wife, to assist her to her feet.

Priscilla grabbed her husband's arm and spoke to Chalgrove. 'I hope you'll excuse us. I must send a few notes to my household and I know my husband must get to his business now.'

She left, a blur of overstuffed skirts and lace.

Left alone, Chalgrove stood and approached Miranda, bathing her in the scent of freshly laundered clothes dried in sunshine, starch and a hint of dried rose petals.

He took her clasped hand and pulled her to her feet. He dropped a kiss lightly above the knuckles and moved to the door.

With his hand on the frame, he lowered his voice. 'For your safety, if you leave, I have men who'll accompany you. The constable recommended it.'

He waited, no longer watching her, but staring as if he tried to see inside himself. 'I can't stop thinking about you and not just about what you're hiding. You've lodged in my mind and I feel that ending this will also destroy the connection I have with you.'

'You would have never noticed me except for the ordeal.'

'It could be,' he mused. 'Which could have been the biggest mistake of my life, yet I would never have known it. Who knows?

'But I have an appreciation for someone tossed aside and determined to make the best of it,' he continued. 'Alone. I admire you, Miss Manwaring, for making your own way. And, yes, for the oddest and most dangerous thing of all—for not telling me your secret.'

'I had little choice in the matter of making my way alone.' She didn't want him misled by Priscilla. She wasn't the loving stepmother, but always grasping for more. Priscilla only breathed to suit herself. Her children next. Anything which might take even a glance which she felt should go to her daughters would be crumpled and tossed away if possible. And in no way did Priscilla feel Miranda was her daughter. Priscilla had considered her an obstacle to be removed.

'You could have married.' His voice rumbled and his eyes assessed her with no modesty, no prurient nature, but showed an acknowledgement of her femininity. 'Married well.'

'My stepmother didn't wish for me to be introduced to society, and I didn't wish to be introduced.'

'Yet you would have been safer, I would think. As a wife.'

'You worry more than the constable.' She stood and moved to the door, planning to leave.

He stopped at the door before he opened it for her. 'Just because I admire you for keeping your privacy…don't be surprised when I find things out.'

The subtle movement of his jaw betrayed an intensity inside him. He touched her chin. His hair fell across his forehead, in touchable strands. But still, he was of the world of her stepmother—the society which had ignored her and she'd been grateful.

'Miranda, you slept in the bed beside me. I listened to you breathe as I lay awake. We've shared too much intimacy for false pleasantries and sidestepping. Besides, when you mean to mislead, you pause before you begin to speak. You must learn to curtail that if you are to deceive.'

'You imagine that. I merely think before I talk. But why would you tell me such a thing when my ignorance of it is to have me at a disadvantage? Secrets are never to be shared.'

'I don't know. I shared my secret of Susanna with you and I don't feel a lesser person because of it. I feel stronger because you listened and didn't condemn. Perhaps it isn't what is in your private life that I want to know, but only that you're willing to trust me with your confidences as I trusted you.'

'I can't. Unless you promise to forget all about the kidnapping.'

'The magistrate is involved.'

'But you pay for the constables from your own purse.'

With one arm folded behind his back, he gave her a brief bow, acknowledging her words. She bit the inside of her lip, but stepped away with shoulders high. Inside, she crumpled.

When she walked with the others to the table for dinner, the flickering light from the candelabrum cast shadows which shaded everyone's face into a forbidding severity, but then she realised the candles had nothing to do with the bleakness.

Everyone sat exactly as she expected. Chalgrove's mother on his right. Her stepmother on his left and Miranda again next to her stepmother.

She checked the candlelight again and knew enough candles flickered in the sconces.

The talk was minimal as the meal began, but her stepmother picked up every thread of conversation and embellished it. The older woman did all but purr as she feasted on the pheasant. She put another bite in her mouth, savouring the flavour.

The Duchess acted as if the food were of no importance at all compared to the people around her, but Miranda felt the Duchess was hiding her intentions as much as anyone else.

Chalgrove ate with little appetite and she wagered he observed them individually, gauging their interactions.

The Duchess tapped a napkin at her face and spoke to Miranda. 'Have you discovered if your job is still available?'

'She chooses to work,' her stepmother answered for

her. 'Because she loves babies so much. Children. Families. She is so intent on being dutiful.'

Miranda glanced across the table, taking in the silver wisps of hair around her stepmother's face, but the hair didn't soften the countenance. Her stepmother had never praised her before. She glanced around the table, but no one seemed overly aware of her stepmother.

'You're a wonder with children. I've never seen anyone so suitable to motherhood,' Mrs Manwaring cooed.

Chalgrove's mother swirled the wine in her glass, not sipping.

'I am so fortunate to have been able to take care of the children.' Miranda's fork rapped against the plate when she released it. 'They are as close as I ever expect to having my own.'

Her stepmother's glass thumped on to the table, sloshing.

'Why, of course you'll have your own children.' The voice could have soothed little snakes.

'Thank you,' Miranda said, keeping her voice regretful for lost years. 'But I am fortunate to be a spinster. Otherwise, I might never have been blessed to know Willie and Dolly.' She paused.

'Dear, you're merely twenty-three,' her stepmother called out. 'That's a young spinster.'

'Twenty-five, I think. No one knows my true age.'

Her stepmother frowned. 'Well, then, dear, you get to choose. Choose the youngest age.'

Chalgrove's mother gave Miranda an encouraging smile. 'I can hardly remember twenty-five, Miss Manwaring. But...' candlelight from the wall sconces flickered across her face '...if I guess correctly, I already had a five-year-old son, Chalgrove, when I was your age. You are indeed fortunate to have the children to care for.'

'Yes. I am.'

'Of course she is.' Her stepmother's words came out with the same emphasis of a sigh. She brushed her thumb over the ornate ring on her left hand. Her gaze narrowed. 'But others' children are not quite the same as one's own. I'm fortunate that my elder daughter has a gentle suitor and my younger daughter will soon be off the shelf. I would like to see Miranda married, as she would make such a good wife in the higher reaches of society.'

Miranda cringed. Every person in the room knew who her stepmother would like to see Miranda married to.

And everyone studied her.

## Chapter Fifteen

The night had seemed the most silent one of his life and the longest. Longer even than when he'd been in the cottage.

Chalgrove kept recalling every instant that he'd spent with Miss Manwaring. Every word he could bring to mind.

After falling asleep in the early hours, he'd awoken to realise he'd missed breakfast and discovered an empty dining room with cold bacon. He could have easily sent for more, but instead he took a rasher and sat in his chair.

He stared at the teapot, but waved away the maid who'd offered to replace it. He'd not wanted any disruption in his contemplation of Miss Manwaring.

Then the constable had arrived and they had a quiet discussion.

The constable told Chalgrove no one at Carlton Trevor's residence admitted to knowing more than Miss Manwaring had claimed. The constable had reassured everyone he spoke with repeatedly that Miss Manwaring had assisted the ducal family and Her Grace had much appreciated it and would be wounded if her hospitality was not enjoyed longer.

But at a nearby house, the constable had uncovered a

servant who'd seen an old woman wandering about and the constable had deemed it important. He'd found out more, although the kidnapping had been kept quiet. Miss Manwaring's reputation was secure.

But the old woman had been seen. Her path had been discovered.

Then the constable, chest proud, said he must get back on to the trail before she slipped away and he trotted out.

'I just saw the constable leaving,' his mother said, entering the dining room.

'Nothing of significance yet, but it is only a matter of time.' Chalgrove stood, then suggested to his mother that she and Mrs Manwaring might enjoy a chance to go shopping.

His mother had considered the statement, then agreed a little too enthusiastically.

She'd suddenly remembered that she must thank the seamstress for the gown she'd sent over and they could do that on the way.

Moving to the library, Chalgrove tapped the nib of his pen against the blotter on his desk.

He waited to talk to Miranda. According to the footman, she'd not been down to breakfast and she had only recently requested a morning tray.

But she was safe in his household—both from what she might not know and what she might know.

Chalgrove waited no longer. He sent for her.

When she walked in, the sight of her caused a strange sensation inside him. He'd somehow forgotten to breathe for an instant.

'I received your message that the constable has been to the Trevor household and found nothing unusual there. I must see the children.' Miranda spoke rapidly.

'You will soon, I'm sure. I've sent for the man and asked him to visit tomorrow.'

'He will be concerned that something is wrong if he is summoned by a duke.'

'And he will be equally reassured if he is reassured by me.'

Relief brightened her eyes. She lifted for a second on her tiptoes.

In the drab, sombre, governess dress, she could be ignored, but then she smiled and everything changed. Happiness flooded her face. 'I'm ready to leave.'

He had to regain his footing, wondering if it was the children or their father who brightened her face so.

In the cottage, she'd been in darkness much of the time. They'd been under duress. He'd hardly been aware she was female. First, he'd interpreted her as an attacker, then as a fellow prisoner, and then he'd found himself attracted to her, but only considered it caused by the need to reassure her.

Holding her had been pleasurable, but he'd refused to feel anything at all for her when she was in such distress.

Now, he saw a different woman.

Almost too much of a woman. Yesterday she'd worn a different style of dress. A completely contrasting garment to the one she'd been captured in.

He'd seen her femininity.

Now she wore that drab garment again, but it didn't matter. She'd changed for ever in his mind.

He stopped, his eyes never leaving her. 'Most servants—governesses—wouldn't mind a holiday. A gesture of thanks. A chance to live in a gentler world.'

'I don't want Mr Trevor to think the family can survive without me. It will destroy me. I can't risk leaving him.'

He took the blow without flinching, unaware of where

it came from, and why he even felt it. Then he realised. Love was in her eyes. Compassion. The things he'd expected from Susanna. Perhaps expected as a matter of rote. But then he'd realised it wasn't as common as he'd believed and far more of a treasure to unearth than any cold gemstone.

'Are you attached to him?'

She bit her lip, thinking of her employer. 'No. I'm attached to the family I have there. All of them. The children. Cook. Nicky. The stable boy is going through a rough patch now. We are all trying to make him see that we've all had losses and he must always be honest with others and himself, because it is truly in his best interest.'

She put fingertips to her cheek.

She'd no idea what she'd missed in not having a friendship with her father and she'd not cared a jot. She didn't mourn or long for a lost relationship. She'd not cared. If he had no use for her, it was fine with her. She only wanted people around her who truly wanted her and who honestly appreciated her.

Being tossed away early in life had taught her not to put her hopes in someone who would shove her aside. Better to be unloved than to trust someone who cared for you as a duty. After her mother had died, she'd been alone, knowing Miss Cuthbert was not to remain in her life, and tempted by the prospect of marriage.

Miss Cuthbert told Miranda that if she let loneliness control her, it was the same as taking a lover who could beat you from the inside out. The words had shocked Miranda and Miss Cuthbert had reassured her that a loving heart and kindness and good works, and a discerning eye, would give her hope for true friends. The worst thing of all was to let people close who didn't deserve friendship. They would drain you dry and the truly good friends wouldn't be able to find you if you'd surrounded yourself with undeserving people.

She called it sullying your heartstrings with wastrels.

Miss Cuthbert had found her the job and told her to escape while she could.

It hadn't seemed like much of an escape at first. More like tumbling into a cauldron of a family, with a baby who always wanted something and could only wail to tell her. Her life had evolved into such a guessing game she'd not been able to do much but constantly guess who wanted what, and how to get it, and what to do next.

She'd not mourned so much, then, and Miss Cuthbert had reassured her that the family was one she could leave. Had it been her own husband, the most she could hope for was more children to tend to.

Nicky had started watching over her and they occasionally talked. He'd spouted yarns and he told her about how he'd dealt with his own children and how she could guide her charges. He'd given her a view of what a little boy might say or think and how to respond.

Then Dolly had arrived and, while the loss of her mother had been sad, Miranda had found the two easier to care for than Willie had been on his own. A wet nurse had helped and the whole house had banded together for the sake of the children.

Willie was a terror sometimes, but Nicky reassured her that the child was much better for having her than he would have been with someone else.

Mr Trevor left them all to their own routines, even though she could tell he found solace in the children. When the children were with him, she'd enjoyed her time alone, or visiting with the other servants. She'd never guessed the world could be so busy and so pleasant, but the children were where she was needed. They had no mother.

Then her grandmother had taken her from them.

'You forget.' She envisaged her life without the children in it. Willie, who had hidden under her bed and scared her out of a year's life, and Dolly, whom Miranda had awoken one morning to discover peacefully curled, sleeping, at Miranda's feet.

She couldn't lose them. She couldn't. Her heart plunged. What if Dolly had awoken in the middle of the night after Miranda had been taken? She might have been wandering alone in the house in the darkness. 'I will have to leave soon.'

She could not bear it if she lost the children.

'I will speak with your employer personally and reassure him you're not neglecting them. If he doesn't arrive tomorrow, I will take you there myself.'

She hesitated, calming. A word from him would make a lot of difference. And she needed to keep him on her side. If he found out she was related to the kidnapper, whispers could totally destroy her chance to remain with the little ones. A few loud questions from a duke could hurt her immeasurably.

Chalgrove would not knowingly disparage her so, but he already believed she knew the criminals.

And, she did know one of them.

When she'd left her childhood home, she'd told herself she would never again stay where she didn't wish to be and she'd meant it.

One step, followed by another, and she would be out the door. In the street, she could begin walking and a hackney would soon pass by. She'd be able to take it to the Trevor residence…assuming her grandmother didn't have henchmen about, waiting to capture her again and trying to secure her an earl this time. Or she could wait and return with him.

'I can see by your face that you want to leave. What would you wish for to make your stay more pleasant? I can have it for you in an instant.'

'I'm worried about the children.'

'Do you not think it might be safer for them, for now, if you were not with them? What if the persons who tossed me into the room decided to come back for you? First, we must see what the constable finds.'

She opened her mouth, but words failed her. Surely her grandmother would not...? But the woman had left her beside the road. 'How long do you wish me to stay here?'

'Until the criminals are caught.'

She faltered.

He studied her face. 'Don't worry. It won't be long.'

'I will be cautious.' She touched the pin in her hair. 'I'll take extra precautions. Extra precautions for the rest of my life if needed. Let us move past this. They could never be caught and I want to resume my duties. I want this behind me.'

'We must find these people. They may fear our memory of them. You saw the men's faces as well as the woman's. They may return. They likely will. I've not uncovered a reason for the crime.'

'You said funds.' Her stomach churned. She was misleading him. Purposefully. 'We escaped so quickly that you don't know if they were lax on finishing up. They're lawbreakers. Villains. They don't make good plans.'

'But she didn't take the buttons on my coat, except for one? It makes no sense... Yet they'd been planning for some time on the abduction. One told me that.'

'They're not well organised. How long could it take to prepare a bolt on the door, cover a window and put food inside, then nab the person?'

'So, they must be hanged or transported. They could do this again. But I've received some news that should keep everyone safe. The cottage has been found. Questions asked of it. It's an old gamekeeper's cottage on the boundary of Earl Rothwilde's land and he doesn't use it any more.'

She remembered mention of an earl when she was a child, but she didn't know which one.

'We found where a camp had been set up, but it was deserted. No one knows which direction they went, but it can't be hard to find. I'm having men sent out to ask questions at nearby homes. The place is so sparsely populated someone will notice seeing the old woman and the cart, then we'll keep asking questions until we catch up with them. The hag will be first to the scaffold.'

Her throat burned as if she could feel the rope.

'But what if she fancied she was doing good? What if she didn't think herself bad?'

'The old woman pinched my arm. I know she was the leader.' His voice soothed, but his eyes locked on hers. 'Maybe she worked with others, but I heard her tell them what to do.' His words softened, but didn't weaken. 'I do not assume she worked alone.' He stepped to her. 'You'll go free, but she won't. If she's blackmailing you, then give me a chance to put her away for ever.'

Miranda was stunned at the suggestion. 'I'm not being blackmailed.' She held herself erect. 'You have to do something to be blackmailed for.'

Then she paused. 'Except once. I spent the night in a

cottage with a duke.' She dropped her shoulders, and shut her eyes. 'I can only hope she never thinks of that.'

Miranda made a fist and put it to her lips before rushing from the room.

## *Chapter Sixteen*

The small table gave the appearance of close friends in the intimacy of a private family dining room. Miranda's stepmother and the Duchess had returned late in the day, burdened down with purchases, and dinner had followed immediately afterwards.

'Oh, you should have been with us. We had such a wonderful time.' Her stepmother radiated goodwill.

The enthusiasm of her father's wife flummoxed her. Perhaps the woman's proximity to the peerage had tempered her nastiness. Possibly she would accept Miranda into the family, although Miranda wasn't certain she wanted to be in the same room with her stepsisters.

'I'm sure she found plenty to do here to keep her occupied while we were gone,' the Duke's mother said and Miranda watched the older woman give her son an appraising glance.

The Duke continued eating without an apparent awareness of the females at the table.

Miranda stared at her own soup, aware of her stepmother, sitting with shoulders proud, splitting gazes of admiration between the Duchess and Chalgrove.

'I think the red you chose will go so lovely with anything you select—' her stepmother smiled at the Duchess '—Marjorie.'

*Marjorie.* Her stepmother was on a first-name basis with the Duchess. Goodness, next—

'When you visit us, you must bring what you've had made,' her stepmother continued.

'I certainly will.'

Then the Duke's mother turned to her son. 'And, Chalgrove, while we were gone, what progress did you make with the criminals you're going to bring to justice?'

'Not as much as I'd hoped, but the constable is confident that we will soon know more.'

'Thank you for providing the extra men to make certain the carriage was safe.'

'Of course.'

The Duchess finished her meal. 'If our guests would like to read in the library or perhaps play the pianoforte...'

Miranda stood, putting her napkin by her plate. 'I hope you don't mind if I retire. I'm not completely recovered.'

'Of course, Miss Manwaring.' The Duchess smiled.

Miranda's stepmother glared for an instant, then was wreathed in smiles as she told Miranda goodnight.

Chalgrove conversed with the Duchess and Mrs Manwaring, but he kept hearing Miranda's words about her stepmother.

If he were to place a wager on integrity, he would bet on Miranda.

The other woman spoke perfectly. A charming guest.

Charm, an asset for a man or a woman. But it really told nothing of the person underneath. That hadn't been an easy lesson to learn.

When the two ladies finished talking and decided to

retire to their rooms, he told them both goodnight, but he took his mother's arm.

She assessed his face and joined him in the study.

He closed the door.

'Mother, would you go to Miss Manwaring's room and check on her before she goes to sleep? I want to make sure she is all right and I don't want the servants knowing.'

'Of course. I don't think she prefers my company, but as you never ask for much from me... Well, other than me finding you a wife. I do have someone picked out.'

'Who?' he asked. His heartbeats increased. She was going to say Miss Manwaring.

'Miss Antonia Redding.'

Chalgrove hid his reaction. 'Who is Antonia Redding?'

'You may not have met her.'

That was the last thing he wanted to concentrate on, but he appeased his mother. 'I suppose I must, then. At least before the ceremony.' After meeting her, he could pick out a few flaws.

'I'll see that you get acquainted, but for now I'll go and check on Miranda. Sad that her heart is taken by two youngsters, but really she's not good enough for you, Chal.'

Chalgrove locked his teeth together. Miss Manwaring was suitable for his mother to call her by her given name, but yet she wasn't good enough? He refused to ask his mother exactly what flaw she had found in Miss Manwaring, or Miranda, as she called her.

A quick rap sounded on Miranda's door and her stepmother immediately walked inside. Her dress fitted her with the same give of a suit of armour covered in flounces and draped in silk. Hailstones might dent, of course, but this woman would never be caught in a storm to find out.

'Well, well…' She paused. 'Well—' Her stepmother made each word sound twice as precise as the one before it. 'The prodigal has returned and has brought her own fatted calf. I have already sent a message to have your things brought here. I said you would not be returning to your governess post.'

'You did not.' Miranda gasped.

Only her stepmother would jump to do such a thing.

She ignored Miranda's words. 'I like your methods. I wish to have a little ducal grandson.' She lifted a candlestick and stared at the bottom of it. 'I expected Lydia to be the one to catch the prize. Not sweet, plain Miranda with the over-large mouth and bedroom eyes. Beautiful golden-haired Lydia whom the elderly baron fancies. I only hope he lives long enough to put the ring on her finger.'

She studied the painting on the wall and slid it askew, examining the signature. 'This is of quality. I like it. When you marry, be sure and ask if you might give this to me.'

'I am not courting Chalgrove and he is not courting me.' Miranda crossed her arms.

'You marry that peer…' her stepmother spoke through clenched teeth '…and we'll all be one happy family. But if you do anything to confound me and I discover you have other ideas, you'll never be able to work as a governess again. No one would let a wanton like you near her children. You disappeared for days with a man. I'll tell the whole world you were in your little love nest with a lover. I'll say you bedded every footman and stable boy in my house.'

'And you'd be lying.' She stared at the woman who'd moved into her mother's house, leaving soiled fingerprints on the tablecloths her mother loved, destroying all the memories, making the house appear as if her mother never existed.

'You have a chance to redeem yourself, you little wanton. Marry him. Or I will see you starve.'

Her stepmother moved backwards because something in Miranda's eyes must have warned her. 'I suppose it will make no difference to you. But it does to me,' her stepmother said.

Miranda knew if she let her, her stepmother would take her over. 'I'll not marry him. I'll not marry anyone. You ruined my chance at marriage when you refused me proper clothing to go about in society. You did everything you could to destroy me, even spreading lies to the one man who considered me, but you did me the greatest favour of all. I'm happy with the job of governess.'

'Ha. Proud words for a little nobody. Fortune has smiled on you now. Take him.' Her gardenia perfume choked Miranda's nostrils. 'Or tuck your tail between your legs and run for the stews.'

Her stepmother chuckled, shaking her head. 'I don't care anything about your courtship—just get the ring on your finger quickly. Men tire so easily. I think his mother already knows you've been compromised. If I spread the tale quickly of your abduction, she'll have no choice but to push for a marriage.'

Miranda's jaw dropped as her stepmother walked forward and actually gave Miranda's hand a squeeze. Miranda recoiled.

'I couldn't have planned it better myself. You're truly a smarter girl than I ever realised.'

She jerked her hand from her stepmother's. 'I am a governess. Men such as the Duke do not marry the governess.'

'We just won't tell him you're a little beggar bastard.' Her stepmother put a hand to her bosom, long fingernails flittering like curtains in a breeze. 'Easton so kindly took you in as his ward simply because his wife wanted to keep you. Use that to your advantage.'

Miranda's voice rose. 'And you so kindly said you'd inform all and sundry of my parentage should I ever step foot in society, along with speaking those hideous lies Royce told.'

'Those were not lies.' Her stepmother moved to stare at her. Even though Miranda was taller, the woman ruffled out, not letting her size diminish her. 'They were not lies. My son Royce does not lie.'

Miranda spoke, unable to control her voice, the rage of years pulsing through her. 'They were lies he wished to be the truth. Your wicked son tried to touch me every chance he got. I couldn't live in the home I grew up in because he is there and he frightens me. And I will not try to force the Duke into marriage. I will not.'

Miranda dodged, but the slap caught her. The sound cracked in the room. Miranda showed no emotion, her jaw stinging.

'You will marry the Duke or I will see you ruined,' her stepmother hissed.

'Well.' The Duchess stood, holding the door open.

Miranda whirled. She'd been so engrossed she'd not known the woman had entered.

'I suppose I should have knocked.'

'This was a private discussion between a mother and her daughter.' Her stepmother's voice dripped sweetness.

The Duchess squinted down her nose. She smiled and her eyes had power behind them. 'In my house. About my son.' She opened the door wide for Miranda's stepmother. 'I'll have the carriage readied immediately for you. Your things will follow. If I hear any aspersions about my son or Miss Manwaring, I will hold you personally responsible.'

She touched where the coronet would have sat on her head. 'I'd think long and hard about stirring up any rumours.'

Mrs Manwaring blustered, 'I meant nothing disparaging.'

'Nor do I and I'd like to keep it that way. We will, or *may*, see each other at future events and I would prefer us both to be cordial and pleased to see one another. Wouldn't you? It would be so ridiculous for this to become the topic at Almack's or one of the Regent's dinners, but I assure you I can keep this private as long as my son and Miranda are not mentioned. And I believe you do have two other daughters to be concerned about.'

'Well, I—I suppose you have a point.' She held her chin high. 'I will be getting back home now. Come along, Miranda.'

She bustled through the door.

Miranda started to follow. She would find a way to return to the children.

The Duchess held out a hand, stopping her. 'Oh, Miss Manwaring, stay. I insist. And I do. You will stay.'

It was not a request, any more than the previous conversation had been.

'The constable may need more information. You will be here for questions.' Then the Duchess turned to Mrs Manwaring. 'I will see that Miranda is well taken care of.' She softly shut the door in the woman's face, with herself and Miranda on the inside.

The Duchess moved to the pull in Miranda's room and tugged it, several times more than necessary.

'Miss Manwaring. Occasionally my guests at soirées have too much to drink and misbehave. These things happen. They are best not dwelled upon. The true measure of good breeding is that you can sweep out the refuse with little more than a wave and maintain the dignity of the household.'

She moved to the painting and straightened it. 'When the maids arrive, please see that they help your stepmother depart.' She stopped at the doorway and looked over her shoulder. 'Sleep well, Miranda.'

The Duchess stalked into the study. 'Mrs Manwaring is leaving. She's ghastly.'

Chalgrove stood. 'Why?'

'I could not trust her another minute.' She poured herself a glass of wine. 'The young woman you were with has more backbone than you'd think.'

Chalgrove could not recall seeing his mother ever pour a glass of anything for herself. Pouring was a servant's job.

'Chal, the young woman can be firm if she makes up her mind. Reminded me of myself.'

'What happened?'

'I cannot speak of it right now. I am incensed. It reminded me of your Grandmother Wincett.' She held the stem. 'Trust me. Your grandmother particularly loved stories of a beheading and she could snag a hem with her shoe, causing another woman to go flying. My own mother wasn't much better. Father had to step between her and a footman twice her size once because she was threatening to throw him out of the window. For sneezing when he opened the door for her. If not for Father, we would have not been able to keep a servant in the place.'

She emptied the glass. 'Both your grandmothers were of the same ilk. Trust me, you never saw the truth of them. You were their chosen angel—and they had plenty of the devil in them. Your father and I had no choice in the matter of our marriage. They decided we were to marry and so we did. Luckily...' she gave Chalgrove a wan smile

'…your father was a stalwart man and one I would have chosen.' She closed her eyes, pleased memories softening her face. 'We had a good run of it.'

She marched to the door, pausing. 'Be aware, Son, graciousness first, swiftness so straight and pounding they never know what hit them and graciousness last. It is what separates us from the heathens. The graciousness. You cannot blame someone for something that they forced you to do. If they'd known better, they would have done better.'

She put down the glass, clucked her tongue and gave a chuckle he'd not heard since his grandmother had been alive. 'Graciousness…'

He moved to the entrance with her. He wondered if she could heft an executioner's axe herself. 'What happened?'

'Mrs Manwaring slapped the girl.'

'Why?' Anger curled in him, spreading like smoke from a stuffed chimney unable to escape.

His mother pulled the chain on her necklace, smoothing it into place. 'I sent her on her way. You will not fathom this. The woman was trying to force her stepdaughter to wed you.' Then she heard herself. 'Oh, goodness, that sounds almost familiar. But I would never, ever slap you, Son.'

She arranged the necklace again. 'It was just horrible. Horrible. Overreaching.' Then she searched his face. 'Do you mind terribly that I have Antonia Redding selected for you? She's had an upbringing suitable for a duchess.'

'As I said, I've never met her.'

'Neither have I. But don't be harsh with our guest. Miss Manwaring is not a bad sort.' She waved her arm, summoning a servant as she approached the door. 'Just has that horrible stepmother. If only…'

She put her knuckles under her chin. 'Miss Miranda flatly refused to consider marriage to you. Flatly refused.

I suppose she understands she is not of your calibre.' She lowered her lids. 'I have to respect her for knowing her place... Or I have to be irritated that she doesn't care what a benefit it would be to her to join our family. That has been more worrisome than I expected.'

She moved on. 'Goodnight, Chal. Don't stay up too late.'

Without making a sound, he closed the door behind her.

This was not the time for marriage negotiations.

He would prefer someone who cared for him, but that came second to integrity.

Miss Manwaring.

He'd not asked her to marry him.

How utterly, blasted kind of her to refuse.

# Chapter Seventeen

The rapping at the door was much softer than the pounding in Miranda's head. The night had been a long one. Her stepmother's outburst had shocked her. And she wasn't certain her stepmother was smart enough to heed the Duchess' warning.

Another rap sounded at the door, more insistent.

'Miss.' The maid held out a silver salver, and Miranda picked the card from it.

She raised her eyes to the maid's.

'He's now in the library with the Duke, miss.'

Miranda didn't speak, but the maid set the tray aside. 'I'll help you hurry, miss.'

The maid had been trained well. She was already at the wardrobe before Miranda could rise and helped her dress quickly.

After she had finished the last brush of Miranda's hair, the maid moved to the doorway, snatched the salver and opened the door.

'You're very well trained,' Miranda mumbled as she moved by.

The maid's gentle laugh of assent followed Miranda as she composed herself and walked to the library.

The companionable sound of men's voices drifted her way as she walked inside.

'Miss Miranda.' Willie's father rushed to her, emitting concern. He wore his brown hair brushed straight back from his forehead, the silver cravat he wore tied to perfection. His thin nose darted out enough to offset the angular tip of his chin. He caught her hands. That movement shocked her speechlessness. She couldn't move.

'Why did you not alert me of the terrible circumstances of your departure?' he asked. 'If the constable had not questioned me, I would still be in the dark.'

Chalgrove waited at the side and he appeared to be interested in the top of the mantel, brushing a finger along the top, checking for ash. Something she was sure he did every day.

'I wanted to, but everything has happened so rapidly.'

His grip relaxed and she pulled her hands away.

'You have no idea how distraught little Willie has been.' His voice was low, as if he didn't want Chalgrove to listen, but she saw a lift of Chalgrove's brows. 'He's missed you beyond belief.'

'I've missed both the children.'

'I assure you, Miss Miranda, they so want to have you back with them.'

Chalgrove's cough interrupted the silence. Her eyes darted to him.

'Pardon.' This was spoken ever so innocently.

'Willie,' Mr Trevor continued, lowering his eyes as he spoke, 'has been unlike himself. He's acted a terror since you've been gone.' He raised his face. 'I fear he found more eggs.'

'Oh,' Miranda commiserated. That was not entirely unlike Willie.

'The horses.'

'Ooh.' She almost groaned, knowing how much Mr Trevor hated it when his horses were dripping yolk and how poor Nicky really detested Willie on occasion. Throwing eggs at the livestock equated to the same treason as throwing stones at the Prince.

'You must return. Immediately.' He gave her a smile. Which surprised her. She hadn't realised his lips could move upwards. 'My carriage can carry you home. I know Mrs Manwaring sent for the trunk, but when I asked the staff to prepare it, they were so downcast and surprised that you would leave without informing them... I suggested that I must make certain that it was your wish.'

Divided inside, she made sure her true emotions didn't show on her face. She beamed at him and, by the reaction he gave, he hadn't known she could do that either.

'I do...want to return to your home.' The words carried the same emphasis as a spinster might accept a proposal from a rich, handsome war hero. She would see the children again. She could regain her old life.

'Miss Manwaring...' Chalgrove's words dropped into the room like little pelts of sleet on a bare face '...you are a witness in a crime. A crime in which serious consequences will be levelled against the culprits. A crime against a peer of the realm.'

The Duke moved forward, stopping near Miranda, and his eyes clamped on the other man. 'We cannot risk her being detained again. I might not be with her next time and who knows what might happen.'

'You were with her?' Trevor sputtered. 'With my Miss Miranda?'

'Not when I was taken. Afterwards,' Miranda reassured him quickly. It would not do for him to think of her having an improper rendezvous.

'*Your* Miss Miranda?' the Duke asked.

Trevor's neck stretched to almost double its length. 'She has been a member of my household since my son was a babe. The word choice stands. Perhaps I should have included the children as well.' His neck didn't retreat and his attention swivelled to her. '*Our* Miss Miranda.'

She hid all the emotion from her face. He had never called her that. She didn't think he'd ever called her anything but Miss Miranda.

'There was a serious crime committed,' the Duke said. 'Miss Manwaring could have been injured. She is protected here.'

'You cannot possibly think she is still in danger?' the older man burst out. If she hadn't swayed away from him, he would have clasped her arm.

At her other side, Chalgrove must have noticed, because he moved closer.

'You were not told because I do not want it bandied about,' she reassured him. 'I could not send such a thing in a note.' She asked her employer for forgiveness with her eyes.

'She has been secluded and I am sure the criminals will be caught very soon.' Chalgrove took her elbow.

Trevor flinched, but his voice intensified. 'I will have guards hired if necessary,' he reassured her. 'My son has been incorrigible. Only Miss Miranda is competent to guide him.' He ended the sentence with a glare at the Duke's hand on her elbow.

She breathed in the masculine scent of Chalgrove. She felt the brush of his coat against her shoulder and the sensation moved beyond the fabric of the garment and deeper into her body.

She almost wished to return to the day in the cottage so she could again be alone with Chalgrove, and have the same feeling of closeness she'd had with him when they had escaped and he'd held her in the rain.

'My employer is quite kind.' She hid the longing she felt for Chalgrove, and instead gave him what she hoped was a bland glance.

His eyes rested on her before he spoke, and it was almost as if they were alone again.

'Miss Manwaring. Your safety. I cannot risk you being harmed,' Chalgrove said, and something in his reply reached deep inside to warm her.

Trevor brushed the hair from his temple, interrupting the moment. 'I have known Miss Miranda some time now and the house is empty without her.' He lifted his view higher. 'One might say desolate.'

'Of course it is,' Chalgrove agreed. 'I commiserate. But Miss Manwaring's safety is foremost in both our minds.' He dipped his head to her when he spoke. 'I'll see that she visits the children.'

Trevor's jaw trembled as he decided how best to respond. He appraised Miranda, then studied the Duke.

The determination in Chalgrove convinced him.

'I find that acceptable.' He gazed at Miranda a second longer than necessary. 'If that is suitable to her?'

Chalgrove, tension in his face, asked, 'Miss Manwaring?'

'I do miss the little ones. But I would not wish to impose on your hospitality. You don't have to travel with me.'

'Of course you miss them,' Chalgrove said. 'But you do not know what might happen if you were to go out alone. Right now, few know she is staying here. This is where she is safest. I can take her to visit the children and will have a veritable army of servants with us.'

Miranda regarded Chalgrove, a man appearing more

solid than a continent. Hesitation flashed from her employer's eyes before he moved a hair closer to her.

'Your safety is foremost, my dear Miss Miranda. The Duke's concerns are serious. We must keep you safe. Will you visit today?' His expression was hopeful.

'Yes,' she said.

'Yes,' Chalgrove reiterated. 'I will go with her.'

'You don't have to,' the older man said. 'She can ride in my coach and your army of servants can accompany us. We would not want to interrupt your many important duties.'

'My number-one duty for the foreseeable future is to make certain Miss Manwaring is safe and that the criminals are apprehended.'

Trevor moved, reticent, but still determined. He managed to take both Miranda's hands while under Chalgrove's disapproving glower. 'It will mean so much to the children to see you, Miss Miranda.'

Then he bowed to the Duke. 'You are indeed kind in providing assistance. I didn't realise until she wasn't there what a difference she makes in *our* entire household.'

*Our* again? Miranda considered that she might have misunderstood the emphasis, but from the scowl on Chalgrove's face, she was certain she had not.


She studied Chalgrove when they were alone.

'He should have brought the children with him…if he was indeed thinking of them.' Chalgrove had already ordered that his carriage be readied.

'They are a handful in a carriage.'

'Miss Manwaring.' He frowned. 'I don't like him interfering with your safety and I don't like the way he ogled you.'

'He wasn't. He was concerned for me.' Miranda had

been relieved, reassured she had a chance to return to her job. And she'd not noticed a single ogle.

'He called you Miss Miranda.'

'Of course.'

'Of *course*?' The word rolled from his lips like an accusation.

'So do the children. *Everyone* in the household calls me Miss Miranda. They always have.'

'That's quite informal.'

'Maybe here, at a ducal estate, but not at the Trevor household.'

He raised a brow. 'Did you know he fancies you?'

She pulled a face. 'He does not.'

'I'll make a wager he does.'

'Oh, my.' She clutched the chair nearest to her. 'I could… If he truly, truly cared for me.' She gulped. 'You think he fancies *me*? That possibility had never entered my mind. *Never.*'

She twirled around. 'The children. I had not credited Mr Trevor seeing me as anything but another employee.' Then she touched her chest. 'It isn't such a huge leap. Manwaring's first wife always introduced me as her dear daughter. So, I am almost of the same standing as my employer is. Not so far beneath him as I had always concluded. And our ages are not as far apart as I'd once thought.'

She rested fingers on Chalgrove's arm, feeling a need to explain. 'The children. They are so precious.'

'I'm sure they are.'

He strode to the window and strode back to her. 'And they do need you in their life. They have no mother and a man with a worn-out hat for a father.'

She put her hands on her hips and frowned at him. 'Those are extremely precious children and my employer has always treated me with the utmost courtesy. And he dresses quite finely.'

'What is his first name?'

She paused, eyes narrowed. 'Carlton.'

'Have you ever called him that?'

She shook her head.

'I could be wrong about his being attracted to you. He would have asked you to call him by his first name if he fancied you.'

'Not necessarily. His wife always called him Mr Trevor and he loved her very much. Everyone calls him that, except the children.'

She considered the situation. Her body relaxed. 'Thank you. Thank you for telling me that he might fancy me. I would never have imagined it.'

She paused. 'And, these last few days, being away from the little ones has been difficult. I understand how important they are even more now.' She put her fingertips to her chin. 'Maybe that's what the kidnapper had in mind. It didn't occur to me.'

She put her head down. 'When she said she was bringing me a husband, I presumed you were the man. But now I see it differently. Perhaps she did think you a tailor and was merely trying to spur my employer on to jealousy.'

His eyes locked on her as if she were the one who'd thrown him into the room. 'Bringing you a husband? She said she was bringing you a husband,' he repeated, eyes tensed.

She swallowed. 'Yes.'

'The woman is cracked.'

'Exactly.'

'Why would she think she had to capture a husband for someone as lovely as you?'

*  *  *

He didn't know why a bird-witted woman would think Miss Manwaring needed any help with getting wed. After all, the old woman had him to help that dolt, Trevor, court her.

That would have to stop.

'You act as if it's hard for you to acknowledge that someone could care for you.' Chalgrove levelled a gaze at her. 'Do you not fathom what a treasure you are?'

She sputtered.

He'd attended many dances in his lifetime. Conversed with countless beauties, but no one affected him like Miss Manwaring.

'Yes,' he insisted. 'You care for a man's children as if they were your own. You work to ensure the servants respect and are fond of you. You were thrown into a house with a stranger and you fought back. You ran through the rain to safety, shivering, and all you cared about was seeing the children.'

'Anyone would do the same.'

'I don't see it that way.'

He took a step closer, standing so near he could have told if she'd had a sip of wine. 'Last night, your stepmother slapped you. I cannot tolerate anyone striking you.'

'Of course, your mother told you.'

She smelled—he paused—like nature. Like a morning when all the best trees bloomed and filled the air with the scent of their blossoms.

'Why are you so kind? Does your heart take up the whole of you?'

'I think the love for the children takes up my heart. I had no choice but to be who I am, if I wanted to survive.'

'Of course you had a choice. Everyone does.'

He put a fingertip to her chin. 'It's not what is good to

us that gives strength to some people. It is what is bad. The trials.'

'I was fortunate. To have my mother. To have the job of caring for two little ones daily. To be locked away with someone who could find a way out of the old cottage.'

'I stand corrected. It isn't what is bad that gives us strength. It is how we react to it.'

He hadn't reacted well to everyone else calling her Miranda. Well, he could rectify that.

'My given name is Robert, but no one has ever called me that, except my mother when she is angry. I suppose that is why I have not suggested you could call me that as I don't associate it with pleasantness.'

'A fine name.'

'I suppose I consider Chal my given name, in a sense.'

'Of course,' she said. 'I can't believe I thought you a Mr Chalgrove when we first met.'

My father was Chalgrove and I had an honorific, but among family and the closest friends I was called Chal. I was assessed as a younger version of my father.'

'Did he mind?'

'No. Everyone acknowledged him as the Duke of Chalgrove and, as we didn't question but that he would live for ever, I was the heir happily one step behind the man. The subordinate who relished being outranked.'

'You don't seem to me as if it would be easy for you to accept a lesser role.'

'It was. And it was easy to step into my father's duties, but hard to lose the man. The jest was that even when I had to take three steps to his one step, I was always with him.'

He remembered playing in his father's shadow and his father stretching out his arms, and Chalgrove had stretched, too. His father had spun so that their arms were the same length, then he'd moved slightly so that their shadowed hands touched. His father had knelt and a shadow of an arm had encompassed his shoulders.

'I didn't understand that a woman would really love children until I met you, Miss Manwaring. It hadn't occurred to me. But if you wish to call me Robert, I would accept it.'

'I see you as Chalgrove. There's nothing wrong with that name.'

'Thank you, Miss Manwaring.'

'Miranda,' she said. 'Though it would sound strange coming from your lips.'

'Just different.' He closed the distance.

He took her hand and pulled the back of it to his lips. 'I am pleased to meet you, Miranda.'

'And I you. Do you grasp how important the children are to me?'

'I can only guess.'

'I was left beside the road for someone to find. Alone. I had no one. No one.' She'd never forgotten those feelings. Even then, she'd been aware that the woman who'd found her must like her or she'd not be kept.

She'd felt so betrayed, but then the nice woman had taken her in and Miranda saw the woman argue with her husband, a man who belonged in the house, about her presence. At first, in the vehicle, he'd only grumbled that they could take the child home, feed it and find it a place to live.

'I had to make the woman, my mother, love me, or I would be tossed aside again.' She'd caused as little disruption in the household as she could, knowing that her future would be determined by the woman's whim.

She'd discovered immediately that the man didn't like her. But the woman wanted a little doll just as much as Miranda did. And Miranda had earned the toy she wanted. She did exactly as her mother requested and the only variances were times she was confused by the differences in her old world and new one and didn't know what to do.

She didn't want to be left beside the road again. Ever.

'You had the governess, Miss Cuthbert.' Chalgrove stood so close she could see the pulse beating in his throat.

'I had to make her love me. I didn't know whether she would toss me aside as well. I was a child. I didn't know. I wasn't born with a place in the world.'

She took what she was born with and cultivated it. If her mother wanted a happy child, then she could laugh. Well behaved? She obeyed.

But the man in the household hadn't wanted her there. She'd known that. And she understood that she could never make him like her. If she was near him, he disliked her more. She grasped that his word had sway in the house because her mother and the servants scampered around him, yet her mother championed her and would not waver.

Earlier, she had had to always take care around the gamekeeper as well. She'd tried to stay away from him because he hadn't liked her. And she had still ended up beside the road.

She imagined little Dolly and Willie beside the road. Lost. Willie was about the same age as she had been when she was deserted.

'I can't leave the two little ones alone the way I was alone. What if their father marries again and weds someone like my stepmother and she doesn't like the children? And she sacks me?'

'You can't know he'll do that.'

'Then I would be lost again. I wouldn't even be able to fight back. I did fight back once,' she said. 'I don't know what came over me. I couldn't control it.' She touched the healing marks on his face. 'I'm so sorry.'

When she brushed the marks, it was as if she could feel

the pain of the wound. Her hand slipped downwards and ran along his cheek, feeling a nick he'd likely received while shaving. He should have looked beaten up, scarred, or injured. Instead, he appeared even stronger and his jawline gave her the impression of touching granite, but with a human heart pounding inside it.

Moving lower, she felt his pulse beating. She couldn't take her hand away.

Gently grasping her fingertips, he kissed each one, spurring her desire.

'I'm not sorry about the marks. Not if it led me to this.'

He put a hand to the back of her head, fingers entangled in her hair, and pulled her close for a feather-light kiss.

Longing sensations infused her body, just from the barest touch, but he didn't linger.

'We must leave if we are to catch up to Trevor's coach,' he said and moved away. He stepped behind a chair, almost as if he had to put an obstacle between them.

'Miranda. Trevor would be a dolt not to want you in his household. Or his bed. And it incenses me that he could be in the same room as you.'

## Chapter Eighteen

Miranda sat in the carriage.

Someone had cleaned Chalgrove's boots, possibly within the last hour, because the scent of burnished leather touched her nose.

Chalgrove sat beside her, sombre as a rector going to a second funeral of the day. He'd told her before they left that he couldn't touch her. He had to control himself. Their encounter could only end with heartbreak. She needed the children.

His arm rested at the side of the carriage, the other hand on his thigh. She would have thought him completely unaware of her presence, but for one thing.

Whenever she moved, his mouth thinned.

And she couldn't think of anything but how solid he felt against her. With another person, there might have been a small gap between them, but not with Chalgrove. He filled the space and she took the leftovers, but she didn't mind.

The carriage slipped over a bump, tilting her body to the side, and she pulled herself back into a firm posture and clasped her gloves together.

All the words had already been spoken.

'Must you sigh at every bump?' he asked.

She glanced sideways. Little lines, whisper thin, at the side of his eyes. And she wasn't certain, but she suspected she saw a few silver hairs.

She stared at her hands clasped in her lap and thought of the children. Every part of her life seemed in a different world.

Lord Chalgrove in one. Her grandmother in one. And Trevor and the children in another.

They travelled along the streets she had walked with the children and stopped in front of the house.

Her heart lightened. 'I'm home.'

The carriage jostled as someone jumped from the perch. The door opened and Chalgrove waited as she stepped out and examined the structure.

Nothing had changed about the household. But she considered it with different eyes, as if she saw it for the first time.

Chalgrove stood beside her, letting her take her time.

A curtain moved at one of the upper storeys. A little face popped into view. Dolly. Eyes widening. Lips moving excitedly. Another head darted beside Dolly. Willie. In a flash the curtain dropped and she imagined the flurry of footsteps as the children disregarded all instructions about not running in the house and tore down the stairs.

Chalgrove put a hand on her back, just as the front door opened and two bundles of energy ran towards her. She knelt and the little girl she'd seen each day of the child's life—but the last two—ran into her arms. Willie followed.

After hugs, she stood, keeping one little hand in each of hers, taking them to the front door.

'Eggs got on the horses and Mr Nicky told Papa. Willie cried and you were gone.' The words burst from Dolly.

'I didn't cry,' Willie shouted. 'Everyone was mean when you weren't here. Everyone. Even Cook. She would not give me biscuits because I made Mr Nicky angry and he told her.'

Dolly's lip quivered and she whimpered. 'I didn't get biscuits either and I didn't throw eggs on the horse.'

'You threw eggs,' Willie asserted. 'You just missed.'

'Well, I hope you both have learned your lesson and you are not to ever do that.'

'Will you not go away again?' Dolly said. 'Papa didn't know any of the good bedtime stories and Willie and I had to tell him what to say.'

The butler stood at the opened door. He beamed.

'Of course I won't leave you again,' she said and her throat caught, her fingertips tightening on the two little hands in hers as they walked inside.

The butler shut the door and she realised Chalgrove wasn't in the hall with them.


Chalgrove needed to smell some muck to get the scent of her lilac or rose or lavender perfume from his nostrils. He wasn't sure of the flower, but he'd never smelled something which reminded him so much of a bouquet and had caused him to get aroused.

Only he knew it wasn't the flowers.

He'd been fighting a battle within himself since she had said her name.

Her name. How could the sound of her own name from her own lips make a man hard? He would have sworn it was physically impossible.

Blast it. She should have been named something less intriguing.

He strode away from the house, viewing the grounds carefully.

'Need some assistance, sir?' He heard the words before he saw the white-haired man with a rake in his hand watching him. 'I'm Nickolas Adams and I'm the stable master.' He had a smile on his lips and a challenge in his eyes.

Chalgrove jolted from his reverie. The man had a tattered hat and a day's growth of whiskers. He wore rough trousers and a rough shirt to keep the hay from attaching itself easily. Even his skin appeared tough enough to repel any nicks or cuts by the work he did.

Chalgrove saw the moment the man registered the ducal crest on the carriage door. Chalgrove raised an eyebrow. 'I'm the Duke of Chalgrove.'

The older man's eyes widened and he removed his hat and his head bobbed in a bow. 'You're the one owns the house where she's been staying.'

Chalgrove nodded.

The man's spine snapped up and his words flowed. 'Miss Miranda is a treasure.'

*Blast it, blast it, blast it. He'd called her Miranda.*

'I would prefer she be referred to as Miss Manwaring during our conversation,' he said, 'as that is how I wish to think of her.'

The man squinted, but then continued. 'I knew something bad had happened to her. Just didn't suspect how bad.' He put his hat back on and brushed a hand over his eyes. 'Thanks to goodness she's safe and unharmed. Isn't she?' he asked Chalgrove.

Chalgrove nodded. 'She's had a trial, but she's not been hurt in any way.'

'A jewel, all the way through, our Miss… Manwaring. Don't know how she puts up with all of us.' He smiled. 'We're thankful to have her back and…' He bowed again. 'Can't say enough words of thank you for bringin' her back to us. Never guessed the stables could be quiet as a tomb, but with her gone, even the horses seemed to notice.'

'You spoke with a constable recently about Miss Manwaring,' Chalgrove said.

'That I did.' The old man propped himself on the handle, the tines of the tool resting on the grass.

'What happened that day she left?' Chalgrove asked. 'Had you seen anything odd?'

'Saw two men a few days before. Suspected they might be thieving, so I watched them, but they didn't stay long.' He contemplated the ground, before meeting Chalgrove's examination and continuing his speech.

'Miss Manwaring is a true lady. She might be a governess and she might be a servant, but she's a lady born and bred. Has a high-on-the-instep father and comes from money. Been tossed out, but she's not letting on. She's a good woman. Don't deserve the family she's had, but it made her strong.'

'Did you know she was abducted?'

'Not at first. Suspected it after the constable's visit.'

The old man leaned forward, voice lowered. 'I dare say they sent a ransom note around to her father and he claims not to have received it. That's the sort he is.' He waved a hand, brushing aside the integrity of Mr Manwaring.

'The other servants say anything else of her?'

He rubbed his chin. 'They think the same as me. She keeps too busy with her charges to have much time for conversation and, if she ventures out for her own amusements, she arrives back in a snap with a book under her arm and treats for us all.' He almost whispered, 'She's the type would creep away at night and read to an old cook who's feeling pained.'

'A virtuous woman.'

He gave a firm nod. 'They could write tracts using her as a guide.'

'No vices at all?'

He leaned in. 'Don't hide her book when she's in the middle of reading it or get between her and a morning glass of chocolate. She can spout a few words now and again.' He chuckled. 'Nothing we ain't heard before, though.'

Miranda could not believe Willie's behaviour. He hopped over to her and she cleaned a smear of jam from his face, then he gave her a hug and leaned against her. He did have to remind her again of how good he'd been most of the time.

'Papa smacked his behind,' Dolly inserted proudly.

Miranda brushed a pretend smack on his bottom and he laughed.

Miranda expected Willie to erupt with some sort of childish display, but he contented himself with toy soldiers after they talked of lessons. Dolly examined the pages of a story book.

Mr Trevor opened the door. His eyes had shadows under them, something she'd not noticed since after his wife had passed away. She knew he was thirty-two years old, yet he appeared closer to forty.

'Miss Manwaring, might I have a private word with you in my study?'

His eyes lingered on hers an instant too long and she took into account Chalgrove's claims about Mr Trevor's affections.

'Yes. Of course.'

He led her into a room desperately needing a woman's care, although she supposed her taste differed from his. The petite room had overpowering damask curtains, too many and too large for the room. And the oversized portraits on the wall gave her the feeling of being stared at.

I'm glad you're home.' He brushed a hand across her shoulder. 'The children have missed you terribly.'

He sat at his desk, the same one from which he'd cautioned her about his requirements for his children's care before she began her job.

He directed her to have a seat in front of him. 'I suppose you heard Willie's story about the eggs.'

She nodded.

'He'd do it again,' he grumbled, placing a flat palm on the papers in front of him.

'I'm sure,' she said and he laughed, although she didn't think him truly laughing at what she said because he'd never found his son's enjoyment of eggs as humorous.

'We must dampen down his impetuousness.' He propped his jaw on his fist. 'Didn't know until you were gone what a rascal he is.'

She nodded, agreeing with his assessment.

'I realise not all the details of your...' he paused '...horrible adventure have been brought to light. But the criminals may never be caught. I've given the matter a great deal of reflection and on the way home I stopped to put in motion a few more details of safety. I have already given the order for additional sturdy men.'

He straightened the remaining sheets on his desk. 'No matter what happens—I cannot forget that a person from my household was taken. It has been a trial.'

Guilt plunged into her even though her birth was not of her choosing and her grandmother wasn't the one she would have asked for.

'I agree. But I know the activity was directed at me. Not you, or your family.'

'Still. My house. My responsibility. I do beg your pardon Miss Miranda.' He stared at the papers on his desk.

Miranda didn't know what to say. Chalgrove's words

that Mr Trevor might have a *tendre* for her resurfaced, but so did Chalgrove's kiss.

The softest brush against her, the smallest movement that could be called a kiss, and it had flooded into her, flashed so deep she could not think. Then it had continued until it consumed her.

She touched her mouth. So feather-light for such a large man. She turned her face away from her employer. And the Duke had said those words about Trevor being a dolt if he didn't want her in his bed and she'd heard the strain in Chalgrove's voice. She warmed, thinking of his voice when he'd said the words.

But her employer's voice snapped her back to the present.

'When I spent more time with Willie, I realised perhaps I'd let him get away with too much,' he admitted. 'I remember your hinting that he should be reprimanded when he misbehaved. I credited him—nicer than he is. And I do feel that little boys should be allowed some leeway for their spirits. But Willie is too spirited.' He hesitated. 'He took a bottle of ink from my desk and I only barely saw him do so. I fear what he has in mind next as I know it has nothing to do with lessons.'

'I've missed them terribly.'

'We've all wanted you home. Especially me.' He raised his eyes, face serious. 'You know how much I loved my wife.'

A voice inside her called out for her to interrupt him, but then a doorknob twisted and Willie ran into the room, one arm behind his back. He scampered to her, held out his hand and she saw the egg. 'I'm putting this back,' he said. 'I wanted you to know.'

She nodded and the child ran out again, leaving the door open.

'I presumed there could never be another like her,' Willie's father continued, 'but now I have changed my opinion.'

Footsteps sounded on the stairs and the butler arrived.

'The Duke of Chalgrove would like to meet with you, sir.'

'Show him in.'

Miranda put her foot behind her and stepped back, moving further from Mr Trevor.

Chalgrove strode in and she realised from the ire in his eyes when he saw the older man that it likely wouldn't have mattered where she stood.

# Chapter Nineteen

Miranda noticed brackets of tension around Chalgrove's mouth when he surveyed the study. He seemed more disgruntled now than when he'd been in the little cottage.

Their host indicated a chair, but Chalgrove stood. 'I hoped Miss Manwaring would be ready to return to my house.'

Trevor smiled. 'And I hoped she might stay.' The quiet words almost echoed from the walls. 'I've added more servants so the house will be secure.'

The two men's eyes met.

'I just told Miss Manwaring how I've added more staff to guarantee her safety,' her employer explained. 'Everyone is to be alert to anything out of the ordinary. I can't risk a repeat of the abduction.'

'You can't be certain that any new person you've hired is trustworthy. I already have staff in place. I'm close to uncovering the criminals. I don't think anyone would doubt the safety of the ducal household. I would suggest, today, it is more secure than the palace.'

'You are welcome to stay, Miss Miranda. Your possessions are here. And your employment is needed. The children. You are the only mother Dolly has ever had.

You truly know how much you're needed here and you understand that I also want the culprits captured. They invaded my property.'

Miranda instinctively knew that if she stayed, Mr Trevor would propose. The idea didn't give her the happiness she would have hoped for. Only a week before, she would have accepted, pleased to be connected for ever to the children she loved and to have a permanent place among the people who'd meant more to her than anyone else since her mother had died.

'I would not want to sway you unduly,' he said, voice persuasive. 'But the children have had enough upheaval… what with the loss of their mother at such a young age. They need you.'

'Thank you for your kind offer,' she answered. 'But I can't accept. Not now. I know the people who took me are still about and I would feel better that the children not be involved in this in any way.'

Chalgrove moved aside from the doorway so she could precede him. He stood, hands clasped behind his back, silent, impassive, and unamused.

'Promise me you will not stay away,' Trevor said. 'The children—'

'I could never leave them,' she said.

The truth of her words hit her deep. She couldn't leave them. They'd given her love and laughter. Tears and smiles. They'd given her so much.

'I'm going to tell them I'm leaving for now and I'll remind them to mind their manners and explain I'll be back soon.'

'Is there anything I can do to assist in helping the criminals be apprehended?' he asked Chalgrove. 'It cannot happen too soon for me. My children need Miss Miranda.'

'No. I have everything under control.'

'Wonderful. I will send several men to assist yours.'

Chalgrove glared. 'That isn't necessary.'

'I'm sure it isn't. It is merely for my peace of mind. And, of course, to alert me immediately to the criminals being caught.' Mr Trevor smiled.

Miranda stared. She'd not suspected a man who could be bested by a little boy would have the courage to stand up to a duke, keep a level stare and have a dare in his eyes.

He stepped over to her and, for the first time ever, took her hand and raised her glove to his lips. His eyes met hers after the kiss. 'I anticipate this being over and our lives, with you in it, resuming.'

Then he weighed up Chalgrove. 'And I realise you must get back to solving the crime immediately. Thank you for doing this for us.'

The Duke gave a long, direct stare of acknowledgment.

Miranda slipped from her employer and his eyes followed her.

The scratches on Chalgrove's temple seemed to be jumping out at her, but she supposed it was merely because he'd moved between her and the older man and taken her elbow to lead her to the door.

She walked to the nursery with Chalgrove at her side and Mr Trevor following. Dolly and Willie were having biscuits. A maid was watching over them.

The farewell and instructions to the children were brief and she hugged and reassured them she would not be gone long. From the corner of her eye, she noticed the children's father was smiling, while Chalgrove wasn't.

Chalgrove had her bustled away almost before she could take her leave.

She kept one hand at her skirt so she could keep it high enough not to trip over the hem and dodged the broken egg on the rug.

\* \* \*

'Chalgrove—slow down.'

His hand still clasped her waist, pressing her along, and his movements didn't lessen.

'You wouldn't be safe here, Miranda, and he had no right to kiss your hand. For all I know, he had something to do with your abduction. That could be why he is so determined to get you back under his roof. I will not have you endangered.'

'Chalgrove. You're jumping to conclusions. I have known Mr Trevor for five years. If he wanted me abducted, I imagine he could have done so at four years or three, or even six months. Waiting five years to throw off suspicion is a bit much.'

'An innocent like you cannot understand the workings of a man's mind, Miss—' His lips parted in surprise and he corrected himself in a rush, or attempted to. 'Miss…'

He swallowed. 'Miranda,' he spoke softly. 'I would very much like it if you would accompany me back to my home.'

She got inside the carriage, confused by the way everything seemed to be rushing at her.

'I saw the egg on the rug. I thought Willie would take it back to the cook,' she said.

Chalgrove grunted. 'I'm sure he meant to, until he skittered into me in the hallway.' He lifted the toe of his boot and she saw a drip of yolk.

'Oh, dear,' she said, recalling the fresh smell of boot blacking she'd noticed earlier.

Chalgrove laughed at her expression and took her hand. 'It's not the worst thing I've had on my boots and children tend to be unpredictable, I've heard.'

'They are such dear little ones,' she said. 'And when I saw them again and saw the love in their faces…'

She sniffled.

Oh, heavens.

She sniffled again.

He reached in his pocket for a handkerchief.

'They're such treas—' She gulped. Composing herself. Taking the silk and kneading the cloth. 'Such treasures. More than anything I could imagine.'

Chalgrove moved beside her, both facing forward. He touched her interlaced hands.

When she raised the handkerchief, dotting her eyes, something caught her attention from the window.

She was certain, as the carriage moved, she saw a bright scarf as an old woman flitted around the side of another vehicle.

She pushed back the edge of the curtain and deliberated on what she'd seen, also watching for a constable or Bow Street Runner, but saw no one who could be of official capacity.

'What did you see?' Chalgrove asked, then leaned across her to peer out of her window. She pulled herself back into the squabs as far as she could, but the upper half of his body crossed her. A lingering trace of his soap teased her nostrils and a more personal scent she recognised as the true scent of his hair and skin touched her.

She didn't move, held in place as he surveyed the scene beyond the window. She tried thinking of anything but him.

The silence was different between them now.

His clothes brushed against her as he leaned back and repeated, 'What did you see?'

'Nothing.' She shook her head.

*Broad shoulders. Hair in finger-touchable wisps at the ears.*

'I saw a bright scarf and my memory of the old woman materialised so vividly I imagined it was her.'

'You saw her.' He didn't ask, but stated.

'I don't know.' She thought she had, but maybe the day's talk had brought the image. 'I couldn't say for certain.' She re-examined the scene out of the window, peering until she reassured herself she saw no one she recognised.

'I think all the conversation of the hat and the abduction just put pictures in my mind. And the sudden movements on the street…'

He took her gloved hand and the warmth infused her skin. She'd not felt her employer's touch through the doeskin.

'I don't know if it was her or not, now that I think of it. It's too dark to really tell. My imagination, I suppose.' It had been years since she'd seen more than her grandmother's eyes glinting through the window or a wisp of grey hair. She wasn't even sure she'd recognise her. The grandmother in her memory was spritely and had dark hair. The voice had remained the same, but the grey hair had surprised her.

'The magistrate assures me she'll be caught,' the Duke spoke softly. 'His best constables are working on this.'

He leaned to kiss her, but she held a hand to his chest, stopping him. 'I must explain something to you.'

Chalgrove could hear the silence between them growing more deafening than the sound of the horses' hooves and the rumbling of the carriage.

'I never told you about my memories…' She faltered. 'The ones I have from before I became the Manwarings' ward.'

He remained silent.

'My earliest memory is of living with my grandmother

and a gamekeeper. She once took a blow the gamekeeper aimed at me.'

'He tried to hit you?' The awareness jarred him.

She reached out, taking his hand.

He thought she tried to soften the blow he'd felt at her being abused.

'I remember being scared. He could get angry fast, but he always made sure we had plenty to eat. That was pleasant. He would bring baskets of fruit and wild game, and sometimes he would be gone for several days and re-appear with a box of provisions. It was like having feast days. That is my strongest memory. Of the food.'

He couldn't recall much about the food of his child-hood. It hadn't changed much, he supposed.

'The woman, my grandmother, played games when we were alone. She told me she could change me into a bear, then she would say she'd turn me back into a girl, but leave the heart of a bear inside me. She told me I would need it.'

She leaned half a fraction towards him, just enough to apply pressure to his arm with her shoulder, and their hands clasped more tightly. 'I don't remember a lot more than that. Just a few things here and there.'

He kept his face to the window. 'When I was about thir-teen, my father had an apoplexy. It became less important for me to learn Latin and Greek and more about collect-ing rent and having repairs made.' He faced her. 'I spent more time with Father's steward than anyone else. Father insisted. "Prosperous tenants make prosperous landlords," he would say, words slurred.'

He'd never told anyone that before. The world had changed after his father had the first apoplexy. At first, one side of his face had been stilled, but then he'd recovered quickly, for the most part. He'd begun drinking so much more then. Always having a glass in his hand or near it.

He'd started sleeping all day and his day began as the sun set. The people who saw him at events would see him for those moments, as a man having his first libation of the day. And while he didn't become completely sotted, he liked to stay, in his words, softly sotted.

'Do you think he drank to cover that? So no one might realise the change?'

He'd never considered it before, but now it seemed to make more sense. His father had tired so easily. Had slept so much of the time. And had insisted that Chalgrove bear down on his responsibilities.

Now, he reconsidered the past and his earliest childhood memories His father hadn't imbibed much then and, while it was common for his father's friends to drink more as they aged, he wondered if there was more to it than he'd first assumed. 'I still miss him.'

She removed her gloves, then returned her hand to his.

'A mother and father. Family. They're so important.' She tightened her clasp.

From the first glimmer of daylight in the cottage he'd realised she was a woman. And something about her fascinated him. At first, when she'd came into view, he'd been shocked that she'd not been brutish. After all, she'd put some decent scratches on his face and seemed like all kick and claw when she'd attacked him.

Then he'd discovered her rather more worried than anything else. Her plain dress had appeared even more so in the dark room and the debacle had taken all the life from her eyes. Even in his anger, he'd felt a deep compassion for her.

He'd had to keep pacing the room to keep from taking her in his arms.

Now, the houses of his neighbours came into view and

he didn't want the companionship of sitting quietly with her, their fingers interlocked, to end.

When the carriage stopped and he helped her alight, a thousand new sensations plunged into him.

At that moment he imagined them married. The sensation of helping her, as his wife, from the carriage and walking into their home enveloped him.

He wrapped her arm around his and they walked into his house.

Just inside the door, he stopped and gazed at her.

She appraised him, and spoke. 'You finally understand…how much Dolly and Willie mean to me.'

He looked into her eyes. 'Now I do.'

# Chapter Twenty

Once inside the house, the pleasantness inside him evaporated.

The butler held a hat… Chalgrove's stolen hat. 'An old woman was walking by on the street. One of the men noticed she'd dropped something, and she'd scuttled away without it. I recognised it. Yours.'

Chalgrove took it. 'Thank you. Has someone alerted the constables?' he asked the butler.

'Yes. We did.'

'Let me know if anything else happens,' he told the servant.

He glanced at her. 'Miss Manwaring, could you please accompany me to the library?'

He held the felt hat, but it was meaningless. Just apparel. Much like his house without Miranda in it. Shelter.

Nothing had ever weakened any part of him, but Miranda did. The knowledge that she could go to that insipid beanpole and be mother to the children she loved—that hit him hard. No one should ever take a mother's children from her. And Miranda, by heart, was those children's mother.

His words rolled so smoothly, and without inflection,

yet he saw Miranda brace herself when he finished speaking, 'My hat. The only one like it in all London. Made especially for me.'

She raised her eyebrows, silently questioning him, unsure of why a hat was of importance.

'I had the hat on when I was taken. The old woman kept it.'

He wanted to reassure her and himself. He reached out. His fingers closed over the soft skin below the hem of her sleeve. 'With the criminals still nearby, we stand a much better chance of catching them quickly. They'll be dealt with. The matter will end. For ever. You'll be safe again.'

He expected relief. Happiness. Instead she breathed slowly. Pensive.

She touched a hand to the back of her neck. 'She'll take everything from me. Everything. She gave it all to me once and now she wants to destroy me.'

'She gave it to you once?' he asked.

'The woman who lived with the gamekeeper was my grandmother.' Miranda paused. 'Yes. She dropped me beside the road. Left me. Knew the woman wanted a child and would likely happen by and take me home. I never heard from my grandmother again, until I received a message that she was dying. Then someone shoved me in the room.'

'I will not rest until she is stopped,' he said, words forced out, but not loud. 'She will be tried and hanged.'

'You can't.' The words wrenched from her. 'She's my grandmother. The only blood relative I have ever known.'

'That makes it all the more wrong of her.'

'I... I don't want her to be hanged.'

'But there is no other option. She knew what she was doing. Knows what she is doing. I would have her hanged a second time if I could. Once for taking you and once for leaving you.'

'Please. I cannot contemplate her…meeting such an end.' Her voice trembled.

'If this is what she does to her granddaughter, there is no other option.'

She clasped both his hands in hers and the touch moved through him faster than a flash of lightning could streak through the sky. 'This is why I could not tell you. I knew…'

He could never look into those eyes and wish to disappoint her. She'd been through so much, but he could not promise to let the old woman run free.

'She cannot be left to do as she is doing. It would not be fulfilling the trust I place in myself to make things better for others. She could do this again, and very likely will if she is mad. Or if she is evil, she will do it for the joy of it. Perhaps she wishes to end her life and she is using me to do it.'

He put his arms around her, holding her. The conversation between the two women. The thrown shoes. It all made sense to him now.

'Will you let me know that you won't hurt her?' she asked.

He paused, pulling away. 'I will let the court decide.'

She touched the back of his hand, ran her fingers over his knuckles. Clasped her fingers around his. 'Please remember that she is daft.'

'I will.'

The strength left his body, yet he felt he could have stretched his arm and clasped the sun without being burned.

This woman, whose fortitude held her up from the inside, didn't waver in her support of a vagabond who'd left her to fend for herself at the side of a road.

Miranda, who concerned herself that two little children who had servants at their elbows might suffer if she were not there for them, and it was true. He knew they would. To not have her would be difficult.

She put her arms around him and he folded himself around her, wanting to be infused with all the goodness of her spirit.

The kiss was light, lingering softly.

He stopped, his lips only a little from hers.

He nibbled softly at her bottom lip, then pressed his mouth gently against hers, and she tasted him—the hint of spiced cider melted on her tongue, but the overpowering essence of maleness faded the world away.

The next kiss slowed time and sound, and everything else.

When he pulled away, she held him to keep her balance.

'We have to go somewhere private. I can't risk you being talked about by the staff.'

She knew she could be making an irrevocable step in her life, but she couldn't release his hands, or take her eyes from his.

'Where else…?' she whispered. 'Where can we be alone?' She wasn't sure if the words were loud enough to be heard.

He paused. Stepped back. 'You should go back to your room.'

'My room…' The room with the roses. With the hint of springtime and summer and beginnings. 'I want you to go with me. I want to make love with you.'

He smiled, lips near her ears, before pulling her into a hug. 'Among the flowers?' His forehead touched hers.

'I can't think of anywhere else I'd prefer to be. For my first time.'

He continued holding her. 'It's too risky for you. Too much of a chance of a child. Of regrets. Of your changing your mind tomorrow, and you'll never be able to wish it away.'

'I won't want to wish it away,' she said. 'I'll hold the memory for ever. It will give me something to treasure of the ordeal we've been through. Something to save in my heart. To have that, I need to hold you.'

He put an arm around her waist. 'Are you certain?'

'Very.'

Taking her hand, he led her to the doorway of her room. Outside, he released her, and opened the door. She went inside, then turned to him, clasping his fingertips, and led him into the room.

Her hand worked of its own accord, touching his cravat. Silk. She'd known it would be. Soft.

Suddenly, she wanted to touch all the tender parts of him. She asked permission with her eyes and he gave it by stepping closer and holding her waist.

His kiss stopped her plans, or enhanced them. She wasn't sure which and didn't care. She only cared that he continue.

Running his hands up her back and then down, he brought her closer and increased the temperature inside her. Desire bloomed, causing her to feel engulfed by the sensations he created and unable to resist her body's request for more.

She pulled back, but only enough so she could skim her fingers over his jaw, feeling the roughness and the change in texture when she found the softness of his lips.

He clasped her neck, his thumb lingering at her jawline,

tracing the texture of her skin and infusing her with the strength she could feel through the light touch.

Hands, soft, but strong, clasped both sides of her face and, this time, the kiss took all of her, surrounding her with an intensity she didn't know existed.

Lips, warm and wet, kept hers, his tongue dipping inside for a taste, and she held on, awash with new sensations, her senses immersing her in feelings she didn't want to resurface from, but to go only deeper.

Then he stopped and the world around her appeared again, but she was lost, half in it, half remaining in the place his lips had taken her.

He clasped both her hands in his, intertwining fingers, but his eyes held her even more solidly, bringing his face into focus.

'You pull my heart closer and not with words,' he said. 'I can see gentleness in you. No guile. Nothing but you.'

'I may be misleading you, if you think that I can take the place of Susanna, or anyone else you've had in your life. The children come first with me and I have to go back to them.'

'I understand. Today, it's enough to be in the same room with you again, alone, and feel the connection of your heart beating against mine.'

She rested her head against his neck, breathing in the scent of crisp linen and warm maleness.

It wasn't enough just to be in the same room with him. She wanted to hug him tighter, hold him closer and become a part of him. She wanted a moment she would never forget in this fairy-tale room with its dream of a happy ending emblazoned on everything inside it.

She stepped away, holding his hand in both of hers. 'I'll never forget you and I don't want you to ever forget me.'

'You have nothing to worry about. I won't.' He covered

the distance between them, bringing them back into an embrace. He murmured, his face against her hair, 'Our first night together in the old cottage ensured that. This night means I'll reflect on you with longing for ever. You'll be the memory that keeps my heart beating.'

She burrowed into him until he clasped her chin and watched her briefly, before he said. 'One last time.'

The kiss could never be the last kiss. He swept her into it, holding her, lifting her to her tiptoes, and she didn't know how she could bear not holding him close.

'Stay with me.'

She replied with an answering kiss.

He slipped aside the shoulder of her gown, trailing kisses from her neck to her collarbone, kissing each trace of skin slowly unveiled.

She attempted to loosen his cravat, clenched her fingers just as he nuzzled her ear and pulled the loop, making it knot.

Instantly, she realised what she'd done and stepped away, but he smiled and his long fingers undid the damage in seconds, his coat, waistcoat and shirt seeming to fall away with the cravat.

He lifted her to the counterpane, under the roses, and undressed her with care, as if holding a butterfly and he could not risk damaging its wings.

When they embraced again, skin against skin, savouring the sensations, he didn't hurry, but took his time, as if he wanted to make their time together last until the end of the world.

Touching the ringlet of her hair that had loosened, letting it slide through his fingers, he said, 'This is the pinnacle of my life, holding you.'

He buried his face in her neck, moving enough to increase the sensations caused by skin caressing skin. 'I can't release in you,' he whispered. 'I can't risk changing your life because I want to make love to you. I want you to have no regrets of any kind.'

His hands traced her silhouette, swirling over each curve, interweaving their bodies into one being.

He rested his hand on her hip, his lips remaining near hers, tasting, tingling and savouring her.

Hugging her tight, he rose above her, observing her, before his mouth took over again, and he trailed down her body, kissing her breasts, their peaks and their softness.

He took her hand and held her palm against his face, breath heating her skin, guiding her to experience his jawline, his neck, his chest, and letting the friction of his hair tingle against her.

She caressed him with a sense of freedom, as if touching an artist's perfect sculpture.

When he rose above her, the second when their gazes locked was the deepest connection she'd ever had. An impassioned statement, from deep within, of their unity.

He gently moved closer, taking his time, easing into her and taking them into oneness.

Thrusting softly, he watched her, aware of nothing else in the world but their togetherness and her reactions. He wanted to give her a release she would remember for ever, and nothing meant more to him.

When her eyes closed and she clenched around him, he savoured the moment and his body reacted. Instantly, he pulled away.

He clasped her, holding on to the moment of love.

When the tempest of emotions calmed inside him, he saw her half-opened eyes and kissed her forehead.

Lying beside her, he thought of how cautious he'd been when he'd tried to make certain she wouldn't have a child.

And all he could think about was how precious a child

of Miranda's would be and how he would like to hold it, hear the sound of the babe's mother's laughter as the infant did what he was certain her child would do. What she'd predicted.

In that instant, he could see the image of togetherness and family stronger than any he'd ever felt and he yearned for that bond.

Only it wouldn't be their child or their togetherness. It would be other children with another man. He would be a world away.

He took her slender fingers and kissed her palm.

He mourned for what he would never have with her. He tried to feel pleased for putting her feelings before his own and pushed away the part of him that was the child inside that wanted Miranda to see nothing in the world but him.

Miranda awoke in the morning, with the memory of Chalgrove kissing her goodnight.

Now a maid knocked. As Miranda called for the woman to enter, she glanced around the room. Nothing had changed. The roses were all in place. The room no different.

'Her Grace has finished her morning meal and would like to speak with you.' The maid stood at the entrance. 'I will wait.'

'Of course.' Miranda rose, dressed and followed the maid.

In the Duchess's room, the older woman sat, another maid rubbing a rose-scented cream into her feet.

Miranda took the delicate curved-back chair, unsure why she'd been summoned.

'Some day a man will invent one of these...' the Duchess waved a hand to the looking glass '...which shows a woman only what she wishes to see in her reflection. And the man will become very wealthy.' She turned away from Miranda and chortled softly. 'But until then I will make sure never to stand in front of one in strong light.'

The Duchess moved around until she sat with her back to the mirror. 'Dear. I have some good news of Chalgrove's courtship. While the two of you were away yesterday, I worked on it. I suspected that after you saw the children, you'd not return.' She lifted a brow. 'I didn't expect to see you again.'

'I care for them greatly, but...'

'Well, that gives me a chance to give you the good news. I've found a bride for Chal.'

Miranda put a pleased smile on her face and leaned forward. 'Oh, Your Grace, how wonderful,' she spoke swiftly, certain she did not want to hear of the Duchess's search for a daughter-in-law.

'Oh, sit down.' The Duchess waved a hand to the chair, exasperation in her voice. 'Nothing can be more important than Chalgrove's marriage. Even catching these cut-throats who so unjustly took his freedom is not as important as his having an heir.'

'Chalgrove's marriage?' Miranda felt a churn in her world and she felt her heart thumping, then it was as if it melted away and left an aching emptiness.

'Yes.' The Duchess tapped her jaw and a maid uncorked a bottle and then dotted some scent on her mistress.

'I let that doxy, Susanna, into my house and served her tea. The best tea—which she was obviously not worth. If not for her, Chalgrove would have fallen in love with someone suitable long before now. She jaded him.'

Miranda stood, wanting to comfort the woman, but wanting more to leave the room. 'You can't blame yourself for whom he loved.'

'He did not *love* her. I am sure of that.' The Duchess's

eyes sparkled with ire. 'Although he might conjure up the idea of himself *in love* with her. She...' The Duchess sighed. 'She had— Never mind. It's over and done, and I blame myself.'

Miranda took a small step towards the door. 'You really can't blame yourself at all.'

'Don't leave,' the Duchess commanded, standing. 'You've spoken with Chalgrove under unfortunate circumstances. Did he mention any regrets at being unmarried?'

Miranda stopped. 'No.'

'I'm not surprised.' She moved closer, taking Miranda's arm and waving her to the wardrobe. 'He appears able to find women willing to share their time with him. But yesterday I spoke with someone about this new woman and she will be perfect.' She held a blue dress and raised it for Miranda's perusal. 'A sweet young woman with impeccable family history and even though I've not seen her, I've seen a portrait. I've sent for her and she should arrive in London today.'

Picking at a thread on the gown, she continued speaking. 'Dear, the dark colours you wear do suit you, but something like this would really enhance your complexion better.'

'My dresses are serviceable. Suitable for caring for the children.'

'I suppose.' She left the wardrobe door open as she took a step away from it.

The Duchess examined Miranda's face. 'Your skin is flawless. Hair needs work, though, but nothing beyond Bessie's skills.'

Something flashed across the Duchess's eyes, but Miranda wasn't sure what to make of it.

'I knew your mother—the one who took you in, before

she married your father and moved to the country. Very reserved. Timid. She was the age of my younger sister.'

'Yes.' Miranda nodded, chin erect. 'To lose her was the worst thing of my life. Much worse than anything else.'

'I would imagine. She surely had great expectations for you.'

'I think she would have been pleased by my choice to be a governess. I know she would have.'

The Duchess huffed. 'Oh, I think she would have wanted you to have children, a family. The normal desires of a mother for her daughter. I rather did like her, even if she hardly spoke.'

'She'd accept my unmarried state. She understood marriage doesn't always bring what one expects.'

The Duchess studied Miranda. 'Of course it doesn't, dear Miranda. Romantic love is a sham and has probably destroyed more marriages than it created. It's nothing more than a gauze draping over one's eyes to keep truth filtered out. Have you ever been embroiled in romantic love?'

'I believe as you do,' Miranda spoke simply. 'Romantic love is…unnecessary.' In that statement's aftermath inside her, she wondered if she lied.

'Well, you do have the life of a wife, almost, without the husband. A family around you and a man left to his own devices.'

The Duchess smiled, and looked at the blue dress still in her hands. 'I did, of course, love my husband dearly. Not romantically at first, but realistically, and I liked him. He could irritate me more than anyone else in the world and he could make me laugh for hours. I'll always miss those days we shared. I've considered searching out a new husband, or pretending to. But first I need to get Chalgrove settled.

The Duchess continued speaking, her gaze now on Miranda. 'Your company pleases me and you have pleasant features, which with my help could be improved upon. A woman of beauty should not have to work—her beauty should work for her.' She waved her hand, flicking the words in Miranda's direction. 'Dear. You could learn so much from me.' The older woman shut her eyes, gave a negative shudder of her head and leaned back. 'Are you returning to be with the children?'

'Of course. Dolly and Willie are important. They have been my life and I cannot let them go.'

The Duchess opened her eyes. 'I certainly understand that.' She moved and the maid at her hand followed her as if they were one, never raising her eyes. Then she stood, got a handkerchief and blotted the Duchess's brow, and moved to the other side.

The Duchess pointed one ringed finger at Miranda. 'I had been worried that your employer might sack you, assuming the worst. And I searched my mind for another job for you. I know a woman who needs a companion. If you were to need employment, please see me. I would not want you to live with your stepmother, although I am sure I saw her on a bad day.'

'That is gracious of you.' Let her fashion the truth she wished for, but she'd not seen her stepmother on a bad day. The offer of employment was kind, however.

The Duchess's face scrunched, then she forced her eyes wide again and her countenance bland. 'Face cream,' she called out, tossed the garment to the bed and moved to her chair, leaning her head back and shutting her eyes. A maid grabbed a pot and smoothed a dollop of a clear mixture at the edges of her mistress's eyes. The Duchess sat straight again and gave a pat under her chin.

'I want you to see the woman I've picked for Chalgrove.

She's now in London and I'd like your opinion of her. You seem sensible enough.'

The last thing in the world she wanted to do, even less than she wanted to live in her father's house, was to meet the woman picked for Chalgrove. She could not do it. She could not. 'I should be here in case news arrives from the magistrate.'

'We'll only be gone a short time. Two eyes are sharper than one. Four eyes are even sharper than two. You'll go with me. It will be a lark. Please wait for me in the library. Chal's there. Just ignore him.'

## Chapter Twenty-One

Miranda noticed the skilled needlework on the arm covers and matching scarf over the back of the armchair in the library. The furnishings didn't appear as severe as she recalled. The absence of a constable helped.

The air in the room alerted her to the fact of it being a masculine domain. She didn't think Chalgrove smoked, but the hint of tobacco lingered and mixed with the bold scents of a man's daily life within walls.

Then her view locked on Chalgrove.

'I wanted to let you know the constable has informed me that the culprit's camp has been located.' He spoke ever so properly. Ever so formally.

Miranda could feel the sensation of claws coming closer, taking her world from her.

Chalgrove poured them both a glass of wine. Their fingers touched when she took the glass.

She saw the wavering of the liquid, took a sip and quickly sat the glass on the table.

This time, Chalgrove shut the door with a click and, as the sound reached her ears, she swayed towards him.

The window light softened the room, but Chalgrove's presence added a blast of life she'd never felt before.

He moved close and she raised her face, and his kiss caught her lips. 'I've missed you. Our making love. I can't stop remembering it.'

'But you mustn't think about it,' she said. 'You mustn't.'

She faced Chalgrove and put her hands behind her back, stilling them. 'We must forget. Everything.'

His eyebrows raised, but he didn't comment on the movement. 'I could tell myself that all day and it wouldn't change.'

'It's the only way I can continue.'

His eyes tightened. He walked to the window, and then returned to stand in front of her.

'Very well,' he said. 'Then you need to know that after the old woman's camp was found, she slipped away. The constable continued after her and found word of a group who've been staying not too far away. The woman has to rest one place or the other. We'll keep giving them surprise visits until we find her.'

'But...' she swallowed '... I don't want to see her hanged or in the madhouse. Can she not be left free?'

Chalgrove frowned at the request.

Miranda turned her face from his, hiding the anguish plunging into her. 'You know how horrible things could be for her.'

'She should be punished. Abducting you. Her granddaughter. Taken by ruffians. Thrown into a room with an unknown man. We cannot let this happen to another woman. Miranda, you're a child in the ways of the world. So much worse could have happened.'

'But it didn't.'

'It's not over yet. As things stand, she should be in Newgate by sunset tomorrow.'

'She'll have no hope if that happens,' Miranda remembered the sticks twined together with a little scrap of cloth tied at the top for a head—the pretend doll her grandmother had given her. The only thing she had with her when she was left at the road besides a length of fabric for her to sit on. Later, her mother had given her other toys, but Miranda had always cherished the recollection of those twigs bound together.

'Miranda.' He moved to the desk, his expression hidden from her. 'For me, the question is not what will happen to her, but what will happen to you? Never seeing you again is a strong punishment for me and I hate the prospect of living the rest of my days without you.'

The back of his head tilted as he raised his chin upwards. Then he moved quickly, as if pulled by an invisible heartstring.

His hand snugged around her waist. His face burrowed into her neck. 'Your ear is cold, but your neck—warm. Delicious.'

'Chalgrove.' Miranda pushed him back, but even as his chest and legs increased their space away from her, his lips stayed nestled.

Miranda could not bear to see the desire in his eyes. She shut her own. 'Chalgrove—your mother has a wife chosen for you. And I am another Susanna, except with an attachment to two children instead of a husband.'

She wanted him to understand. She could not desert the children. She could not give them the uncertainty she'd felt each morning when she woke and wondered when her new mother would give her away and where she would find herself.

'If Mr Trevor asks me to wed, I will accept.'

'And if I were to ask you?'

She believed she'd misheard, until she saw his eyes. Her voice left her at first, but she forced speech from her lungs.

'You must never ask me such a thing. The children. I

have promised myself to remain with them.' The words were true and they were crueller than any lie she'd ever heard. She could almost see them slicing into the air between them and creating an invisible, unrepairable chasm.

He stepped away. Light changed behind his eyes, darkening. 'I understand.'

Moving slightly away from her, he agreed again, with the same tightness of his lips that would have appeared had he spoken an oath. 'I understand.'

'I'm leaving soon to go with your mother to meet the woman she has chosen for you. Please don't find needless flaws in her.'

He did not move. 'If we were having a duel, Miranda, that would have counted as a disabling blow.'

Nothing showed in his face when he turned away. He left the room and the walls seemed to close in on her from all sides—he'd delivered the fatal blow in the duel. The fatal blow to her heart.

She collapsed in a chair. She tried to summon the two faces of the children to her mind, but all she could see was the look on Chalgrove's face and the bleakness inside her.

She put her clasped hands to her forehead, trying to block out the flurry of emotions she experienced.

Remaining with the children was the right thing to do. The only thing. Best for everyone. She was a part of the household and her whole life was within those walls. Her whole life. Except the man she loved.


Miss Antonia Redding entered the room on the arm of her aunt, gently guiding the woman to a throne of a chair near the Duchess and Miranda after introductions were made. The walls of the room boasted an abundance of art—all of terriers. Even one small rug had a canine influence.

'So nice of you to call.' The aunt moved to the chair slowly, studying where she placed each foot. 'And I'm doubly pleased for you meet our Antonia.'

Miranda took stock of the girl. Ringlets. Fair. If the miss ever ventured out doors, she kept her parasol, gloves and bonnet in place. No rays of sun had touched the girl's skin.

'Do you play pianoforte, sing or sew?' The Duchess's eyebrows fluttered in innocence and her words clicked out with no subtlety about them.

'A bit.' Antonia met the mother-general's stare effortlessly.

'Our Antonia did the portrait of my dear Ambrose,' her aunt inserted, waving to the watercolour on the wall. A terrier, eyes almost glistening with joy, pranced in the portrait.

'Very accomplished.' A hint of awe sounded in the Duchess's voice.

The aunt continued. 'Her parents were indulgent and terribly over-demanding of her. Did not take into consideration her delicate sensibilities. Sent for a music teacher for her when the child was too small to know what she was doing.' She spoke to her niece. 'What was the name of the family he was related to?'

'Bach.' Antonia practically shrugged the word away.

'Excellent tutor. He claimed Antonia learned more in a fortnight than most students learn in a year.'

'Aunt, please, let us talk about something more interesting. I would love to learn more about your guests.'

Miranda sat, listening as the ladies discussed Antonia's near perfection. The light laughter of the others touched her ears as she realised they were laughing about poor Antonia's flaw. Unfortunately, she wrote letters to her aunt with such a small hand her aunt had to have someone else read them aloud. Of course, her aunt claimed, 'Antonia does not want to waste paper.'

Miranda could imagine Antonia on Chalgrove's arm. This woman would be the perfect match to stand at his side.

Miranda couldn't think of a woman standing near Chalgrove without feeling a choking sensation.

The evening continued with mutual admiration flowing around the room, and practically drowning Miranda in the happiness that jabbed her from all sides.


Finally, the Duchess stood to leave.

When the carriage door shut behind them, the Duchess clasped Miranda's arm with both hands. 'The search is over.' The Duchess's words rushed from her mouth. 'What do you think?'

'She's lovely. Perfect.' It hurt to speak and the smile she gave ached even more.

Antonia was as close to perfection as a woman could be. She would make a suitable companion to Chalgrove. The woman was too good for a king.

'Very perfect,' the Duchess said, musing. 'Even I was not *that* suited to be a duchess.'

'You are an example she would do well to emulate,' Miranda said.

The Duchess put a finger alongside her cheek. 'Dear Antonia. She is exactly, exactly, exactly exact and would be a fine daughter-in-law. To be fair, it is almost as if she were raised to be a duchess and needs no example at all.'

The carriage rumbled along, the only sound Miranda heard until just before it stopped at the town house.

'It's settled, then,' the Duchess said. 'I will drop some hints to my son. The kind that he can't ignore. I'll tell him that he should consider courting and marrying Antonia.

They'll make a lovely couple and have many accomplished children.' Her voice lilted, then dropped. 'My job is done.'

Miranda's body jolted as the carriage came to a complete stop. The driver opened the door, but the Duchess didn't rise. She studied Miranda. 'I need a new project and I think it will be you.' The Duchess touched Miranda's arm.

Miranda shook her head several times before she spoke. 'That is indeed gracious of you. But there's no need. I can't leave the children. I must be their governess.'

The Duchess touched the side of the coach as if to rise, but instead of standing, she calculated Miranda. 'He is unwed? Their father?'

'Yes.'

The Duchess gathered her skirts to exit. 'For now. I must be invited to meet those lovely children. I'm sure no one would mind if a duchess takes notice of two youngsters.'

Miranda took in a deep breath.

The older woman said. 'I must let the world know how heroically you saved a duke.'

'I did no such thing.'

Her Grace put a finger to her lips and made a shushing motion before making a light fist at her chin. 'My son will never publicly contradict me and you shouldn't either, Miranda. Only two people were there… You. My son.'

Miranda didn't speak.

'The constable told me that you were on your way to see an ill person. At some point, you realised some culprits had abducted the Duke to hold him for ransom, but he escaped and you managed to… Managed to get that respectable farmer to return you both to London.' The Duchess secured Miranda's arm. 'Your reputation is secured and enhanced, and what devoted mother would not want to reward such an act of kindness?'

'But there is no need.'

'You are right, of course. And with you wed to Mr Trevor, you will never have to worry about anyone becoming those children's stepmother…but you. I will see that it is accomplished. Think ahead. You'll be the perfect bride for him.'

Chalgrove knew the old woman was in his grasp. He stared across his study at the constable's face.

'I can't let you be harmin' her. I mean, if you do, nothing will come of it. But just the same, I can't let you.' Wiggins sat in Chalgrove's study, ensconced in a chair, fingers clasped at his belly. 'Takes a special kind of man to do the dirty work.'

Chalgrove's eyes raked Wiggins. If someone would have yelled fire, Wiggins would have not raised a brow and his reaction would have been with the same rapidity he would have given to pulling a book from the shelf.

'Got the Runners, if we need them,' the constable continued. 'An old woman's harder to apprehend than street vermin. Not my favourite thing—an old woman. They swear worse 'n anything.'

'Do you know where she is?' Chalgrove asked Wiggins. Chalgrove twisted his fingers on the stem of the brandy glass, rotating it back and forth.

'I can have her caught if you give me a nod of your head.' The constable raised his chin, lowered his eyelids and stared at Chalgrove. 'We got her where we want her. All you have to say is the word and she'll be tossed into gaol.'

'I want to talk with her. To find out why she did as she did. And more.'

'Best let me handle that. Easier for you if you don't see how questions get asked.'

'No.' He stood. 'I want to be the one to talk with her. The woman had me ambushed.' And she'd pinched him. 'I have no wish to harm her.' He stopped, sitting the glass upside down on the tray. 'I don't. Her crime was heinous, but…' He wanted the old woman punished for Miranda's sake, but he couldn't, because it would hurt Miranda most.

'You can't get tender-hearted.' The constable watched Chalgrove's face. 'If we let her go, she could do the same to someone else and, next time, they might not be so lucky. I might find them later with their skull caved in by a spade. It's not my concern about your abduction, because you're safe and sound. The noose will protect other gents and ladies.' He sat back in his chair, slouching, his fingers interlaced. 'Just the way of it. You can't break an egg without losing a baby chick, but I like my eggs.'

'That doesn't make sense.'

'Gotta hang 'em to kill 'em and make the world a better place.'

'Criminals run the streets.'

''Cept those with rope cravats. They never commit another crime.'

'This old woman, if I think she'll harm anyone else, I'll tell you,' Chalgrove said.

'You've not the mind to judge. Takes a professional. Course if she does harm someone else, then she'd hang as she should have, I suppose. It's not like the line to the gallows is getting any shorter. Last hanging, people started leaving early. After a dozen or so—kind of tiresome.'

'I've never seen one.'

'You should.' He crossed his ankles. 'You really ought to attend a hanging—of course, the show's really in the people watching. I mean…' he raised his brows '…some of them takes a mite too much enjoyment out of it to be normal.' He shut his eyes and sighed. 'Sometimes it's hard to get a good hangman, too. Sad state this world's comin' to.'

Chalgrove imagined the bystanders jeering at the old crone. On the other hand, he could imagine her being transported and somehow swindling the other criminals out of whatever they might have.

'I wish to talk with her.' Chalgrove said forcefully. 'Today.'

'Suit yourself.' The man shuffled to his feet, rubbing his fingertips in a massage under his hat. 'I have nothing better to do.' He gave Chalgrove a wink. 'She's got to hang for her own good. Best thing for her.'

Chalgrove called for a vehicle, grabbed the hat at hand and they left to get into the carriage.

The town coach rolled along the cobbled streets, veering right or left to avoid pedestrians and carriages, but suffering through the cracks in the street.

'You don't have a wife, do you?' the constable asked, giving a cross-wise glower at Chalgrove.

'No.'

'I do. Married me a widow woman. Said she poisoned her husband. *Well,* I said, *he must'a been a bad 'un. No,* she said, *I just didn't like the yellow hat he wore that day.*' He crossed his arms and shut his eyes. ''Course it wasn't nothing like yours, I'm sure.'

'I had it on when I was kidnapped. I want to make sure the old woman sees it.'

The man moved his shoulders about as if trying to get comfortable. He didn't even open his eyes. 'With respect, Your Lordship, I am surprised you were taken with that on.'

'Thank you for informing me.'

# Chapter Twenty-Two

Chalgrove saw her standing beside one of the wagons before his carriage even came to a full stop. He clenched his teeth.

'I wish to talk to her alone.'

'If you're sure, Your Grace.' Wiggins let his head fall back against the squabs. 'Shout if you need help. I usually wake up. Always have after I've been asleep.' But instead of shutting his eyes, he stared out of the window.

Chalgrove jumped out of the carriage, muscles stretching after the ride and ready to explode into action against the criminals. They'd captured him last time and this time they would suffer for it.

Instead of seeing a band of culprits suitable for the drop from a trapdoor, he saw one female vagabond, humming to herself and shuffling around a fire with a pot bubbling over it smelling of stew. A child ran away in the distance. Horses stood tied among the trees. The old woman wasn't truly alone, but she appeared abandoned.

Chalgrove heard the clunk as she dropped the last of the wood on to the fire pit.

She surveyed him. 'A little late, aren't you? But there's still plenty to eat.'

'You knew I'd find you,' he said as he strode towards her. She considered him as if she'd invited him.

'You do look familiar. The seal on the carriage helped.' She laughed, a joke of her own. 'And your constable...' She pointed to the window of the carriage. The constable waved at her. 'We've met before. Several times. The man does not trust me, but then I've never given him a reason to.' She grinned. 'I don't trust him either.'

She indicated the stump someone had provided as a seat. 'Sit. Be a guest of Ella Etta in my mansion of no walls.' She chuckled. 'Yes, sit. I don't like craning my neck to see you, Your Grace.'

'You aren't very proud of that neck or you'd be watching over it better.'

She stared at him. 'After all I did for you. I gave you a beautiful woman to woo. A cottage. A feather bed.' She smirked. 'I guess I should have taken one look at the hat and known you couldn't see a beauty in front of you. That hat was so ugly my mule wouldn't wear it.'

He ignored the jibe. 'I wouldn't take advantage of a woman.'

She pursed her lips, then moved to fetch a three-legged stool which hung from the side of the wagon and sat it beside him. He ignored the movement.

The sun dappled through the shade of the trees, illuminating the worn clothing she wore.

'I'm here to take you to Newgate.' Chalgrove put a foot on the stool.

She scowled. 'You can't be serious. It's not for me. Nasty place. You really visited because you missed my good bread and my sweet voice.' She laughed and studied his face. 'You're looking better than when I saw you last. Except—' Her eyes moved to the top of his head.

'Tell my fortune, old woman?' he challenged. 'I'll tell you yours.'

'I have no fortune for a duke. The title gives him enough.'

She inclined her head away from him. 'Coffee?' Without waiting for an answer, she went to a pot hanging at the side of the fire pit. She poured some into one of the cups sitting at the edge of the fire, then brought the cup to him. 'Can't seem to find good tea in the woods.'

'You can be hanged, or, if you give me a reason for what you did, you may be only transported.'

She touched the sleeve of his jacket. 'Wouldn't want to ruin our good friendship by your doing such a thing to me.' She held out the cup.

He stared at it, grasped it, then took a sip, surprised at the earthy flavour.

'You can take me to hang and I won't speak a word. Or you can sit and have a sip with me and I'll tell you all.' The woman rummaged around in a basket until she found another cup.

'I'll decide,' he said. 'You are daft and have no choices.'

'You two were more trouble than I expected.' She examined him from head to heel. 'But I guess it's my lot in life to take care of others.'

'By kidnapping?'

She nodded, pouring her own drink. 'With whatever means is at hand.' She raised her brows.

'Why'd you risk your life for a few coins, while lugging food and water to us?'

'I'd never met a duke?' Innocence poured from the words.

'Why me?'

'A man wearing a hat like yours, I guessed you wouldn't put up much of a fight. But you didn't make it easy,' she mused as she sat down on the stump and crossed her ankles 'I'd seen you from a distance. You have a shadow that blocks the sun and the night in your eyes. I liked that. And your servants don't complain about you…much.' She viewed her boot laces, sat her cup on the dirt and tied one of the worn, mismatching strings.

She grinned. 'My scrawny Child grew into being a Miranda. It's a suitable name. She fits it.'

'Makes no sense. Abducting the two of us.'

'I don't have to make sense. I'm addled. I'm old. I'm so old I don't even know how old I am.'

'You could hang.'

She shrugged. 'You want me to hang? To let this be in the newspapers. To ruin the girl? Child would not let me kill the hare eating our beans even when I told her we would starve.' She frowned. 'For her, I had to get a dog to scare the rabbits away so we could eat. I'm sure the dog ate meat and we ate vegetables.'

'Abducting me is enough to send you to the gallows. I don't need to spread tales about her.'

The old woman nodded. 'I hoped…' She pulled the shawl tight and he heard the sound of beads clicking together. 'I'd hoped to guide the governess to marriage.' She lifted her cup. 'I wanted the best for her. That's how I picked you.' Her stare wavered. 'Against my better judgement. But no matter. I saw it in the stars.' She gazed overhead. 'But I can't really see the stars at night any more. They've faded. So maybe I imagined it.'

She wriggled her boots out in front of her and he noticed the loose sole on one.

'You should find yourself some new boots.'

She tapped the toes of her boots together, the sole flapping. 'I like these.' She grinned up at him. 'I'm saving funds for my dowry.'

'Why do you act as you do?'

She let out a deep breath, and stared at the ground, disgusted. 'My eyes are so dim, I can barely see the lines in a palm, so I just tell the people whatever I want to say.' She held out her arm as far as she could, studying the inside of her own hand. 'I'd have to have the palm this far from me to see it and who would believe I could see into the future if I can't even see my own hand? So, I bumble along and do what I can.' She gave him a smile. 'I say what I wish and everyone is happy. I found you a bride and I caught Child a husband.'

'You call your granddaughter Child?'

She chewed her bottom lip, smiled, and said, 'I don't have a true granddaughter.'

'Miss Manwaring.'

Staring at her boots, she spoke. 'She is my granddaughter by heart, not blood.'

'Why do you say that?'

'Drucie. That was the name her mother gave her, but I just called her Child or Grandchild. Seemed to make us a family. Her true mother died when she was just a little one and her real father possibly a rich man.' She stared at him, death in her eyes. 'Made me angry to see a little babe, running and laughing and her true mother dead, and no one but me to care for her and her as innocent as everyone else wasn't. I couldn't toss her away. Then...' She examined the sun. 'The stars told me I could get her dressed in silk.' She laughed. 'I just preened, wondering if I could do such a thing.'

This woman truly was for Bedlam.

'Or I dreamed it.' She sniffed. 'There was a story about a babe left in a basket.' She cupped her chin. 'So, I studied the world and I knew where Child belonged,' she continued. 'I put Child in her best dress. Did her hair nice and put smudges beneath her eyes. I sat her beside the road where Manwaring's wife—not the flea-ridden mange he beds down with now, but his first wife—went to Sunday Services.'

'You were risking a child's life.'

She sneered. 'Manwaring was rich. His wife was childless. I'd read her fortune and told her she'd discover a child soon that was to be her reward. Told her how a brown-eyed child would bless her.'

Then the old woman's eyelids dropped, but not before he saw the determination.

'I'd heard this story about a little boy being left floating in the stream and a princess found him and took him in and made him a leader. Long ago in a faraway place. I had the spare child. Decided it might work.' She chuckled, and her face brightened. 'It did. Almost.'

The woman met his glare. 'Child's mother was the daughter of the gamekeeper. So, we met. Not long after the babe was born, they stayed here. Talked about the babe's father. Then the daughter ran off and left Child with me. Died soon after.' Her eyes tightened. 'I didn't like that babe being so alone, so I took Child.'

Wind whispered through the trees.

'Manwaring's wife, not the most sensible, but she always paid me well when I read her fortune. Her brain not much bigger than my little finger, but her heart bigger than ten of mine and she could give the little one a home. So, I read her fortune that way.' She shuffled her shoulders. 'She wanted a baby. I gave her one. I don't think Manwaring thought it was as good a plan as I did. The toad.'

Then she tossed the dregs of her coffee away, sat the cup on the ground again, and snapped the shawl into a knot. 'Then the woman went and died.' She huffed, shaking her splayed fingers. 'That nearly killed me. I had to scramble around when I knew that Child was without a mother to protect her. Not only once. Now a second time. I didn't know what to do. Took me some time to work on it.'

She chuckled. 'So, then I read about twenty fortunes at no cost, finding out what I could where I could, and I found a rich man, Trevor, who had a sickly wife who wasn't expected to live. I read Miss Cuthbert's fortune and told her about the governess being needed. Once his wife died, I decided the man would trip over his own feet falling in love with Child.'

The toes of her good boot touched the ash of the fire before she reared back and moved her feet closer. Her glare pinched. 'Wouldn't you have expected the man would have fallen right away in love with her? Any man with a grain of sense would.'

He didn't move. 'Yes.'

'But she's not getting any younger and when I read the fortune of the scullery maid I found out about the stories of the house where Miranda is a governess.'

She moved her hand as if wiping off crumbs. 'Only tales of that house's master was of him being distracted and not by Child. Her praises went high and wide, but no secret looks between her and the master and no whispers of the servants about how the two of them might be carrying on. Only carrying on was by the cook and a stableman. I had to do something, Child is turning into a spinster.'

The fortune-teller held up her chin. 'I had to get her a husband. What if something might happen to me? Who would watch out for her then?'

She glared again to the sky and seemed to talk to it, holding her hand high. 'Three times now. Three times I have had to guide the blasted stars.' She composed herself, then scratched the loose skin of her neck. 'I figured you were my last chance to get her settled in gold and you would have eyes enough to see her value.' She spat at the ground. 'I didn't call that one right.'

He studied her.

She scowled at him. 'I was fond of having her around, but then I decided she deserved better than rags.' She sneered. 'Perhaps you believe I should have left her in tatters.'

'You are to stay clear of her,' he said to the old woman.

She shook her fist at the sky, moving her head in a negative shake, then spoke to him as she raised both palms. 'I give up on her now. She's alone in the world. Just like the rest of us.'

'You *will* stay clear of her.'

'I wash my hands of the brat. I would have done better to have found her a job as a scullery maid. I keep trying to turn her into a silk purse and she keeps finding sow's ears.'

'You wished for me to marry her? That's why you trapped us together?'

The woman frowned. 'By that hat, I knew you didn't have a woman around to guide you. And you might be simple-minded enough to fall in love with her. I call her a beauty, although she's not much to look at, but it was dark enough in there.' She squinted. 'No. You'd expect a peer's daughter. Not a mindless simpleton Child. Not a woman who wastes all her time caring for a rich man's children.'

Anger flared in him. 'You could hang.' She dared criticise Miss Manwaring.

'I should. One simple task and I could not complete it. I wanted Child to have a home of her own. A family. Marriage.' She kicked at the dirt.

'You can't be tossing people into a room expecting them to marry.'

'Yes. You can. I did. It didn't work.' She straightened her shoulders and puffed out her chest.

She held out her palm again, and studied it. 'Doesn't seem to work like it should. Maybe because I can't see the lines any more.' She spat into the fire. 'What use am I if I can't make up nonsense to give people hope?'

He looked at the old woman. Every servant in his house dressed better than she. And his butler and man of affairs had spectacles.

And she spoke of giving people hope. This tattered vagrant in a camp of thieves.

'You truly should hang, you know.'

She raised her shoulders. 'I'd break the rope.'

'You probably would. And would claim it magic.'

She smiled. 'Of course I would claim that. I claim the sun rising as magic and, if we need rain and it rains, I say it is all my doing. I lie, but it makes people happy. Particularly me, when they pay for my nonsense.' She held out her palm. 'I would like to be reimbursed for introducing you to the lovely woman.'

'Your payment is that I will not see you hanged.'

She folded her palm back under her shawl. 'I'll take what I can get.' Then she laughed to herself. 'Not everyone can say a duke chose not to hang them.'

'You will let her live her life as she wishes.'

She kicked at the dirt. 'It was tiresome doing all the work to get you with her.' She shrugged. 'I knew you'd find a way to get out. You did, didn't you? You always find a way to get out. Of marriage.' One eyebrow quirked when she said the word marriage.

He didn't need her to read his palm. He saw it in front of him. A lonely existence, if he married someone besides Miss Manwaring. His future. As routine as his sister and cousins lived their lives and he would continue to live his life and work long hours trying to move the country forward.

The country would move forward, but his life would be left behind.

She picked up a ladle and found a bowl, placed some soup into it and put the bowl into his hand. 'Best to drink it,' she said. 'I've no spoons so I chop the vegetables finely.'

He wanted to make London a better place so little children wouldn't starve and old women would have shoes. He expected other people to take care of the details. This woman didn't. She took care of her own particulars.

Chalgrove took the soup and held the bowl to his lips. The broth and the vegetables satisfied. The old fraud could cook.

For an interval they talked and ate, and she offered him a hunk of bread to take with him.

He didn't want to take food she might need, but then she smiled. And he took it and made his way back to the carriage.

'Well?' Wiggins asked when Chalgrove crouched to enter the vehicle.

He broke the bread in half, gave Wiggins a share and the constable took a bite, nodding.

Chalgrove settled himself on to the leather seats and raised his hand to thump the roof. 'She's the most daft old crone I've ever seen. Forget about her. Not the right woman.'

Wiggins shut his eyes and his head dropped to the side. 'They never are.'

But Chalgrove knew who the right woman was. She just loved someone else. Two someone elses.

## Chapter Twenty-Three

Chalgrove left the door closed in the library, staring at it. But in his mind, he saw Miranda's eyes and lips. Dark eyes. Bright lips.

And his irritation grew when he remembered the old woman criticising Miss Manwaring, but he suspected the harsh words had been well aimed to raise his defence of her.

Now he could think of nothing else. His mind was wrapped around Miss Manwaring.

Chalgrove watched as the door opened. Before he saw who it was, he knew. Everyone else knocked—but not his mother.

She stepped inside and he saw her eyes search his face. 'It is a shame you were not here right after I paid a call on the lovely Antonia and her aunt earlier.'

'I had business.'

'None so pressing as arranging your entire future, I hope.'

'I found the person who abducted me.'

His mother clutched the nearest chair. 'How long before the hanging?'

'It might be some time, Mother. An old woman, with a

few ragged people around her afraid to ignore her orders. The woman's soles are falling from her shoes. She's got enough problems.'

His mother lunged forward, glaring. 'What?'

He took her shoulders. 'It's fine. I'm fine. She's daft. I can't hurt her. The woman who instigated this says the stars told her to take me.'

Her fingers shut, clasping air.

'Stars? She listens to stars?' Her fingers opened again. 'People don't listen to stars. They don't listen to clergy or parents or well-wishers. Why would they listen to stars? And she took my son. She should hang.'

'Mother.'

'She must hang.' She folded her arms across her chest. 'I plan to be in the country that day.' She shuddered. 'It's enough for me to simply know she's done for. It's not as if I want a piece of the rope as a memento.' She considered what she'd said. 'Well, maybe a small one.'

'Mother.'

He stood and recognised the tiredness in his jaw which told him he'd been clamping his teeth for some time. He relaxed the clench. 'She will go free.'

She stepped closer. 'She got away?'

'In a manner of speaking.'

'Another woman can get stars to talk with her and I have to pull words out of my son.'

'Mother. All is well.'

'What is wrong in this world?' She patted her cheek as if to wake herself.

'I would give you answers, Mother, but I don't know them myself.'

'Don't be surprised if we have some changes around here.' She rotated on her heel. 'You need a wife to take you in hand. Championing a woman who did such a thing. Unthinkable.'

He examined the lines of his palm, wishing they could show him answers. 'I never told you, but you were right. About Susanna.'

'I have no doubt about it. I just didn't know if you'd ever discovered it.'

'She was everything you concluded and probably less, I suppose.'

'It didn't ease me to be correct about her. But not to worry.' She preened. 'I've found you a wife, Chalgrove.'

'Mother. I've reconsidered my plans on marriage.'

'But I wish for grandchildren. And you must keep the bloodlines strong. You must assess this woman Antonia. She is the most perfect female in the world. I admit, even I was impressed at her flawlessness. I can hardly wait until you see her and how you'll react.'

'I've changed my mind. I won't marry a woman you've picked out for me.'

'I feel certain you will.' He saw the set of her shoulders. 'Antonia is… You have to see her to appreciate her beauty. It's perfection. She is the best the country has to offer. I have verified it. She is well mannered. Only a few women like this are born in a decade. Quite perfect and you know I would never say that lightly. I have not even said such a thing about my own children.' She softened her voice. 'You must see her and you'll agree.'

He had to discourage his mother, but from the determination pointed at him, she wasn't going to listen.

'You don't have a choice,' she said. 'Neither does the fishmonger or the street urchins. We're born into our lives and we make the best of them. And my children are fortunate to be able to do so in lovely surroundings.'

'This woman you've chosen may be impeccable—but…'

He could only think about Miranda. He put fingertips to his forehead. He could only think about her.

'You must meet Antonia. She is the best of the *ton*. Manners to spare. Skilled in everything she attempts. Dripping with beauty so deep you can't ignore it.'

'I'll think about it.' But he didn't have to.

His mother's brows were drawn in a harsh line. 'Mark my words, Robert Quincy Andrew Aubrey, Duke of Chalgrove, Antonia truly is perfection and you must see her to believe it. She will open your eyes to what is in front of you.'

She linked her arm through his and moved ahead with the strength of a bulldog. 'We must go before your carriage is unhitched. Her aunt is having a small dinner party and we're going to be late as it is. I accepted for both of us. I hope you don't mind. What with your promise and all.'

Antonia Redding was all his mother had said and more. But one thing she was not, and could never be, was Miranda Manwaring.

The evening passed and he watched the smiling faces and the polite manners. This was the world he belonged in and the world he would always live in. His place in it could make another world even better—the world of little children without someone to care for them.

He applied himself to accepting his role in life and in making the people around him feel better and keeping his own feelings hidden away.

He'd never had to do that before, but now he did.

When the eternity of the night ended, they left, travelling to his house, with him hoping he would still find Miranda inside.

As his mother left him at the top of the stairs, she gripped the railing. Her knuckles shown white. 'Think about your promise. You'll have lovely children and, if you aren't fond of them, you'd hardly have to see them until they became well mannered. Which might not be until the grandchildren arrive. Could happen.' She beamed. 'I will see you married to the right woman.'

When the door shut, he just had to be thankful his grandmothers weren't alive and still making their plans. That many meddlers would be too much for any one man to handle.

He had to make a decision.

Miss Manwaring. Miranda.

The word kept floating through his mind, unable to be shoved aside. Miranda. Now he knew of her past and he cared even more for her.

He didn't want to be away from her any longer. He'd promised he'd tell her when he found the woman and he would.


Miranda heard the knock on her bedroom door and opened it.

Chalgrove stood on the other side. She took his hand and pulled him into the room, closing them in together.

'You've been to see the old woman?' She knew even before he answered.

He gave a short nod.

'And what did she say to you?'

'She said she spouts nonsense more than a cloud gives rain, but that you are her finest creation.' He held out his hand, palm up, and she moved closer.

He clasped her and she held close the sensation of having him near. Without her planning it, she rested against him, complete in the feeling of his arms being around her. Basking in the safety his presence gave her.

This was someone she could find shelter with, in a way she had never known, but two little faces popped into her mind. Two faces that she'd given comfort to, time and time again. They had to come first. She had to give them the family she'd only had briefly.

'Tell me what she said.' Her words were little more than a whisper.

'Apparently, she needed a duke and a governess to complete her scavenger hunt and she wanted a prize for you.' His arms tightened.

She assessed him. 'I had guessed that. What did she win?'

'She planned to win you a family.'

'I'm not surprised. She said she was bringing me a husband. My grandmother does as she wishes and to the devil with all else.'

Miranda could see intensity in his face, hesitation and words he didn't want to say. She waited.

'The fortune-teller claims you're not her granddaughter.' His voice roughened. 'Your true mother left you before she died and the old woman kept you.' He spoke softly. 'You, a babe. Alone. With no one. If what she said is true, she saved your life.'

'She's not my grandmother?' Instead of flying into the air with happiness, the ground seemed to dissolve beneath her. Nothing, no one, had been her own. The childhood memories had been a lie. The grandmother she knew was someone else's grandmother, or maybe even no one's grandmother.

'Claims she's not related by blood.'

'Who knows if that is a lie? And my name? Did she tell you what I had been named?'

'Drucie. She called you Child because she didn't like the name. She planned, she said, even from the first on getting you a new name and a new family. It just took her longer than she expected. She finally told me it was hard to give you up on the day she left you, but she knew she must for your sake.'

She didn't know what was true. Except her grandmother possibly was adding more lies to the mix in order to keep Miranda safe. Better to be an orphan than be a grandchild of a fortune-teller, a fraudster and a swindler.

She searched her memory.

She could remember several other people calling the old woman Grandmother, but she couldn't feel they were her relatives. She couldn't recall why she called her Grandmother, or if she'd ever been told anything about her history. Her true relatives. She'd been given the notion that she could have a real doll and it had been described over and over so that when her grandmother had left her at the road, she'd not cried…right away.

And it was true. The china doll came first.

Years later, she had explained to Willie that they were going to get a little doll in the family, but it would cry and wet and some day laugh and play and he was to be the biggest, best thing of all in the world, a big brother. Willie had taken one look at the baby and called her Dolly. The name stuck. Miranda had truly received a doll.

She couldn't lose her.

'All I can count on with her is my memory of the cold. In the winter, the cold made my feet hurt so badly, the fire could never warm them. They would ache from the cold and sting when I tried to warm them by moving near the flames. I've never once been as cold since I left. Never once.'

'Winter doesn't last for ever.'

'It does when you're a child. When my grandmother had so little fuel to burn to keep us warm.' An image she'd lost returned to her mind. Of her grandmother huddling in front of the little fire, Miranda clasped in her arms for warmth and a cover from the bed wrapped around them, while her grandmother blew out breaths and showed her how they could see them in the air.

'In her own way, I believe she loved you. Loves you still.' Chalgrove released her.

She stared into his eyes. 'You think she does?'

'Yes.'

He ran a fingertip across her almost ringless hand, a stark contrast to the weighty cheap jewellery on the old woman, then he held her against his side and considered her palm, seeing the lines, wondering if there was any truth to being able to see what was inside a person by looking at their hand. 'You don't like jewellery, do you? Only one ring. One hair pin.'

'If it doesn't have sentimental value, it seems to get in the way.'

'What if it were something for this finger? Would it get in the way?' He touched the third finger of her left hand.

'I'll—I'll be leaving in the morning. I need to get back to Dolly and Willie. Even if the old woman does change her mind and come after me again, Mr Trevor has extra staff and everyone will know where to search for me. I won't leave the household without one of the men with me.'

'I agree you shouldn't. But I'll still be concerned about you. And I'll wonder. Wonder what our lives could have been like together. With children of our own.'

He understood she intended to be gone in the morning. But he couldn't walk away from her. She had to be the one who left. He wanted her heart to be beating close to his for as long as he could have it near.

She had moved to the open door, one hand on each side of it, her eyes unwavering. 'I will go to the children.'

Before she'd finished the sentence, she'd not been able to resist closing the distance between them again.

As gentle as he'd cradle the stem of a goblet, his hand circled her waist and he pulled her back inside his embrace.

His fingers moved up her back, feeling the small buttons as if they were a ladder to her heart.

'I will—' He stopped, gathering his words. 'Memories fade. This was an adventure you can tell your grandchildren some day.'

His slid his hands slowly back down the path they'd come. 'Yes. It's best for us if we forget this for a time, but inside me, I'll never forget it. Forget you.'

'Thank you.'

'Miranda.' His voice almost failed him. 'You're Miranda to us all and so much more. The nights we were together, I cannot get them from my mind. Two. One night of us alone on a bed. As distant as the moon, and yet it is as if I touched you then. And I did, when we left. In the cold rain. And I never felt so warm…having you in my arms. When I held you, my life changed for ever.'

'You have a chance to wed Antonia. Someone who will fill the needs of a duke's wife.'

It didn't matter how perfect Antonia was, or what her skills were, or even if she were a princess. She wasn't Miranda. 'I can't marry her. It wouldn't be fair to her.'

'She's so perfect. I'm sure you could tell her you don't love her and without blinking an eye she would agree to marriage.'

'I don't need or want that in a wife. I want you. I love

you.' The words sounded as natural as if he'd been saying them every day and he felt them to his soul.

She didn't move.

'I so wish we could marry, Miranda.' He said her name aloud, again. An endearment to him. 'But I can't ask you to wed.' The children. They needed to be in her life. And, if Trevor married again and she could not see them, it would devastate her and it would be because of him.

She stood before him, slim, wavering, voice cold. 'Do you really want me to give up the children I love?'

'No. I wouldn't want you to give up anything that you care for.'

He stepped away, giving her room to think and keeping himself from taking her in his arms.

He wished he could turn back time to the days before she had become a governess. He would have courted her and pursued her and, if he'd not been able to sweep her off her feet, he would have told her over and over again how— But, no, he couldn't have done that. The children needed her. Their mother had died.

He'd been an adult when his father had finally succumbed and he had lost so much. Without Miranda, and Trevor mourning their mother, the children would have been almost alone.

'They need you. More than I do. I'm...' He'd wanted to say he was mature. But his heart felt as broken as a youth's. There would be no recovering from this, even in the countryside.

He stood against the bookcase, his shoulder touching it, keeping the world from whirling away around him.

'I'm pleased you understand.' She spoke softly, her eyes on his feet.

'Part of me does and I hate that part of myself right now. But you're right. You'll not be able to forget and you'll feel you betrayed the little girl who was left beside the road.'

'No. It's the children.'

He straightened. 'For me, it's Child. The one who was left and I don't want her betrayed. Even by her own wishes.'

'Your mother expects you will court Antonia.'

'I don't trust Mother really wishes for me to wed Antonia,' he said. 'She's tossing Antonia my way as a distraction. She really sees you as my wife. And if she doesn't, that's too bad.'

He waited a second. Touching her chin, he said, 'I have a fascination with you. It goes beyond love. Love is a giddy feeling. A feeling of drunkenness. Distraction.'

He wasn't distracted by Miranda, he was consumed by her. And, he realised that nothing was going to change that. Not distance. Or months or years. In just a few days, she'd woven herself into the fabric of who he was.

Perhaps he'd fallen in love the morning he discovered the wildcat who had clawed back at him wasn't a beast, and those first few moments of light had illuminated a fragile wisp who hardly emerged as able to stand on her own two feet, much less kick back.

She'd accepted the situation. Studied it. In the darkness, she'd fought for her life. The daylight appeared and he saw a meek lamb. Then, when the old woman had appeared and off had popped the shoes, the delicate wisp had disappeared and the fire had shown in her eyes and her arms.

When he'd pulled her through the roof, the rain beating down on them, and held her in his arms for that second, with all the uncertainty surrounding them, he'd felt complete. She'd not hesitated, running with him into the darkness.

Telling him which road to take. Not complaining. Only going forward. Not back.

He contemplated what it was about her that made her different and it was the direction she took. Always forward. Never back.

A woman thinking of the future and of the people she wanted in it. Children she didn't want to desert.

He could only respect that. And her. But he couldn't ignore the anguish roiling inside him in a life without her.

'I love the children so. You've always had a family, Chal, and known they'd be there for you. I've made my family at the Trevor home. I can't leave them. Do you understand how I feel?'

He reflected on his words before he answered, 'Almost. Even though Susanna didn't make me happy, I enjoyed her presence. Having a partner for the quiet times. Someone to talk to after the party was over. But when I discovered she truly wasn't what I saw…' His voice became flat. 'I saw inside myself. I didn't really care that she was married. It wasn't as though either of us were innocent virgins when we met. But she couldn't tell me the truth of her past. And she had betrayed me by telling my confidences.'

None of the things she'd told had wounded him, but that she had told them had been the cutting blow.

From her husband's words, she still visited him when Chalgrove was at the country estate. As the man knew the times that Chalgrove was gone, he had to believe him. He'd felt betrayed and when the truth had registered—that he was angry with a woman who'd betrayed him…with her husband—that had been a bitter pill.

'I decided the truth was more important,' he said, 'than the lies. To build a life and future based on truths, even if it meant not sharing my life with someone.'

Better to be alone, than together with an illusion.

'You have a family you can trust.'

He took her wrists, sliding to hold her fingertips. 'The things you were told might have been lies. But the things you don't acknowledge are the truths. The love. The old woman loves you. Her eyes sparkle when she mentions you. Your mother loved you. I'm sure Miss Cuthbert loves you. The children love you. Nicky loves you. Trevor loves you. And I love you.'

'Perhaps I'm making a wrong decision.' She clenched her hands.

'No. You're making the right decision. One based on a family already there and who loves you. I couldn't expect you to give that up. I'd never want to see two little children lose the only mother they've ever known.'

## Chapter Twenty-Four

'Do you recall when I held you in the mud and rain?'
Chalgrove asked.

'Yes.'

'I knew then I held someone special.' His lips moved
closer with each word and ended with them against hers.

She moved one foot back, but somehow her body tilted
closer to him.

Her fingers slid through his hair, nestling against his
head and holding him.

She couldn't let go. Her fingers wouldn't move away.

His lips moved lower, caressing her, and his hands
cupped her breasts, filling her with warmth.

Miranda felt more tugs at her back, lower. Her words
caught in her throat.

She intended to catch his attention and her hands
clasped the sides of his cheeks, feeling the roughness of
his beard. When his eyes closed, she pulled his face to
her lips.

When their lips touched, their bodies aligned.

Chalgrove's hands had pulled her close and she knew,
knew from the way his arms around her lowered, and he
held her firmly, then gently slid her against his hardness.

She meant to give him one last chance for reason. One last chance to rescue himself, but his tongue touched against her lips and she didn't know how to speak in such a situation. And when she tried to think sensibly, her mind became mixed and her body responded by struggling to get closer to him.

He cupped her bottom, pulling her to him. He wasn't satisfied with only kissing her lips, but trailed along the edges of her mouth, moving lower.

She pulled away, breathing, and rested her head to the side and pulled her chin up so he could graze his teeth against her neck.

'The bed,' she whispered.

He'd turned her from the bed and she faced him as he'd leaned down and the hooks of her dress were undone. The dress had fallen open and his lips were lingering at the slipping bodice, managing to create sensations in her body she hadn't known existed.

The only wisp of a realisation which floated through her mind was that her clothes were falling away and she'd never known how easy it could be to disrobe.

The chemise moved up her legs.

His hand touched her thigh, and hooked under her leg, with nothing between his fingers and her skin. He pulled her up, so that her knee was bent, and he grabbed the other thigh, lifting her against him. She grasped his shoulders and he stepped forward, lowering her to the bed.

She still wore her corset and chemise and he lay alongside her, breathing in deeply. By his expression, she knew neither of them were in the same world they'd woken in.

She felt the pulls of her corset strings in the back loosening and each tug brushed her breasts against the fabric between them, heightening the sensations.

Arms around her, he tugged and tugged, and she took in his burning eyes.

Miranda realised he'd managed to grasp the shoulders of her chemise and slide it down, taking her corset with it.

She raised her hands to his chest and knew she had to get the clothing from his body. He must be suffocating wrapped in so many layers.

Chalgrove's shirt slipped easily over his head with the smallest of pulls from her. The boots were removed and she heard a clunk when he slung them to the floor. His trousers hit the cheval mirror.

Skin. Soft skin over hardened muscles accepted her hands better than her own would have.

His hands traced her body and his lips followed, caressing her breasts, her nipples. Then his mouth found hers again and he pulled her close.

He stopped. Completely. With his eyes, he asked and, with her lips, she whispered, *yes*.

He grasped her hips and the tip of his member pressed against her, moving inside. Filling her with the magic of lovemaking.

The pulsating thrusts of his body, gentle yet overwhelming, and his breath against her ear while he told her how much he loved her brought her to completion, turning the relentlessly strong yearnings inside her into a fulfilling tranquillity while he released.

They lay, still intertwined, side by side, and holding on to each other, trying to get even closer than before.

He lifted her hand to his lips, and kissed her knuckles. 'I just realised a lie I believed. That I could be happy without you. I can't.'

The same knowledge simmered in her. Without him, she would only have half a life, but it would still be giving Dolly and Willie the world she had craved, and they would have memories of their childhood to hold dear the rest of their lives.

The last words her mother had said to her was that she didn't want to stay for herself, but for Miranda.

Miranda had reassured her that she would be fine, then a pang of guilt had sheared her when she'd seen the hurt on her mother's face.

She'd tried to take the words back with the truth by telling her mother that her life would never be the same without her, that her mother had truly given her life by rescuing her.

Her mother had smiled and drifted to sleep, holding Miranda's hand.

'I know there will be a time when the children will be grown and go off on their own, but now they need me. Everybody deserted me when I was a child. I don't want them to face the same fate. Their mother died, leaving them. Just as mine did. And, at this age, I can't risk their father marrying someone who will treat them as my stepmother treated me.'

She slipped from the bed and observed the man contemplating her.

'You say it is the children.' He touched the bed where she'd rested. 'I'd never given it much consideration on how a woman might feel regarding the matter because I'd naturally assumed any woman in my life would be caring for my children.'

She remembered hearing her stepmother and stepsister talk of a woman who'd missed an event to stay home with a sick child and how meaningless that had been when the lady could have obviously used a chance to be relieved of her duties. After all, there was nothing the mother could do but depress the situation more, and the little one was up and about the next morning and no better for having its mother at hand.

She wouldn't have thought anything of it because she'd been sick when she was with the fortune-teller and the woman had left her alone for a day. Miranda had been told not to leave the bed. That evening, the dimming sky had worried her, but before darkness fell, her grandmother had bustled in with food and had the world humming around Miranda in no time.

She'd expected the same when she'd become ill at her different home. It had felt odd when her new mother had asked if her pillow was comfortable and put a tray beside her bed with a bowl of broth, and returned over and over to check on her.

She'd pondered on that the rest of the day and decided she'd not tell her mother that she could manage being ill on her own.

But she didn't think Willie or Dolly could.

## Chapter Twenty-Five

Chalgrove searched the dining room when he went in for breakfast. His mother sat, a newspaper beside her and her teacup in her hand. She put down the cup and stirred it, tapping the spoon against the china before placing the utensil at the side.

A maid put a plate in front of him, with a rasher of bacon, some butter and bread.

'Well, Chal, I guess I should invite Antonia for tea as I loaned Miss Manwaring your coach so she could leave. She left the house this morning.'

'She told me—yesterday.'

His mother gave one long meaningful blink, as if she knew exactly when Miranda had told him. She probably did.

'You look like you've been up all—yesterday.' She sipped her tea.

'I was.'

He sat at the table. He'd hoped Miranda would be there. Would be there to tell him she'd changed her mind.

Deep inside, he wondered if she'd really meant it when she said she was leaving because of the children.

'She's pleasant enough.' The Duchess picked up the newspaper she'd been reading.

'As a child, she was abandoned.'

'I know.'

'Wants to stay with those children. Their blasted father.'

'Mmm.' His mother sipped from the cup and turned a page. 'We talked before she left.'

'What about?'

His mother blinked again, set her cup down and covered a yawn. 'The weather. Boys. And how they grow up to be bigger boys…um, I mean, men.' She turned the page again.

She definitely couldn't be reading that fast.

'I gave her some motherly advice, wisdom and the loan of a carriage.' Another blink. 'Women talk. It's exactly like men talk about when they're alone except we talk about nonsensical things like feelings, people and the future. We hardly ever cover how many hands high a horse is or the size of a bosom. Much too important for us to discuss.'

'Your motherly advice is always appreciated.'

'Thank you. Some day it may even be taken.'

'Any advice for me?'

She didn't answer, just blinked and kept not reading the newspaper, and he kept not eating his breakfast.

Miranda stood beside the road. Again. The Duchess had been kind enough to loan her the carriage.

'Miss Miranda.' The shout startled her. Nicky ran out to check on her, a bucket of water sloshing in his hand. 'I saw a carriage and wanted to make certain everything was fine.'

Miranda hugged Nicky and he reddened. 'You only do that to embarrass me.'

'How is Cook?'

'Finer than a frog hair split five ways.'

'I hope you don't tell her that.'

'As a matter of fact…' he sat the bucket on the ground '… I don't. That's what she tells me.'

'I'm back,' she said.

'You sure?'

'It depends on Mr Trevor. I can't leave the children. I just can't. And I'm afraid if I return, he might expect me to marry him.'

'I wouldn't worry much about hurting him. Although you'd make a fine mother for the children and a good wife for any man. And our employer is of good character as well. You've been right under his nose. Of course he'd notice you.'

'That's not flattering me.'

'You don't need empty praise. It's true. We all care for you. Always will.'

'I had to come back. The children. I love them so much.'

'I understand. But you have a right to a life, too. If you're attached to that duke who came around asking about you, then ponder it. Even if you were a natural mother to the children, they'd grow up and make their own way. They'll leave as well. It's nature. Think about that before you choose the children over anything else.'

'You're the second person who has told me that today. But, I can't leave them as I was left.'

''Course not. You've been abandoned twice. Turned you right into an evil witch, didn't it?' He winked at her. 'I'd say it ruined your life something terrible being abandoned.'

'It was difficult.'

'You've been with Willie the first five years of his life and it won't be long 'till he's going off to school. Little fella's choosing his own path already. And Dolly's got her mind made up to be a good child.'

'You make me feel unneeded.'

'No. Mr Trevor needs you. For a wife. And you'll have other children with him.' His lips straightened. 'Another Willie running around. Maybe two or three. Throwing eggs.'

'He's just high-spirited.'

'That he is. And disorderly, boisterous, lively and a hellion…all before he even has his morning toast. Are you sure Willie's father should bring more children into the world? I think he should stop while he's behind.'

'Now, shush.'

He laughed. 'A lot of boys start out like Willie, Miss Miranda. He's a little more noisy than most, but he's not a bad child. And we owe all his goodness to you.'

She left Nicky and the stables and found her way to the study.

Knocking on the door, she opened it after Trevor called out to enter. He waved away his man of affairs and waited for her to speak.

She took a breath and said, 'I don't think I can return. My heart belongs to someone else.'

He rose. 'That's a respectable reason not to come back,' he said, standing behind his desk. 'I saw the way Chalgrove gazed at you and saw the way he glowered at me. I realised then I'd made a terrible error. I'd been caught in my grief so long that I'd not noticed what was in front of me.'

'Your wife was a good woman and you do her memory justice.'

'I really will never forget her and I don't believe anyone else will ever take her exact place in my heart, but you would have made my life whole again. I don't know what we'll do without you.'

'I have a former governess, Miss Cuthbert. I'll contact her, if you think you might be interested in hiring her.'

'I would. And if she is recommended by you, I'm sure she will be a good governess.'

'I was hoping I still might be able to see the children often. To be an aid to Miss Cuthbert. I can't bear leaving the children, but I know I can't continue to live here and a new post was offered to me this morning. Caring for an older woman.'

'You're taking on two jobs?' he asked.

'Well…' she laughed '…the other is not really paid. It's room and board and I'm to be a companion to a lady who doesn't want one. I'm hoping to convince her.'

The Duchess had already sent a letter of introduction. She had it in her reticule. 'It's only three houses over from here and I can be a help to Miss Cuthbert while the children are growing older.

That afternoon, Chalgrove knew his valet would have preferred tying the cravat with a knot strong enough to choke him. He could see it in the man's jaw and fluttering fingertips.

'You may have the rest of the day off,' Chalgrove told the man in atonement for the bear he'd been when he'd woken up after an hour's sleep.

Instead of a properly subservient display of gratitude, the valet huffed out a tortured agreement.

'I've had a rough morning,' Chalgrove spoke. 'It took me hours to get my mother to tell me what she and Miss Manwaring had spoken of.'

'The Duchess so enjoys the back and forth. Exemplary of you to provide challenges for her.'

Chalgrove lifted the hat that had been returned. If he were going to describe the hat, he would have compared the texture of the wool similar to what he might guess a rodent's fur might feel like and the colour…perhaps similar to the inside of said rodent's stomach on an ill day when it had been eating pale egg yolks.

He flexed the brim, trying to push it back into shape.

Wheaton's eyes widened, before he slid back into his role. If Chalgrove hadn't been watching, he wouldn't have caught the movement.

'What do you think of my hat?' he asked.

'An incredible example of creative craftsmanship on the shape. And a particularly inventive colour. The brim is unlike any I've ever seen.'

'Do you like it?'

'Only you could make such headwear show to its best.'

'I'm pleased you like it.'

'I am a great admirer of your fashion choices.'

'And you always tell me the truth.'

'If you listen closely, I do. Sometimes, I suppose you must listen very closely.'

Chalgrove tapped the hat. 'I have been thinking of ordering one for you.'

'It would certainly please me for you to take my tastes into consideration, sir, but not a hat like that in this lifetime. Perhaps the next. Yes, the next, depending on which direction I might take after life. If it is not the preferred course, that hat will be suitable to wear.'

Chalgrove took the hat, held up an index finger and spun the felt. 'This is even uglier than the last one, I'd say.'

'I'd agree.'

He tossed it to the valet. 'Don't let anything happen to it.'

The valet held it dangling between two fingers. 'I will

happily save it for you. In fact, you could be buried in it, should you pass on before I. You would have no worry of the fiery fiend accepting you as he would not want that hat to disgrace his premises.' He clucked his tongue. 'I don't know how the angels would react, but the task of convincing them it is fashionable would be your burden and you seem adept at it.'

'It's useful. It's almost as if I can read palms. When I have the hat on and ask someone if they like it, I can tell if they are telling the truth. If they smile and say it is a fine hat, generally I know them to be a liar. Some are good liars. Some fair. Doesn't work with close friends as much, but that's why they're close friends. Close friends would ask me what had happened to the poor horse that had caused him to become so ill to leave such residue behind, but it was indeed kind of me to wear his waste on my head as a memento…only they never say it in those exact words.'

'You should value those friends.'

'I do.'

Chalgrove spoke to the valet. 'My father wasn't as foxed as he seemed. He pretended to be drunk to hide how much the apoplexy affected him, didn't he?'

'He demanded that the decanters around him never be filled completely and he never regained as much of his strength as he pretended. He insisted he was a duke and for him to admit what *he* perceived as weakness hurt him terribly. Yet he was the strongest man I knew.'

'Why didn't you tell me?'

'Nothing to tell. Your father was as he was. If he preferred you to think he was foxed, then I was not going to contradict him. He was my employer. A good one.'

'You can contradict me.'

'No, I can't.' He smiled.

Chalgrove glared at him.

'Perhaps, Your Lordship, it is much better for the both of us if I am agreeable. And that hat is as fine as any residue I've ever seen.'

'Thank you. I believe I'm going courting. Would you select a suitable hat?'

'Yes, Your Grace. I will keep that one safe here for you and I will choose a different one.'

Mrs Miles had read the letter three times, then she'd folded the letter, unfolded it, smiled at Miranda and said, 'Of course you may live here.' She dotted her handkerchief to her eyes. 'So sad. You growing up motherless, and those little children close by here without a mother and you not in love with their father.'

A knock sounded at the door, even as a crack of thunder faded into the distance.

Mrs Miles folded her handkerchief this time into a square shape. 'I'm not expecting anyone. For me.' She sighed, but her eyes were shining. 'As your first duty, would you see who the housekeeper is letting in?'

After Miranda moved to the top of the staircase, she saw Chalgrove stepping inside.

Even with the cloudy day behind him, he created a light within her.

'Miranda.' He removed his hat, a few drops of water dripping from it.

'I thought I should let you know. Mother believes she has the perfect potential daughter-in-law.'

'I suspected she had. Antonia.'

Chalgrove crumpled the brim of the hat in his hand. 'That was only the distraction, while she positioned her selection where she wanted her.'

Miranda didn't move.

'In my aunt's house.'

The voice of Mrs Miles interrupted them as she stepped behind Miranda. 'Oh, my, it's Chal. Well, this is a surprise.'

'I would like to speak privately with Miss Manwaring, if you don't mind, Aunt?'

'Of course. Of course. Of course.' His aunt practically sang the words. 'Miranda, why don't you take the Duke to the sitting room? I believe I will have a lie down in my room. This is indeed serious if he has his father's hat.'

After Mrs Miles left, Miranda reached out, running her fingers over the damp brim and his knuckles, before pulling her hand back. 'I thought—I hoped—it might be you. At the door.'

One side of his lips turned upwards. 'I couldn't put it off any longer. I have to ask. Will you marry me?'

'Would you mind if I continued to live here?' she asked.

'Not at all. I own the house.'

'Then, yes, of course, I'll marry you.' She jumped forward, throwing herself into his arms, and he took a step back, bracing himself to catch her and swing her around.

He laughed and hugged her tightly, the droplets of water on his coat reminding her of the first time he'd held her close, when he'd pulled her through the roof.

'This is your house?'

'Yes. But I think of it as my aunt's. And I would have to have her agreement before I moved into it.'

'You have it,' a shrill voice called from above, startling Miranda.

He took her hand and pulled her outside the house. He held his hat over her head, letting it drop around her ears, and it shielded her face from the light rain.

He spoke softly as the breeze surrounded them, leaving a fine mist on their clothes.

'I told myself I'd never trust my feelings again,' he said, 'and I realised I'm not. I'm trusting what I see. I see a woman who chose not to be damaged by the faults of others. You don't care that the people who tossed you aside aren't perfect, you only want your life for yourself. You put the children's needs first.'

Before she could answer, a creak sounded. Chalgrove's eyes darted up and she realised a window had opened above them.

He reached out, took Miranda's hand and lessened the distance between them, holding their clasp at his heart. 'I'm sure you will be welcomed into my family.' He bent close to her ear, his forehead almost dislodging the hat. 'And that may take some getting used to for you.'

She laughed, reaching with her free hand to hold the hat in place. 'Willie may take some getting used to as well.'

'If you will agree to do your best to keep him away from my horses when he has eggs.'

'I will.' The weight of all her sad memories of the past vanished.

'I'll ring for tea,' a voice called from above and the window slammed shut.

'We should tell your grandmother of our plans to marry.'

'But she's not really my grandmother.'

'Not by blood, but by heart,' he said. 'And she is peering from beside the house to my left and a constable is behind her, and one of my stablemen is to the south of her.'

'I'd always concluded hardly anyone noticed me.'

'Everyone notices you. They all want the finest for you. It will be best for everyone if I keep you close at hand so they will be reassured and can sleep soundly in their own beds.' He took her wrist, placing a kiss in her palm. 'Aunt falls asleep at dark. I'll be back after that and we can discuss wedding plans, if you'd like that.'

She laughed. 'I suspect we will have a lot of guests. Invited or not.'

He put his face against her hair, breathing in the warm feminine smell of her he loved so well. Her skirts swirled around his legs as he swayed their bodies. He wanted the world to know—they were to be married.

# Chapter Twenty-Six

'Mr Manwaring is at the door,' the Duchess said. 'He's heard that there is to be a wedding today and he asked if he might see his daughter.'

'He said *daughter*?' Miranda touched the fichu she'd chosen to wear on her wedding day. The cloth was the only part of her old life she had. The piece of silk the old woman had told her to sit on and wait beside the road. And she'd kept it, always, and decided she must have it for her marriage. A memento.

The scarf, faded by time. Carefully mended by her mother. She ran her hand over the tiny stitches.

She felt as if someone had pressed the air from her lungs. She hoped her father did nothing to mar the day. He'd barely tolerated her for years and looked at her as if she didn't belong in his house. Which she'd not blamed him for, because she'd been dropped on him. It seemed he'd mellowed when he'd visited her at the Duke's house the first time, but she'd heard nothing more from him.

The Duchess smiled and put an arm around Miranda's shoulders. 'It is your decision whether you see him or not, but I hope you do. You have a new family now, but you'll always wonder what he might have said if you don't see him. If he says something that you don't like, smile, be gracious and leave the room, and step forward into your new life and place in our hearts. You'll likely never have to see him again.'

Miranda saw the support in the Duchess's eyes. 'I would like to see what he has to say.'

She headed to the library, unsure of the encounter.

He sat, dressed in black, his head bowed, but when she entered the room, he stood. 'It's good to see you again.'

'Thank you.'

'Did the old woman tell you…about me?' he asked.

Miranda shook her head.

'I met your mother. I was married and chose to forget it. I was young and felt invincible. She told me she was going to have a child and insisted I pay her to keep quiet. I was angry because I realised that had been her plan all along. I gave her the money she wanted. Then, and twice more when she asked. Two years after your birth, I realised she'd not asked for money in a far-too-long stretch and I searched for her. I found out she'd been ill and someone said she'd moved, but no one knew where she'd gone.'

He tucked his fingers of his left hand over his thumb, and his knuckle cracked. He shrugged. 'Then I was driving home from Sunday Services and my driver saw something moving beside the road. Of course, we could not leave you and, of course, my wife fell instantly in love with you and I knew this child looked exactly like my younger sister had looked. My wife refused to find another home for you. Told me she would take a poker to me in my sleep if I didn't keep you.' He folded his arm across his body and clasped his elbow, rubbing it. 'She'd never raised her voice before, or hinted at violence.'

'The woman who treated me as her own—was tricked

into raising her husband's bastard child.' Miranda felt the heat of anger within her. Her mother hadn't deserved such deceit. The woman who'd treated her with such love and compassion had been lied to.

'She knew. She'd found the letter asking for money to keep quiet.'

'What was my real name?' She had to know he wasn't saying he was her father just because she was marrying a duke.

'Drucie. And you're really a year younger than you know. You were born on October third.'

'That's my real birthday?' She paused. 'And I'm not twenty-four. I'm twenty-three.'

'My wife didn't want it easily connected that her ward might be the child of a woman I'd known. You were big for your age and smart, so she just made you older.'

'I think I'll keep the birthday and age Mother gave me.'

'She would prefer that.'

Her adoptive mother had given her a name, a birthday and a new life. 'You really believe she knew?'

'Yes. I sent the money to keep your mother silent, but my wife found the letter.' He snorted. 'I didn't burn it. I didn't know my wife had found it until later. She just packed up and moved to our country home. She said after her anger subsided, she couldn't let it rest. She asked her cousin to search out your mother. He befriended your mother before she left London and found out all he could about her life.'

'And you didn't know?'

'No.' He shook his head. 'Your mother was really a gamekeeper's daughter, which I didn't discover until my wife told me. He wanted nothing to do with you even before his daughter died, but a woman who lived with him kept you. She sometimes travelled to fairs and told fortunes. My wife would seek her out from time to time after you were born and give her much too much money for some nonsense. I didn't know anything about it until after we found you along the road. I discovered that hell hath no fury like a childless woman whose husband fathers a babe and abandons it, and the babe shows up almost on the doorstep. She fell instantly in love with you that day and never felt I deserved you. She was right.'

Miranda remembered her mother running her fingers through her hair and saying it was just like someone's hair she used to know.

Their eyes locked. 'My hair. It's like yours.' Miranda touched the knot.

He nodded. 'When your mother first took you in, if I walked into a room, she would call you and start combing your hair. My wife wanted me as far from you both as possible. And over the years, I became accustomed to it. You seemed to do fine on your own. I thought Priscilla would be a mother to you, but I didn't understand the relationship between the two of you until you were leaving for the governess position and it seemed to make you happier than you'd been since my wife died.' He looked at his feet. 'You seemed to do fine.'

He coughed. 'And, should anything happen to me, I wish to ask a favour.'

She waited.

'I'm not really married to your stepmother. Old habits die hard, but I am faithful to her. My man of affairs has my will and I've left another copy with the Duke. Please take care of your stepmother, if I die before her, if she needs it.'

Miranda could not find it in her heart to brush away everything he'd done as if it had never happened. But his irresponsibility had given her life. She'd been raised by his wife and had been given the home and a mother she would have chosen. Now she was to wed the love of her life.

She might never see him as a father, but she would give him a chance to be in her life. 'And if I were to have children? What relationship would they have with you?'

'If you would allow it, they would be the grandchildren I never expected to have and a treasure I do not deserve.'

'Would you like to stay for the wedding and the breakfast?' she asked her father.

Nodding, he said, 'I'd like that.'

They walked into the room where the old woman stood in the corner. She had on one new boot, one old one.

Miranda rushed to her side. 'The cobbler only made you one boot?' she asked.

'No. Two.' She lifted the hem of her skirt. 'But this one wasn't worn out yet, so I'm saving the other.'

She reached into the bag she had slung at her side and pulled out a packet.

Miranda unwrapped the parcel. A small ring. She turned it over.

'Your gift,' the fortune-teller said. 'From the button. I'm fortunate to know someone who can melt gold.' She grinned widely. 'I have friends with many talents.'

Miranda slipped it on to her smallest finger where it fitted perfectly.

She held out her hand and the woman chuckled. 'I can't see it that well.'

'What about the spectacles Chal purchased for you?' Miranda asked.

The woman groaned. 'I see too much in them. All the way into the future. Everyone is older. Have more lines to read. Too much knowledge for my old brain. Except I see a happy future for Child.' She patted Miranda's hand. 'Even though I had to catch a husband for you.'

'Yes, I—'

'You did not have to catch me for her,' Chalgrove interrupted as he stepped into the room. 'We only needed to be introduced.'

After the festivities ended and the world calmed around them, Chalgrove took Miranda into his bedroom. She gasped and put her hand over her mouth. Roses. Real ones. Everywhere. They scented the room.

She couldn't speak.

'And I've a hat collection. I thought the flowers might soften the blow.' Chalgrove went to his dressing room and pulled open the door, motioning her inside.

Hats. Hats, and more hats. This was not so much a collection, but a swarm.

She turned to him. 'You like hats.'

He nodded. 'My father's. My grandfathers'. Even some from my uncles. It started when I kept my grandfathers' hats as mementoes, then it just grew over time. I don't really like hats, particularly, but they seem to find me.'

She stared, open-mouthed.

'What do you think of my collection?' he asked.

She walked over and picked up the most hideous hat. The one he'd had on when they were taken. The one the old woman had returned.

She put her hand inside and twirled it on her finger, smiling. Then she stood at his dressing table, contemplating his reflection in the mirror. She held the hat high, as if she were going to wear it.

'I'm having a bonnet made in just this colour, with perhaps a dress to match, and I shall wear them with you when you go outside with this hat on.'

He grinned, eyes twinkling. 'Are you sure?'

'Positively. No one will ever question why you married someone not in society. Instead, they will close their eyes and mutter about how perfect we are for each other.'

He picked her up in his arms, walked into the next room and placed her on to the tester bed. She still gripped the hat.

He took it from her hands, swirled it to the far corner of the room and dropped beside her, kissing her. 'Just like the old woman, you've a plan.'

'Of course. And I want to stand out under the stars with you, night after night, and I don't even have to make wishes, but just be grateful for what I have been given.'

'Then we will be together and thinking the same thoughts.'

He kissed her again. 'Would you really wear a hideous outfit at my side?'

'If you wear the hat.' She moved away from him. 'But for now, we have a journey to take.'

'Yes,' he said, standing. The room was cleared of all his personal wear but the hats. He strode back to the dressing room and picked out one, held it up and she nodded approval.

Then he took the little parcels, a gift for Willie and Dolly, and one for his aunt.

'I'm ready to meet the children,' he said, 'and later embark on a honeymoon trip.' His things had already been moved to his aunt's house.

'My steward has a son who has agreed to help his father manage my affairs while I'm gone and the extra help will make it easier for me to spend more time with you when I return.'

'The house is smaller than what you're used to,' she said.

'I know. When Dolly and Willie are grown we can return to my estate. But Aunt's house is plenty big enough for us, Wheaton and, perhaps later, our children. My aunt has told Mother she is moving in here with her. She said she fears her reputation will be diminished if I am seen near her wearing one of my hideous hats.'

'I can understand that.'

He chuckled. 'What about your grandmother?'

She shook her head. 'She claims the stars won't let her move and she must have them close at hand.'

'My wife is what I must have close at hand and our children,' he said and dropped a kiss on her hair. He imagined holding their child for the first time and the joy he'd have in his heart. 'Today. Tomorrow. And until the stars stop shining.'

\* \* \* \* \*

*If you enjoyed this story, why not check out
these other great reads by Liz Tyner*

Redeeming the Roguish Rake
Saying I do to the Scoundrel
To Win a Wallflower
It's Marriage or Ruin
Compromised into Marriage